Frank Dumont

The Witmark Amateur Minstrel Guide

and burnt cork encyclopedia

Frank Dumont

The Witmark Amateur Minstrel Guide
and burnt cork encyclopedia

ISBN/EAN: 9783337223526

Printed in Europe, USA, Canada, Australia, Japan

Cover: Foto ©Andreas Hilbeck / pixelio.de

More available books at **www.hansebooks.com**

THE WITMARK
AMATEUR MINSTREL GUIDE

AND

BURNT CORK ENCYCLOPEDIA

By FRANK DUMONT

OF DUMONT'S MINSTRELS

Philadelphia, Pa.

PRICE, CLOTH, $1.00

M. WITMARK & SONS

CHICAGO   NEW YORK   LONDON

Contents.

SECTION VI.
END GAGS, CROSS-FIRES, STORIES, ETC.

SECTION VII.
MONOLOGUES, CONUNDRUMS, STUMP SPEECHES, SQUIBS, POEMS, ETC.

SECTION VIII.
FIRST PARTS, FINALES, CAKE-WALKS, MUSICAL ACTS, ETC.

SECTION IX.
TRAVESTIES, SKETCHES, AFTER-PIECES, ETC.

SECTION X.
SHADOW PANTOMIMES, ETC.

"GENTLEMEN, BE SEATED"

AND PAY ATTENTION TO A FEW WORDS BY THE AUTHOR.

A MINSTREL entertainment gives the young amateur rare opportunities to display talent in the vocal, comedy and dancing lines. No form of entertainment is so replete with comedy, nor gives such universal satisfaction when well represented. It affords vocalists a chance to *come out* in solo or concerted work, and the young comedians or dancers excellent opportunities to *shine forth* and give full vent to their humor and wit. Minstrelsy is the one American form of amusement, purely our own, and it has lived and thrived even though the plantation darkey, who first gave it a character, has departed. The dandy negro has supplanted him, but the laughable blunders are still incorporated in the negro of the present time. The ballads of Stephen C. Foster, breathing of slave life and the cotton-fields, have been laid aside for the modern love song with a dramatic story or descriptive ballad,— yet the minstrels sing them and the change from ante-bellum days to the darkey of the present time, has been accomplished without perception. Minstrelsy is the most popular form of amusement and is always selected as a vehicle to present the talent of a club, college, school or association. With this in view, the present book is compiled and arranged to instruct, suggest and prepare a minstrel entertainment, perfect in all its details—from the "blacking up" of the artists to the fall of the curtain upon the concluding burlesque. Everything is arranged in the most simple manner to assist the aspirants in their preliminary efforts, *detail* being the watchword. The ladies have not been forgotten, for be it recorded that it is quite the fad for ladies to "black up" and give a minstrel show. Valuable suggestions are offered to the ladies in their minstrel efforts, such as how to prepare themselves for the performances and the providing of suitable sketches, monologues and burlesques wherein ladies appear. There are also entertainments for both sexes, outlined in a comprehensive manner, giving full directions for a complete performance ; especially the *cake walk* and *shadow pantomime*. A collection of up-to-date jokes, conundrums, gags, monologues and bits of reparté will prove valuable to professionals and amateurs alike, for all may refresh their stock of "Chatter" from these pages and select from the abundance of *funnyisms* and humorous material enough to equip them for a long time.

It has been the aim of the writer to provide for the young amateur a gold mine in which to delve and draw forth "chunks" of fun, to spring upon his audience, and he has also endeavored to make this book a veritable encyclopedia of everything appertaining to minstrels ; at the same time he has not forgotten to build a work to which the reader can turn and peruse, when seeking funny literature, or a remedy for that tired feeling called *ennui* or the blues.

It is with feelings of pleasure that the author acknowledges the many valuable suggestions advanced by Isidore Witmark, Esq. The hours of collaboration and exchange of "ideas" to benefit and place this work beyond anything ever attempted in its line will ever be pleasantly remembered by him.

In conclusion, he sincerely hopes that THE WITMARK MINSTREL GUIDE AND BURNT CORK ENCYCLOPEDIA will do some good somewhere, assuring those interested that all the material contained in the book has been given before very refined audiences, and thoroughly tested by DUMONT'S MINSTRELS and other first class troupes of America.

Sincerely,

FRANK DUMONT.

FRANK DUMONT has devoted a lifetime to minstrelsy, and in writing for it, in all its phases. He entered the profession as a mere lad, and has been connected with all the famous troupes during his career. With Birch, Wambold, Bernard & Backus' San Francisco Minstrels, in New York City, he produced many burlesques on current events. His burlesque on "Patience" ran for one hundred and fifty nights at the San Francisco Opera House. While with Duprez and Benedict's Minstrels (then in the zenith of their popularity) he wrote many sketches and burlesques, which achieved great popularity, notably, "My Wife's Visitors," "The Polar Bear, ' "Red Riding Hood," "Black Robinson Crusoe," "Il Trovatore Done Over," and a score of musical burlesques on popular comic operas of that era.

For the ELEVENTH STREET OPERA HOUSE he wrote "Helen's Babies," which ran nearly an entire season. Then his burlesque on "The Mikado" ran for fifty nights. This is still a favorite piece with amateurs, for which Mr. Dumont has arranged many comic plays. He was connected with the first complete minstrel company that crossed the Plains directly after the railway to San Francisco was finished, and was in the Indian attack upon the troupe, the news of which created quite a sensation when it reached the East, where the members were so well known. Hughey Dougherty, then its comedian, was reported killed and scalped. Mr. Dumont's writings for the minstrel stage cover a wide range—from end songs, monologues and sketches to elaborate burlesques—original or on current fads or follies. The best known are "Scenes at Wanamaker's," "Broad Street Station," "International Yacht Race," "Camille," "The Steal-the-Alarm (burlesque on Still Alarm)," "Fedora," "Heart of Maryland," "Secret Serve-us," "The Blizzard Hotel," "Atlantic City

Storms," "The Trolley-Car Party," and hundreds of minor sketches upon passing events, as the ELEVENTH STREET OPERA HOUSE presents burlesques on everything that is "talked about."

Mr. Dumont has been the purveyor of amusements at this noted home of minstrels for many years. He thoroughly understands his audience, and knowing that people come to the minstrels to laugh, he furnishes food for merriment in abundance. His comic work is noticeable in productions of greater pretensions, such as "The Book Agent," from which "The Parlor Match," for Evans & Hoey, was elaborated; "The Rain-makers," for Donnelly and Girard; "McFadden's Elopement," for John and Harry Kernell; "The Cuban Spy," for Maude Hillman, and a dozen dramas which achieved popularity at the time of their production. He has collected the latest and best effusions of mirth for this book, and there is no doubt of its triumphant success. Every amateur, college student and professional comedian will find it of the greatest value as a book of reference to "think up" and construct monologues or gags at remarkably short notice.

ELEVENTH STREET OPERA HOUSE,

PHILADELPHIA, PA.

WHERE DUMONT'S MINSTREL COMPANY IS PERMANENTLY LOCATED.

IT'S HISTORY AND SUCCESSFUL MISSION.

SEVERAL generations have come and gone since the ELEVENTH STREET OPERA HOUSE first opened it's doors for *laughing purposes only*. Its mission from the start was to amuse, and no other place of entertainment in the world has more successfully accomplished its purpose, nor can point with pride to its banner upon which is emblazoned : *Veni, Vidi, Vici*. It came, it saw, and it conquered melancholia and gave merriment in abundance. The ELEVENTH STREET OPERA HOUSE was the 31st place of amusement in Philadelphia. It was opened by Sam Cartee, Dec. 4th, 1854. He made alterations in the building and called it Cartee's Lyceum. The Company was called the "Julien Serenaders," or Minstrels. In this company were E. F. Dixey, Ben Cotton and others who became popular ; but Cartee soon gave way to S. S. Sanford, who began April 23d, 1855, with Sanford's Minstrels. The opening bill contained the names of Cool White, Sanford, Kavanagh, Lynch, Dixey, Von Bonhurst and others. For a long time Sanford occupied this house of burlesque, and to a past generation catered successfully in every respect. In 1862 Carncross and Dixey assumed the reins of management, and under their guidance it continued to amuse, delight and interest Philadelphians. Upon its stage came a rapid succession of local burlesques, which has made this opera house famous the world over. After over a quarter of a century of successful permanency at the ELEVENTH STREET OPERA HOUSE, Carncross retired and was succeeded by Dumont's Minstrels, which constitutes the best minstrel talent in the country, and distances all its predecessors in the elegance of its vocalists, the humor of its burlesques, the attention to details, *mise-en-scene* and general appointments, to such an extent as to make it one of the front rank amusement attractions in Philadelphia to-day. Upon the stage of this familiar resort famous comedy and singing stars have received their first instructions and graduated. Among them may be mentioned : S. C. Campbell, Wm. Castle, Chauncey Olcott, Lew Dockstader, Weber and Fields, John C. Rice, Edwin Foy, Press Eldridge, Gordon Thomas, the basso, and a host of former favorites now gathered to the silent majority.

All these received a finished education in stage craft, which is absolutely needed in the work of presenting and portraying characters in the great burlesques written for this opera house, which is truly styled the "Fountain Head of Minstrelsy," where originated almost everything humorous which one sees transplanted into the many pro-

ELEVENTH STREET OPERA HOUSE, PHILADELPHIA, PA.

ductions that visit our city or that are given elsewhere. The great burlesque hits of this house of minstrelsy, still remembered with pleasure by its patrons, include the popular travesties, " Pinafore," "Mr. Mikado," " Peck s Bad Boy," "Helen's Babies," " Wanamaker's Restaurant," " Broad Street Station," " Yellow Kid," " The Girl from Paris (Green)," "High Lung Chang," "Duke of Marlboro's Wedding," "Mrs. Bradley Martin's Ball" and hundreds of local sketches, which created their share of laughter, and were then laid aside, as the "mill" is constantly grinding out merriment here, its prolific promoters believing in *onward evolutions*. Rehearsals are in progress every morning, but no labor of any kind is permitted in the Opera House upon the Sabbath. The history of minstrelsy is closely interwoven with this famous place of amusement, which is known throughout the world. The present lessee, Mr. Geo. W. Barber, has been connected with the Opera House since 1876. The business manager, George S. Hetzell, has been here the same length of time. Both are indefatigable in their work for the comfort of patrons, the excellence of the entertainment and all its details. Frank Dumont has been here for years, and his work as an author and producer is well known to Philadelphians. THE ELEVENTH STREET OPERA HOUSE is noted for the character of its entertainments, is patronized by clergymen, and is a household word among local and visiting pleasure-seekers.

IMPORTANT INSTRUCTIONS

FOR THE MIDDLE MAN AND STAGE MANAGER.

IN rehearsing the gags with the end men, be careful to impress upon them the necessity of selecting those of a varied nature in order to avoid similarity of subjects. One end man may represent the enlightened, sarcastic darkey; another, the dense fellow—jolly, but ignorant. Still another, the imitative or declamatory darkey, whose *forte* seems to be poetry or recitations; then, again, you can have a sleepy, blundering fellow, mispronouncing words and totally at sea concerning etiquette or history, there being material enough in this book to suit all. Do not use dialect, nor allow it to be used, as it spoils the stories and is often unintelligible to the audience. It is for this reason that the gags, etc., have not been written in dialect form.

A mannerism of speech can be assumed without using the thick dialect of the Southern darkey, which is seldom heard among the latter-day children of Ham. Have the entire company participating in the opening chorus, on the stage five minutes before, prepared to be discovered standing before their chairs when the curtain rises. See that every member is correctly attired, and, above all, that collars, cuffs, shirt fronts and white vests (if used) of the gentlemen are spotless. Often the members of orchestras will not "black up," which naturally would prevent them from sitting behind the circle. It is much better to have them seated in front, if it can be arranged, as the leader can then observe the singers, and the vocalists in turn can watch the leader. The musical conductor should always be seated in front to direct both singers and the orchestra, should the musicians even be seated on the stage. Every eye should be upon the director throughout the musical numbers of the first part. The middle man should have a list or routine of the gags and songs written upon his fan for his own safety and so that he can refresh his memory. He may arrange same something after this manner :

1.	Overture.	
2.	Squibs and Cross-fires, by	
	Kane & Chase.	
3.	Comic Song by Platz.	
4.	Ballad by Singem.	
5.	Gag by Williams.	

6.	Change of end men.
7.	Song by Robbins.
8.	Ballad by Triller.
9.	Gag by Howard.
10.	Comic Song by Rufus.
11.	Finale.

of course using the matter of his own programme. This list will enable him to know exactly the routine of every song and gag in the first part, and by whom it is rendered, thus avoiding serious mistakes which are apt to spoil an entire performance. It is also a good idea for the middle man to jot down the first few words of each gag as a *cue* in the order they are told.

Instruct the leader of orchestra to lay out all his music in the rotation in which the songs will be rendered, and also mark the "encores" in each orchestral part from where such encore is to be taken. This saves delay and dangerous mistakes. Be sure to rehearse each "encore" as you would your solos and other musical numbers, and thereby insure a smooth and perfect performance. Where the Witmark Minstrel Overture is used, the middle man's cues are already marked and opening speeches incorporated. Such as : The chorus before rise of curtain—Introduction of end men—"Gentlemen be seated," etc. All these features are arranged in this overture, which is replete with novel features, chorus selections, and innovations, making it one of the big successes of the famous minstrel companies of America. Now, where this overture is not used, the interlocutor will exclaim, "Gentlemen, be seated," and when seated announce "Overture." After overture, and to give the musicians time to change instruments, or turn pages of music, the end men and middle man indulge in a few squibs. These will be found in Section VI. A few conundrums may also be added after the overture. Then the middle man announces the first ballad somewhat after this style : "*The popular tenor, Mr. Blank, will render Ford and Bratton's ballad success, 'Don't Ask Me to Forget.'*" (Future ballad announcements are delivered in about the same manner, changing the style of language to avoid monotony). Then may follow a gag from one of the inside end men. (The outside end men have, as a rule, the last gags and songs). By a careful perusal of Sections V. and VI., the comedians may each be able to select a line of good gags which they can easily dove-tail by introducing a little original "patter" relative to the gags. It is advisable to have only a little patter—*a very little*.

After this, interlocutor announces : "*Mr. Dash will sing the latest coon ditty, by A. B. Sloane, 'You've got to Play Rag-time.'*" (Similar announcements for other coon or end songs). If you have a change of end men, which is a prevailing novelty, rise and announce in this manner : "*I now take great pleasure in introducing the Kings of Momus and Jesters, par excellence, Messrs. 'Ha-Ha' and 'He-He.'*" As soon as this announcement is made, the outside end men leave the stage quickly to make room for end men just announced, who enter from opposite sides and cross to their seats, bow and sit down. (NOTE.—End men who have just retired, can, in the meantime, be dressing for parts in the finale). The new-comers begin with a gag or a song which will be announced by the middle man. So the first part is kept running—song and gag—until all have had their innings. Then the finale is presented. Selection can be made from material in Sections VII. and VIII. It is very often necessary to drop a scene in first grooves in order to set the stage for the finale. In that case the interlocutor announces a quartette or a sextette or some specialty that can be done in one to consume enough time for the change of scene. As soon as announced, the singers step to the front and the drop is lowered. It is advisable *not* to place two tenor ballads one after the other in arranging your programme. Have a baritone or bass solo between ; it will be more effective. One of the most essential points is the proper selecting of varied songs. The publishers of this book will be pleased at any time to give advice on such matters upon application.

Each comedian should have a *guide* of his own to study or make selections from for his individual work. This will expedite matters. The stage manager will arrange and prepare the programme for the printer and correct the proof, time each act, song and gag at rehearsal and will thus estimate the length of the performance. Avoid too much pomposity and the constant repetition of the word, "Sir." Be natural. Talk distinctly and loud so as to be heard by your audience, especially where a point is to be gained by the comedians.

REMEMBER—"Brevity is the soul of wit," so do not have your show too long, as it may become tedious.

SELECTING THE TALENT AND ARRANGING THE REHEARSALS.

AN EXHAUSTIVE TREATMENT.

THE most important item in the beginning of your minstrel preparations will be the appointment of a competent and strict stage manager. The old saying, that "too many cooks spoil the broth," is true in this case, as it would be in the culinary department of a hotel. *One* must conduct and direct the rehearsals, and it is better to have that *one* conversant with music, as it will aid in the rehearsals of the overture and other musical numbers, especially the playing of the Tambourines and Bones, which, while seemingly simple, require a vast amount of practise, (if more than two "end men" participate) to get the movements and taps alike, where to rest and fill in the time with graceful movements, or rising from chairs, going to centre of stage, and with graceful evolutions return again to work up a spirited climax for an emphatic ending. All this must be rehearsed carefully under the direction of the stage manager. A very clever and original idea in Descriptive Overtures has been prepared expressly for this part of minstrelsy. It is entitled, "The Witmark Minstrel Overture and Opening Chorus," composed and arranged by Isidore Witmark. No detail is lacking in this overture. Instructions for every tap and every move are distinctly and comprehensively given. It has been a grand success with the professional troupes, and is within the ability of every amateur, both in its vocal and musical arrangement.

In selecting your Middleman, it would be best to have one with good delivery, deep voice, good memory, and if he can be *impromptu* in his replies, it will greatly aid the Comedian. He can have the "cues" for titles of songs or jokes pinned or secured upon his fan, where he can glance at them unseen by the audience There should be frequent rehearsals for the End Men and the Middleman, whereby the jokes and dialogues can be thoroughly gone over and memorized. Call special rehearsals for the principals only, and announce your date for *all* rehearsals two or four weeks in advance of the time of your performance. There will be no excuse for your members to make other engagements when dates are thus arranged. Demand full attendance at rehearsals, and, more than any thing else, *strict attention.* Stop all talking in the entrances, idle gossip and side remarks that may annoy the stage manager and those intent upon their work. It is essential to secure a good pianist to teach the music to ladies and gentlemen of the "chorus," and to assist the stage manager, who will be directing the "business."

It will now be necessary to select the talent in all departments to form a complete minstrel company. First, choose the singers comprising the vocal corps. An ordinary male quartette is composed of a First and Second Tenor, Baritone and Basso, (for female quartette,

First and Second Soprano, First and Second Contralto), but for minstrel part singing the "Male Alto" is a valuable acquisition for solo work, as his voice "stands out" well in ensemble. Having selected a number of voices, you will next turn your attention to the Comedians. This is a very important matter, as nine out of ten beginners imagine they are "funny," without having the least reason for thus guessing. This can best be determined by the manner in which they sing comic songs at rehearsal, or the manner in which they render a humorous recitation. A few tests will soon show the ability of the aspirant, who should abide by the decision of the stage director. The pages of this book will supply him with comic anecdotes and jokes, also the lines and suggestions for enacting the characters in Burlesques, etc.

Having secured your opening chorus, the selecting of popular ballads and funny coon songs is in order. These can always be found

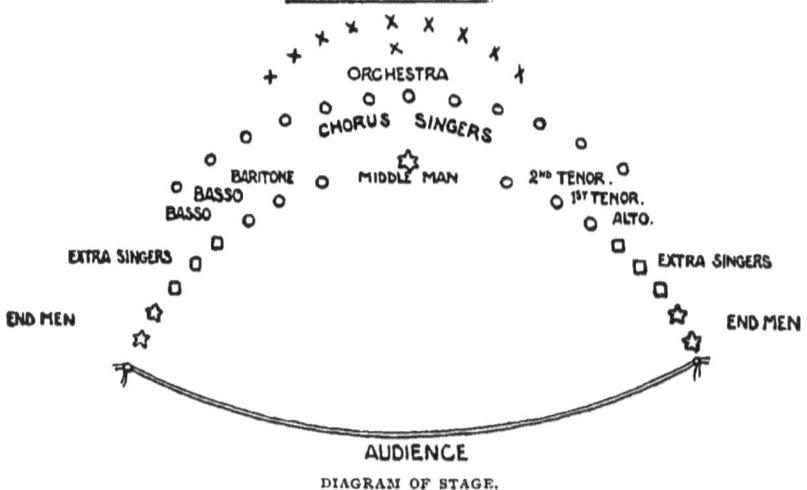

DIAGRAM OF STAGE.

in the extensive stock of M. Witmark & Sons, who are continually keeping strictly "up-to-date." A special catalogue of catalogues, entitled "Are You Interested In Amateur Affairs?" embracing interesting suggestions of the latest vocal and instrumental hits of all kinds, will be sent on application. With your rehearsals of ballads and comic songs, you will have taken the first important steps in your minstrel rehearsal. You must next determine the styles and settings of your "first part." You will find in section IV., several suggestions. These are described and a sample program is given to each as a guide. The Finales, Olios, Specialties and Burlesques suitable for them will be found in sections VI., VII., VIII., IX.

Be sure to rehearse with "props" and *on the night* have them in their proper places.   A special man should look after them and see that every character requiring "props" is taken care of.

The position of the gentlemen in the circle is outlined in the diagram on preceding page, but changes can be made to suit the conditions.

In arranging the first part select a handsome palace, conservatory or columned interior for the set of the above "First Part." You place the musicians behind the circle of singers and comedians, upon an elevation or staging, high enough to be over the heads of the front circle, when seated, also second circle, if you care to have one.   The "set" above described is for a handsome interior "First Part," in which the costumes may be of regulation evening dress suit, court dresses, or any costuming suitable for *interior pictures.*

From the ideas thus advanced the amateur will be enabled to frame a "first part" of his own liking and costume it from the resources at his command.

HOW TO BLACK UP.

AN INSTRUCTIVE INTERVIEW.

A REPORTER of the *Evening Star* called upon Mr. Dumont last evening in his dressing room of the pretty Eleventh Street Opera House, wherein Dumont's minstrels nightly hold forth. The members of the company were preparing their "faces," to appear as darkies in the first part, and were applying the burnt cork. All this was a revelation to the reporter and a peep behind the scenes, a privilege granted but to a few. "What is that you are putting on your face, is it black paint?" "No indeed," replied Dumont, "it is burnt cork, a very simple preparation, but nothing has ever been invented to take its place. First, we get a lot of champagne corks, or remnants of cork from a cork stopper factory. These are placed in an o'd tin pail —which serves as a furnace—and then ignited. A few holes in the pail which furnish draught for the blazing corks. When they have been thoroughly burned, they are crushed and reduced to a powder by hand. Then this powder is moistened with water, and we run it

BLACKING UP AND ADJUSTING WIG.

through a small paint mill to grind it fine. Then we place the paste thus made into tin boxes and it is ready for use. You moisten with a little water the quantity you need as you are applying it to the face. We do not mix any thing else with it, although I have seen various recipes calling for vaseline and other ingredients." "How is it applied?" "Take some into the palm of your left hand, rub it over the palms as if about to wash your face; then smear it over the features as if applying a cosmetic. Carefully apply it around the eyes and about the lips." "Do you paint the lips red?" "No, sir; when you have applied the cork and left the lips in the natural condition they will appear red to the audience. Comedians leave a wider white margin all around the lips. This will give it the appearance of a large mouth, and will look red to the spectator. Having blackened my features, I now take my sponge and with it wipe the palms of both hands. This is for a double reason. It represents the real color of the colored man's hand; at the same time cleans that portion of the hands for the remainder of the make up for the stage. Thus you can handle the white vest, bosom of shirt, collars and ties without soiling them.

"You will notice that in 'blacking up' I use an old under garment commonly called an 'undershirt.' This is used to keep spotless white, the bosom of the article in which I appear before an audience. Now, you will observe that I am all 'blacked up.'" "Yes," said the reporter, "but what has often puzzled me is how do you fix, or paste on your face, the white hair to represent old darkies?" "That is quite easy to represent, after blacking up, we use chalk. Drop chalk we call it, and it is obtained at the wig man's or your drug store. You just outline eyebrows with it, chin whiskers or a grey beard. It's all done with this chalk. A 'bald' wig with just a fringe of grey wool is placed on the head, and large brass rimmed spectacles on your nose, and you've got an old 'Uncle Tom,' and the picture of an aged colored individual." "Then it's all in the wig and a bit of chalk?" "Yes,

ADJUSTING OLD MAN'S WIG, BEARD AND EYEBROWS.

sir; excepting you desire to adjust a bare gray beard which can be had of the wigmaker or costumer.* Now you see I am blacked up and I take a small soft brush, which also get at wigmaker's, to rub off the particles of cork from my features to prevent them from falling on my white shirt front and white vest." "I see, I see!" "Now, sir; I put on my creamy white shirt, after I am thoroughly blacked up; then a paper or celluloid collar, a small black tie—some use a white tie—then my cuffs, either of paper or celluloid. Now I put on my white vest. Here my clean hands do not soil the vest as I button it." "Now I see why you used your sponge upon the palms of them." "Certainly; now I put on my swallow-tailed coat, with a flashy flower or 'boutonierre' in its lapel, and I resemble a perfect Beau Brummel, do I not?" "You do," said the reporter, "and those satin knickerbockers?" "They are a compromise between the old and new style of dress. I do not use the silk and plush costumes here, so we wear black satin knee pants, black stockings and low cut patent leather shoes.. This is very genteel, dressy and in keeping with minstrelsy. It is also full evening dress as adopted by the 'Four Hundred,' so you see we are 'in it' so to speak." "I understand that it is quite the fad for ladies to give a

* See directory back of book.

minstrel entertainment." "Yes, indeed; it is more popular than ever. Why this season I have furnished material for several entertainments, given by ladies only." "How do they blacken up?" "Pretty much as we do. It would'nt do for them to put on their complete costumes first. That would surely spoil them. No, they commence as we do, then attire themselves in their stage costumes. Where they wear short sleeves they do not blacken the arms, but wear long black silk or ordinary gloves, and, by the way, we sometimes do not blacken the hands, but wear black gloves or white ones. I have my minstrel company blacken the hands, especially musicians, who cannot wear gloves for such instruments as violins, flutes, clarinets, double basso, etc. Therefore to 'look alike' we blacken our hands. The ladies, however, all wear black gloves except the 'end men.' You see I call them 'end men' even if they are ladies." "One thing more," said the reporter. 'Now the cork is on, how do you get it off? Scrape it off with a knife?" Mr. Dumont laughed of course at the scraping part of the make-up. 'I just remove all my finery,' said he, 'also the make-up shirt, and with a sponge and a cake of soap I go at it. I make a good lather and smear it over my face—then with the sponge well soaped, I go over the face and neck, and presto. the cork has almost vanished. No hard rubbing is necessary. Plenty of lather and a sponge. Then go over the face once more and then rinse your "features" in a bucket of fresh water—if you can get it—and once more you are a Caucasian ready to take up the 'white man's burden,' instead of the coon's. You can catch the idea from my explanation, but if you wait until after the show, I will be pleased to give you a practical demonstration,—how simple it is. It's easy to take off if you do so properly. After you are washed and features are dried with a towel, use a little powdered magnesia upon the face." By this time Mr. Dumont and his troupe were ready and they descended to the stage. I heard the bell ring and the curtain arose upon the handsome circle of minstrels. The Interlocutor said, "be seated, gentlemen." They bowed, sat down, and then began their "First Part."

HOW TO RELATE JOKES, OR TO TELL A "GAG."

THE NEWSPAPER MAN "AT IT" AGAIN.

"Pardon me, Mr. Dumont," said the reporter, "but here I am again to bother you." "No trouble, sir. What is it?" "I want to know if you have a system or a method for telling gags, relating jokes such as you and your end men do nightly in your Opera House?" "Well, that is rather a peculiar question, but one that has often been asked," said the minstrel manager. "There is certainly a style and a jolly manner to be assumed in relating a story, especially while seated as 'Bones' or 'Tambourine'. Imagine a blank-faced fellow telling a very funny story with features immovable, looking sad, expressionless and as if he didn't have a friend in the world. How can he expect his audience to show signs of mirth with his funereal countenance and slow delivery, especially in this age of rapid transit?" "That's very true, Mr. Dumont." "Now, Hughey Dougherty and myself begin our fusilade of chatter as if we enjoyed it, and I confess that we do. Once or twice your newspapers remarked that the middle man had to laugh at the jokes, consequently they were fresh and funny to him. That was a compliment and a truth. Dougherty is one of the cleverest, funniest and most witty of comedians. He is spontaneous, and most of our gagging is *impromptu*. I start in speaking of some local fad or happening and Hughey turns it into ridicule. Before several nights we have a roaring joke or gag constructed. But all jokes or gags are not evolved in this manner. The comedian writes them out and studies the points, delivery, inflection of voice, and the words leading up to the finish or climax; as on that he depends for his big laugh to terminate his story or gag." "Then," said the reporter, "it's very much like studying elocution?" "It is harder; you can't learn to be a poet, nor can you learn to be a comedian. You must have some natural talent and a sense of humor. Some men in a circle of friends will relate an anecdote which in its brevity and mimicry or tone of voice will be funny to all listeners. Then others will begin a story, a long, tedious preface, useless words, a story long spun out, and when the climax is reached, you yawn and laugh, a hollow laugh, just to be polite; but you're mighty glad the bore or drowsy story-teller has finished. He can't tell a story, and yet he inflicts it upon you, if he gets a chance." "I have met the man you describe," said the reporter.

"Well, sir, the comedian telling his gag, studies to avoid that and must avoid it. Everything depends upon his jolly manner (unless he assumes a sorrowful or sarcastic manner, which is necessary in telling some gags), the quick reply of the middle man, and the emphasis here and there upon certain words, especially when he plays upon words. Don't rattle off your story like a poll parrot, nor smother your voice when coming to a point. Keep the voice up. Don't let it drop in concluding your words, wherein lies the point of your joke or story. That is natural elocution. We do not need the *ultra* dramatic idea of speaking for minstrel business; not a bit of it! Speak naturally, without dialect, as it is not used by the end men. Keep the dialect for your imitations of colored preachers or old darkies. Dialect spoils the story and detracts from it." "I wish you could give me an idea of how to tell a gag or joke," said the reporter. "I do not know that I can give you a lesson or rather a kindergarten idea of how to relate a gag; but, if you will listen, I'll run through a short story and you can gain an idea of how to deliver a few lines in the joke department. For instance, the end man will commence laughing as if he had just thought of something. I say to him: 'What seems to amuse you? Tell me; let me enjoy it also.' He says: 'Something funny happened to me. I was standing on the corner and along came a policeman, and he says: 'Do you play *checkers*?' I say 'Yes.' 'Well,' says the cop, 'it's *your* move!' I moved or he would have *jumped* me right there!' Now, that's simple, isn't it? But do you see where I raised my voice or made certain words prominent or emphatic? Relate the above without punctuation or emphasis and it would be very flat indeed." "It would," assented the reporter. "And now for a bit of mimicry," said Dumont. "Two cross-eyed men on bicycles ran into each other. Oh! what a collision! They sprawled all over the street; one cross-eyed man said to the other (imitating his voice): 'Why don't you *look* where you're *going*?' The other cross-eyed man said (imitating angry man): 'If you'd gone the *way you were looking* this wouldn't have happened.' Do you note that I kept the tone of voice up as I neared the conclusion of this short joke? I imitated the tone of voice of the two angry cross-eyed men also." "You certainly did," said the reporter. "And now to relate a sensational story, thus: I heard the cry of fire and saw a woman at the third story of the burning house. I rushed upstairs; it was your mother-in-law. I took her in my arms and carried her all the way down stairs and landed her safe on the side walk." The middle man says: "What nonsense! My mother-in-law weighs nearly three hundred pounds. You couldn't lift her off the floor, and you certainly couldn't carry her down from the third floor in your arms!" The end man sees that he blundered, but is going to stick to his lie and bluff it out, so he says: "I knew what I did, I saved your mother-in-law. I carried her down. I was there when I did it." Middleman says to him: "You did nothing of the kind; you couldn't lift her on account of her three hundred pounds in weight. So *how could you carry her down?*" A gleam of satisfaction shoots over the end man's face, as if he had just thought of a brilliant lie or excuse. He turns and says to me, 'I made *two trips* of it; I went up *twice after her!*' He says this distinctly and in a triumphant, laughing manner, pointing his finger at me and in slang parlance 'giving me the laugh.' That, sir, is how to successfully relate a joke."

Section III.

A VALUABLE DICTIONARY OF STAGE TERMS USED BY PROFESSIONALS.

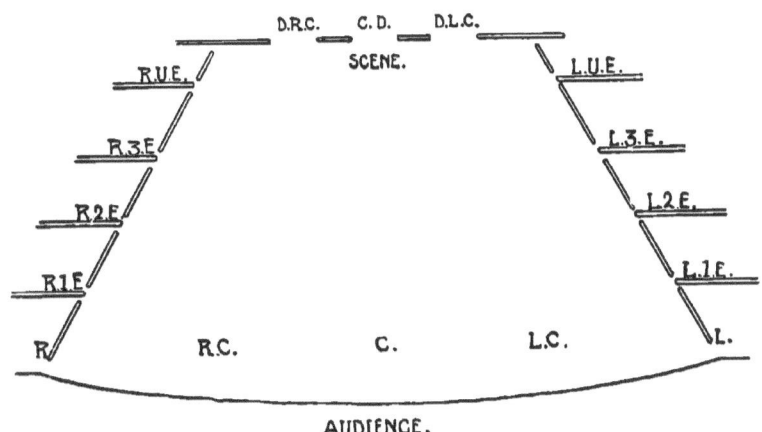

DIAGRAM OF THE STAGE.

L. 1. E.   Means left first entrance.
R. 1. E.   Means right first entrance.
R. U. E.   Right upper entrance.
L. U. E.   Left upper entrance.
C.   Means centre of stage.
R. C.   Right centre of stage.
L. C.   Left centre of stage.
C. D.   Centre door.
D. R. C.   Door right centre.
D. L. C.   Door left centre.
Door F.   Means door in flat.
Flat.   Is a scene of any kind, where canvas is stretched on frames.
Drop.   A scene that can be rolled up or let down like a curtain.
Tormentors.   The first set of wings (or drapery painted wings) down front—acting a " picture frame " for balance of scenery.
Grooves.   The upper slots wherein the flats or scenes are fitted when pushed out upon the stage or drawn into entrances.

Borders. The drapery above such as " sky," " wood," "'foliage " or " interior" borders, etc.

Backing. Is used behind open doors ; sometimes it is a garden scene which is seen through open doors, or a chamber or any in-door or out-door scene, placed beyond an open door arch, or other scenic opening.

Mask in. Means to conceal the article or screen from view by other bits of scenery, such as using a wing, or a door, curtains, tree, or screen, to hide the principal object until it is revealed in the course of the play.

Closed in. Means that the scene is closed by lowering a " drop," or moving on " flats " to thus end the farce or burlesque.

Set in One. Means scenes in the first grooves, down near foot-lights. These " Scenes in One " are generally used when the stage is being set for another scene.

Set Cottage. Means a practical house, cottage or other habitation placed at an entrance and braced to keep it in position.

Set Waters. These are pointed waves or " water " scenes which rest on the stage and are used in sea-shore or marine farces. Sometimes one or more rows are used, when boats are drawn on or between them.

Set Fire-Place. An opening in the scene or set piece to represent a chimney-place or a grate fire.

Brace. Is a long or short pole with a twisted iron at one end to hook into rings or screw-eyes, and an iron at the other end to enable it to be secured to the stage. They are used to hold up scenes and set pieces, to " brace " a cottage, a wall, a fence, "waters," trees or any stage objects.

Battens. Narrow strips of wood to which drops are tacked either top or bottom. This enables them to be pulled up by ropes, or secured to the stage by screw-eyes.

Props. Means all articles used in the farce, burlesque or comedy, such as : Bread, knives. pistols, clubs, clock, table, chairs, etc.

Stage Screw-Eyes. Iron screws with rings. These are screwed into the stage by hand to hold objects or braces.

Grass Mats. These mats are simply ordinary cocoa mats dyed green. to imitate grass or shrubbery. They are invaluable to the stage manager to place about tubs of plants or for "Lawn" effects in out-door scenes.

Foot Lights. Lights at the edge of the stage.

Border Lights. Lights swung above ; across the stage to illuminate the top of scene.

Up Lights. Means to raise the lights.

Lights Half Down. Means to lower them to have a half darkened scene.

Business. Anything done upon the stage while speaking or acting. " To remove a coat," " move a table," "shoot a pistol," "seize and pummel any one," "hiding behind a screen and peeping over," "showing fright, joy, surprise, anger," all come under the head of "business" This is one of the things hardest to explain properly, illustrate or teach the young beginner. He or she must closely follow the directions of the stage manager during his arduous labor to convey his meaning, etc., to his company. In holding a play book to rehearse, remember that you are always facing the audience.

Bus. Abbreviation for "business."

Straight Business. This is a part wherein the genteel character "feeds" the comedy, and it is generally the educated man enlightening the ignorant intruder or companion in the sketch or farce. The genteel character is also known as the "Walking Gentleman" of the dramatic stage.

Ginger. To perform in a lively manner.

Patter. The "talk" or "chatter" used in a monologue, or between verses of songs. The "patter" is generally applied to all descriptive dialogue used by *Raconteurs* (story-tellers).

Feeding. This is where a character talks with the express purpose of having the comedian reply in a humorous manner, or to lead up in dialogue to the "points" in his speeches.

Points. The emphatic part of a speech, pun or retort wherein the laugh is expected from the force of the remark, or its explanation. This is also frequently the ending of a joke or recitation where the full force of the story culminates.

Cross-fire. A running "Talk" between the two End Men or Specialists, in which they indulge in repartee—questions, short squibs, satire, sarcasm and jokes—at each other's or the middleman's expense.

Climax. The grand ending or conclusion of a speech or piece of business. It is frequently applied to a forcible situation in a drama comedy, or burlesque.

Ad. lib. Abbreviation for *ad libitum.* At discretion.

Exit. Means to leave the stage. An outlet from the stage.

Exeunt. All exit.

Enter. Means to come on the stage from some entrance described in the play-book, Right or Left.

Omnes. Means everybody—all the characters.

Cross. Means to cross the stage, but be careful not to do so in front of any one unless the "business" is arranged by the stage manager, as it is considered one of the worst breaches of stage etiquette.

Aside. In dialogue, means that portion not to be overheard by the performer who is being addressed, or, rather, a bit of dialogue intended for the audience, such as: "Now for the borrowing of the money," or, "He doesn't recognize me," "Well, I'll get out of this."

Aloud. Resuming dialogue in the natural voice and addressing those on the stage.

Cue. Is the important ending of a speech where the next person to whom this " cue " is given—will speak his or her lines. It generally consists of a few words written thusly: ———— *shall go home*, and this is a " cue " to the one having the words in the part or book. Cues for " business " or " music " are given in a similar manner. Everything is done upon the stage by cues, and particular attention must be paid to them.

Discovered. Means that a person or article is on the stage when the curtain is raised or when flats are drawn.

Tag. The closing words uttered by a character or characters in any musical or dramatic performance.

Encore. To repeat by demand of an audience the song, speech, or recitation just given.

Under dress. Means to have a costume for male or female beneath the one in view. This is done to save time and to hurriedly change costume when the part calls for it Often several " under dresses " are necessary.

First Part. Is the initial portion of a minstrel entertainment where the circle is formed with singers, comedians, orchestra and middle man. It generally concludes with a musical comedy or burlesque called a " Finale."

Finale. Means the ending number of the First Part of a minstrel performance. Under this caption local or musical burlesques are introduced.

Olio. This is the portion following the first part or minstrel circle. Under the title of " Olio," all the specialties, sketches, dances, monologues, solos, etc , are grouped, and it marks the division of the entertainment in a vaudeville or minstrel performance.

After-Piece. The concluding numbers of a programme and generally a pretentious burlesque introducing nearly all the company. (See Sec. VIII.)

Interlocutor. Another name for the middle man.

HOW TO PRODUCE STAGE EFFECTS.

COLORED FIRES, THUNDER, LIGHTNING, CRASHES, HORSE, WIND AND RAIN.

ALL the above effects may be used in a minstrel performance, as the Burlesques frequently call for them. Therefore, the young amateur and stage manager should become familiar with each and every "effect" needed. Colored fires are used for Tableaux, Battle Scenes, "House on Fire" and Patriotic or Allegorical Illuminations. They are made of the following ingredients, and can be manufactured by the young amateur or purchased from "Fire Works" stores.* The materials needed can also be had and compounded at any drug store.

RED FIRE.

Strontia,	8 ounces
Potash,	4 ounces
Shellac,	2 ounces
Lycopodium,	¼ ounce

BLUE FIRE.

Nitre,	8 ounces
Sulphur,	3 ounces
Charcoal,	½ ounce
Antimony,	1 ounce

GREEN FIRE.

Nitrate of Barytes,	62½ parts
Sulphur,	10½ parts
Potash,	23½ parts
Orpiment,	1½ parts
Charcoal,	1½ parts

These fires are burned on an ordinary coal shovel or pan, and can be ignited by a quick match, or cotton cord soaked in oil, if a quick match cannot be obtained. Hold the pan over the head as the fire is burning; this will illumine the surroundings much better.

RAIN.

To imitate rain, place a lot of dried peas or almond shells in a long box, so you can tip it up and down like a see-saw. In the bottom of the box nail bits of wood as obstructions. The peas or shells falling over these produce the sound of rain. You can place this box in a hanging position and work it up and down with ropes. Dried peas shaken on the head of a bass drum will also give the desired effect.

WIND.

Bits of old silk drawn over the edges of the bass drum, or a board, will make a whistling sound. This effect is not used very much in minstrelsy.

* See directory at back of cover.

THUNDER.

Suspend long piece of sheet iron from "flies" in first entrance, and shake it vigorously. This will make a good substitute for thunder. Pounding on a bass drum will also give the booming sound of thunder or firing of cannon.

LIGHTNING.

Lightning is furnished by lycopodium. It can be purchased at any drug store. Put the lycopodium into a small box, in the top of which many small holes have been made like that of a pepper box. In the centre of this box is soldered a small cup or receptable, into which cotton soaked with alcohol is placed. This is secured by a bit of wire to keep it from falling out when this box is moved to and fro. At the bottom of this tin box is another tin socket, into which is placed a piece of wood or part of broom stick to serve as a handle A small opening can be made in the side of the box to pour in the lycopodium, and then cork it up. Here is the illustration of what is called a "flash" torch with which lightning is made:

THUNDER EFFECT.

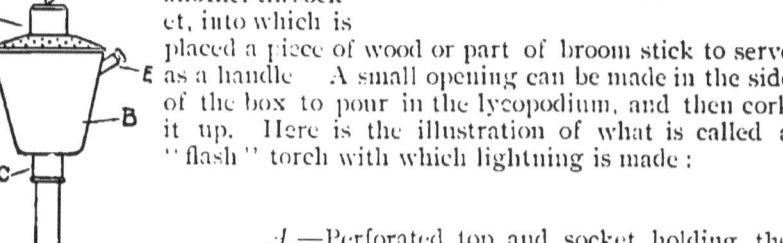

LIGHTNING TORCH.

A.—Perforated top and socket holding the alcohol-soaked cotton.

B.—Bowl or box to hold lycopedium.

C.—Socket to hold the wooden handle.

D.—Handle.

E.—Tube to pour in the lycopodium.

Strike forward with this torch and "lightning" will follow.

GLASS CRASH.

Get a pail filled with broken bottles, glass, old crockery, etc. Empty this into another pail by elevating the pail of crockery quite high and spilling it into the empty one, and *vice versa*, as length of crash is required.

WOOD CRASH.

WOOD CRASH.

Numerous bits of old lumber thrown violently down will produce a "wood crash." Sometimes it is constructed like a large "rattle" and turned by a crank. This is arranged on an upright or a frame, and is very effective in imitating a terrific crashing or the fall of some one. See cut.

RAILROAD EFFECT.

Take a piece of sheet-iron and place it upon a small table or box, then beat upon it with two "whips" of wires fashioned like egg-beaters. Beat a tattoo upon the sheet-iron and by a little practice you can easily imitate a train at full speed or slowing up. The "whistle" can be made by an "organ pipe" or by the voice.

HORSE EFFECTS.

The clattering of hoofs, announcing the rapid approach of a horse, is a very effective trick, and by a little practice can be done in a manner to imitate a horse galloping in the distance and drawing nearer and nearer, or *vice versa*.

A small oaken or maple board about a foot and a half long and a foot wide, suspended in front of the person by a strap, will serve as the "table." Upon this you beat with two round or oblong pieces of maple, to which are attached little straps, for the purpose of giving the hands a secure hold upon them. With little practice this effect can be readily accomplished.

HORSE EFFECTS.

A LIST OF STAGE DON'TS.

A GOOD IDEA FOR THE STAGE MANAGER IS TO HAVE THIS READ TO
THE COMPANY OCCASIONALLY; MORE FREQUENTLY WHEN
NEARING THE PERFORMANCE.

Don't cross your legs in the "first part."

Don't make visible efforts to recognize your friends out front.   Remember that it spoils the picture.

Don't fail to watch the musical director in all chorus work.

Don't speak to your neighbor while sitting in the first part unless it is absolutely necessary.

Don't keep the stage waiting; rather be at the theatre or hall an hour earlier than a minute late.

Don't sit forlorn looking or with a bored expression upon your face. Look pleasant and enjoy what is being said and done without being too demonstrative.

Don't be eager to suggest or try to *teach* the stage manager his business.

Don't think you are the whole show.   There *may* be twenty others in the same circle.

Don't grumble, because you haven't the best parts.   Remember that while everybody cannot play "first violin" in the orchestra, *everybody* is important in a minstrel show.

Don't look slovenly or careless in your attire.   Very Important.

Don't pull out your watch (if you have one) to note the length of time.   That will be regulated by the stage manager.

Don't interfere in any way with the rehearsals, if a bright thought strikes you; wait and suggest it later on.

Don't turn around and giggle if anybody makes a mistake or a string breaks on an instrument.   You wouldn't like to be laughed at in public, would you?

Don't have any friends or outsiders present at a rehearsal.   This should be strictly enforced.

Don't pass remarks about any thing in the course of rehearsals or when a person is striving to learn a part.   Remember, we can't all be as smart as you are?

Don't smoke, Gentlemen, on any part of the stage.

Don't leave the stage unless it is your duty or necessary to do so.

Don't expectorate upon the stage, Gentlemen.   During performance carry 'kerchiefs for that purpose, and lastly ;

Don't monopolize *all* the hooks, nails and space in the dressing rooms.

NOVEL INNOVATIONS IN FIRST PARTS.

THERE are a number of ideas advanced in this book that have never been published nor produced elsewhere. At considerable expense, thought and many months of labor, these brilliant first parts are arranged in this work and given to the amateur minstrel for the first time in the history of stage publications. In connection with these first parts we present illustrations that will aid those desiring to take advantage of these novelties in arranging their pictures, costumes. scenery and general grouping of each innovation, remembering, however, that these are *only suggestions* and need not be strictly adhered to, as there are unlimited possibilities to elaborate upon.

Another very important item is the sample programme which accompanies each First Part of this book, suggesting the songs, (which can be had of the publishers), olio specialties and after-pieces of the evening's entertainment. The first we offer is entitled "Our Navy."

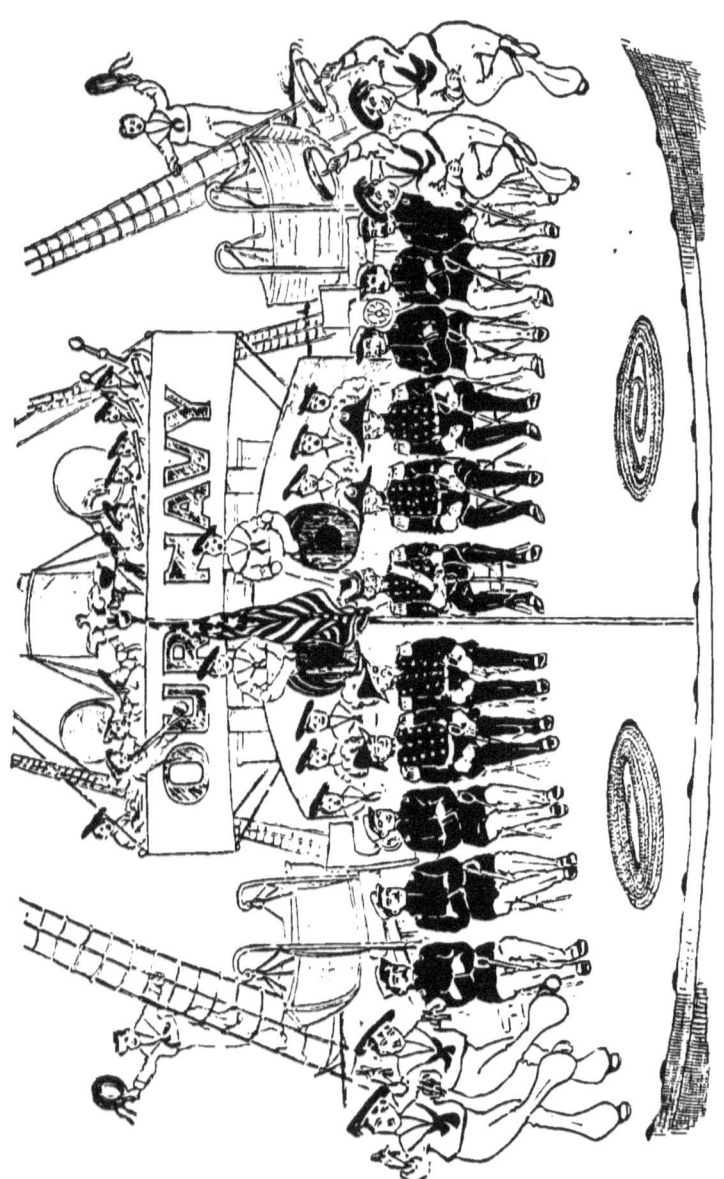

"OUR NAVY." (FIRST PART.)

PICTORIAL FIRST PARTS.

"OUR NAVY."—FIRST PART.

(See Illustration.)

Scene represents the deck of one of Uncle Sam's Cruisers or Battle-ships. Horizon at back. The wings are painted to represent the rigging leading up to a mast and a part of the bulwarks of the vessel. The officers, gunners and crew form the circle of the "First Part," which can be seated upon platforms as used for interior scenes. The middleman is the "Admiral," the singers are the officers, the endmen are "rapid-fire" gunners. All are dressed according to uniforms worn in the United States Navy.

NOTE.—This first effective in either white or black face.

PLAN OF FIRST PART.

o   o   o   o   o   o   o   o

Orchestra   o   Leader.

Men Behind the Guns.

o   o   o   o   o   o   o   o   o

Admiral.
o

Bass.   Baritone.   (Mr. Dewey Shootwell.)   2d Tenor.   1st Tenor.

Officers. o o   o o   Officers.

Extra Singers.   ooo   ooo   Extra Singers.

"Rapid-Fire" Gunners. o o   o o   "Rapid-Fire" Gunners.

OPENING CHORUS—"The Witmark Minstrel Overture," . . . . "OUR NAVY" MINSTRELS
SYNOPSIS.—1. Curtain Raiser. 2. Introductory, Bones and Tambos. 3. Opening Ensemble. 4. "Anvil Chorus" (Trovatore). 5. Waltz Song, "Mary." 6. Drinking Song. 7. "My Dainty Cigarette." 8. Sleighing Chorus. 9. Whistling and Humming Interlude. 10. Coon Refrain. 11. Finale.

Sea Song—"Bounding," . . . . .Mr. R. U. Warbling
Neat End Specialty—"Willie off the Yacht," . . . . Gunner Smith
Bass Song—"Deep, Down Deep," . . . . .Mr. Campanari Roberts
Coon Song—"Mandy from Mandalay," . . . . .Ragtime Gumper
Waltz Song—"Sweet, Sweet Love," . . . . .Mr. Vocal Chords
Comic Novelty—"She Knew a Lobster When She Saw One," . . . . Gunner Rigging
Ballad—"In Fancy You Are Ever By My Side," . . . . .Mr. Retrospect
Drinking Song—"We'll Drown It in the Bowl," . . . . .Rear-Admiral Ofomnies
Song and Refrain—"Where is My Boy To-Night?" . . . . .Mr. Bowsprit
Negro Shout—"Ram-a-Jam," . . . . .Gunner Boozy
The Intensely Amusing Finale, "THE WONDERFUL TELEPHONE," or a Long Distance Experiment, by Admiral Shootwell, Gunner Jenkins and Gunner Smokeless.

PART II.

OLLA PODRIDA OF NOVELTIES.—The Celebrated Musical Experts,

PLINK and PLUNK,

In their laughable interlude, called "The Musical Convicts," playing on many known and unknown instruments, depicting the pleasant life of jail birds, if "Harmony prevails."

DECK ORATION.—BOATSWAIN WINDY GUFF,

Reviewing the exploits of heroes, past and present (Section VII.), also the fads and follies of the times.

"THE MEN BEHIND THE GUNS."—MESSRS. SHELL and DYNAMITE.

In a laughable melange of up-to-date happenings, wise and otherwise. (Can be made up of matter contained in Sections VI. and VII.).

PICTURE SONGS.

Beautiful Views Illustrating the Popular Ballads, "A Letter from Ohio," "Gold Cannot Buy a Love Like Mine," etc., sung and introduced by MR. R. U. WARBLING.
(For list of Illustrated Songs and particulars, see Directory.)

Concluding with the Laughable Burlesque,

"A PLEASANT EVENING."

(See Section IX.)

Another good terminating burlesque would be "THE LOBSTERSCOPE." (See Section X.)

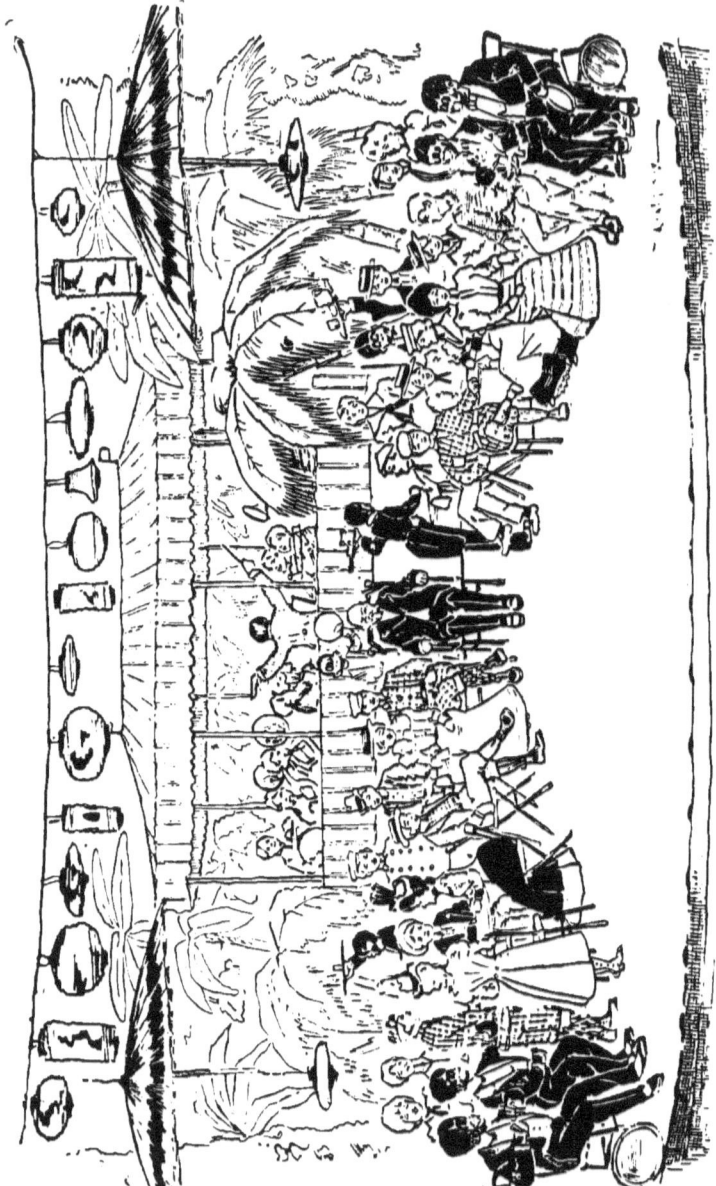

"THE LAWN PARTY." (FIRST PART.)

"THE LAWN PARTY."

Scene represents a garden brilliantly illuminated. (See illustration.) Part of a mansion L. U. E. can be shown. Place a number of shrubs, plants, etc., in tubs about the stage, and here and there some grass mats. Use camp chairs for vocalists, rustic chair for middle man, wooden chairs for the endmen, who are supposed to be the waiters or household servants. In this circle can be placed several ladies in order to get the chorus effect of mixed voices. The costumes can be handsome golf or bicycle dresses, with here and there an outdoor costume of colors. The endmen can dress in the regulation evening dress suits. The Telephone Finale or the Shadow Pantomime can be introduced to bring the First Part to a climax. If you select the Shadow Pantomime, use a front scene in order to get your "sheet" and lights ready. Here the vocal corps will render selections in the front scene in order to prepare the pantomime.

Extra Singers on the
o   Porch or Veranda.

The Guests.   The Host.   o
    o   o   o
o   o   o   o
Singers.   Middleman.   The Guests.   o
o   o   o   o
                                       o   o
                                          o   o
                                       Singers.
                                          o

Bones.—Attendants.   o   Waiters.—Tambos.
o   o
    o   o   o
        o   o

PROGRAMME.—PART I.

OPENING CHORUS—"The Witmark Minstrel Overture," . . . . . . LAWN PARTY MINSTRELS

SYNOPSIS.—1. Curtain Raiser. 2. Introductory, Bones and Tambos. 3. Opening Ensemble. 4. "Anvil Chorus," (Trovatore). 5. Waltz Song, "Mary." 6. Drinking Song. 7. "My Dainty Cigarette." 8. Sleighing Chorus. 9. Whistling and Humming Interlude. 10. Coon Refrain. 11. Finale.

Soprano Solo—"Don't Ask Me to Forget." . . . . Miss High C

Coon Song—"I'm the Warmest Member in the Land," . . . . Waiter Rufus

Song and Chorus—"When you were Sweet Sixteen," . . . . Mr. Uppertone

End Song—"Tell It to Me," . . . . Attendant Sam

Harmonized Ensemble, with half darkened stage—" My Little, 'Lasses Candy Coon,"
Solo by Miss So and So

Dialect Shout—"I Love Ma Little Honey," . . . . Waiter Ephraim

Dashing March Song—" Miss Divinity," . .   ' ' . . . . Miss Flighty

Baritone Solo—"Because," . . . . Mr. Voche

Ethiopian Novelty—"You Got to Play Rag Time." . . . . Attendant Jim

Ballad—"Just as the Daylight was Breaking," . . . . Mr. Great Solo

Mixed Quartette—"Some Day You Shall Know" . . . . { Misses High C and Round Tone
                                                         { Messrs. Velvety and Smooth.

NOTE.—Drop sheet after Quartette are announced and introduced or when "chord" is played by musicians.

Finale—"THE WONDERFUL TELEPHONE."

PART II.—"Mixed Pickles."

Select from our Monologues, Sketches, etc., for this Olio.

To terminate the bill "THE CAKE-WALK," "A PLEASANT EVENING," or "ILL TREATED TROVATORE," will be found very effective, as they can be played by ladies or gentlemen. (See Sections VIII., IX. and X.)

"OUR BOYS IN CAMP." (FIRST PART.)

"OUR BOYS IN CAMP."
A MILITARY FIRST PART.

Scene represents an encampment on the banks of a river, or use a bright landscape. An effect can be gained by not using the raised platforms, thus showing a number of tents painted on the scene; plenty of guns stacked, drums, campfire, etc., to give it a realistic effect. (See page illustration.) The Middleman is the Colonel commanding; the Staff Officers are represented by the vocalists; the End Men are the Rough Riders. The entire First Part can be in white face, except the End Men, and all should be in military uniform.

Orchestra.

o o o o o o o o o o o o o o

Guns Stacked.	Extras.	Middleman.	Extras.	Guns Stacked.
X X X X	000	o	000	X X X X
Officers.	Major.	Colonel.	Major.	Officers.
o o o o o	o	o	o	o o o o o

Rough Riders.—Bones.   Rough Riders.—Tambos.
      o o   o o

PROGRAMME.—PART I.

OVERTURE AND OPENING CHORUS—"Off to Camp,"........ ....OUR BOYS
    N. B.—Baton juggling can be introduced here, if one of the Company is proficient
          in that direction.
Coon War Song—"Lazy Bill," ....Rastus Hash
Ballad—"Sing Me a Song of the South,"......................George Cartridge
End Song—"Hats off to the Boys Who Made Good,"...........Soup Ferguson
Bass Solo—"At the Sound of the Sunset Gun,"... ....Spencer Griflat
Mock Ballad—"A Large Front Room on Broadway,"................Hava Shot
Descriptive Song—"Just as the Sun Went Down,".................Fast Retreat
Ethiopian Medley—"Witmark Coon Songs,"....... ....Pepper and Salt
Song Novelty—"The Little Tin Soldier Army,"....... .... Onthe March
"THE DARKEY CAVALIERS,"—Military Finale.................Entire Company
    N. B.—Stage Manager can arrange an appropriate drill for this.

PART II.—"Picket Varieties."

Select from our Monologues, Musical Act or Individual Sketches to make up this Olio. Sections VII., VIII., IX.

To conclude with the roaring Military Burlesque entitled,
"THE WAR CORRESPONDENT."
See cast and full description Section IX.

BERT COBB

"OUR GIRL GRADUATES." (FIRST PART.)

"OUR GIRL GRADUATES."

This First Part is arranged for ladies. You can use the platforms and the diagrams for stage setting as shown in the previous First Parts. (See illustration for appropriate scene.) All wear the collegian mortar-board hats and gowns. The ladies acting as the "End Men," or "Terrors" of the school, and principal can wear the same in white, or add large collars, white vests and small dress coats over their gowns. The musicians can wear the same in another color; red would make a bright effect. A very humorous Finale will be found in "Girls at School," as it is arranged for female minstrels, in this collection. The Shadow Pantomime, to terminate the performance, will be found easy for lady amateurs, and especially "funny," as it keeps the audience guessing as to the identity of the performers seen in silhouette attitudes. For ladies' minstrels, would advise a piano in orchestra.

Orchestra.

o o o o o o o o

Principal.

o

Students.   Students.

o o o o   o o o o

Bones.—Terrors.   Terrors.—Tambos.
o o   o o

PROGRAMME.—PART I.

OVERTURE—"The Witmark Minstrel Overture," GIRL GRADUATE MINSTRELS
SYNOPSIS.—1. Curtain Raiser. 2. Introductory, Bones and Tambos. 3. Opening Ensemble. 4. "Anvil Chorus" (Trovatore). 5. Waltz Song, "Mary." 6. Drinking Song. 7. "My Dainty Cigarette." 8. Sleighing Party. 9. Whistling and Humming Interlude. 10. Coon Refrain. 11. Finale.

Ballad—"Always," . . . . Miss Vassar
Southern Lullaby—"Honey Little Black Boy Dan," . . . Miss Wildy
Song and Refrain—"Open Your Mouth and Shut Your Eyes," . Miss Normal
End Song—"I Won't Play Second Fiddle to No Yaller Gal," . Miss Noisey
Waltz Song—"Only a Dream," . . . . Miss Student
Comic March Song—"Cinderella," . . . . . . Miss Shouter
Contralto Solo—"Just as the Tide Went Out," . . . Miss Lowvoice
Swell Coon Song, introducing Cake Walk—"My High Stepping Lady,"
Misses Picture and Pose
Song—"The Turn of the Road," . . . . . . Miss Solemnity
Oriental Novelty—"Two Little Japanese Dolls," . . . Miss Spouter
Quartette—{ a. Zenda Waltz Song, . . . } Misses Tone, Melody
{ b. "Mammy," } and the Sisters Harmony

——: FINALE :——

"GIRLS AT SCHOOL." See Section VIII.

PART II.—"Examination Day."

Select from our long list of timely Speeches, Sketches, Monologues, etc., to make up this Olio, closing with the Scenes in Shadowland, "FROLICS IN THE MOON," or "THE LOBSTERSCOPE." See Section X.

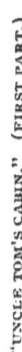

"UNCLE TOM'S CABIN." (FIRST PART.)

"UNCLE TOM'S CABIN."

SCENE—Represents a cotton field, landscape or river scene. Orchestra is composed of " field hands " and seated on platform. Directly in front of them are female cotton pickers or "shouters." Then comes the Circle in which Simon Legree is the Middleman. The three " End Men " on each side are represented by Topsy. Marks the lawyer. and Aunt Ophelia. To Legree's left are George St. Clair, Deacon Parry, The Major and Eliza. To his right are Uncle Tom, Phineas Fletcher, Sambo and Cassie, house servants. A little girl to represent " Eva " can be announced and sing a ballad during first part to make it effective and introduce the character.

```
                         Orchestra.
            o  o  o  o  o  o  o  o  o  o  o
                    Female Cotton Pickers.
          o  o  o  o  o          o  o  o  o
                      Simon Legree.       .
                           o
            Uncle Tom.   o      o   George St. Clair.
    Phineas Fletcher.    o      o   Deacon Parry.
         Sambo.       o              o   The Major.
    Cassie.        o                      o   Eliza.
  Ophelia.    o ⎫                      ⎧ o      Ophelia.
  Marks.    o   ⎬ Ends.        Ends. ⎨   o      Marks.
Topsy.    o     ⎭                      ⎩        Topsy.
```

NOTE.—Would suggest to give the names of the cast with the names of the participants, as is done on a regular programme of the dramatic production, viz.:

CAST.

(Here substitute real names.)

Uncle Tom	Ben Johnson.
Simon Legree	Chas. Hartway.
St. Clair	Fred. Dwight.
George Harris	John See.
Eliza Harris	Laura King.
The Major	Sam Lightfoot.
Deacon Parry	Tom Jeffreys.
Cassie	Sarah Joyce.
Sambo	Cal. Tompkins.
Topsys	(Bones) Sally Smith, (Tambo) Maud Glenn.
Marks	(Bones) Joe Jones, (Tambo) Jack Norman.
Ophelias	(Bones) Clara Brown, (Tambo) Caddie Booth.
Little Eva	Baby Spencer

PROGRAMME.—PART I.

OPENING CHORUS—"The Witmark Minstrel Overture," . . . Entire Company and Orchestra
Synopsis : 1. Curtain Raiser. 2. Introductory—Bones and Tambos 3. Opening Ensemble. 4. Anvil Chorus (Trovatore), 5. Waltz Song ("Mary "). 6. Drinking Song. 7. "My Dainty Cigarette." 8. Sleighing Chorus. 9. Whistling and Humming Interlude. 10. Coon Refrain. 11. Finale.

End Song—"Home was Never Like This,"	Marks Jones
Ballad—"The Girl I Left in Dixie Waits for Me,"	St. Clair
Comic Song—"Miss Cadenza Brown,"	Ophelia Booth
Bass Solo—"Laugh and the World Laughs With You,"	Uncle Tom
Coon Song—"Who Dat Say Chicken in Dis Crowd?"	Topsy Smith

Introduction of Little Eva.

Song—"My Sunday Dolly,"	Little Eva
Mock Ballad—"Honest John Jones,"	Marks Norman
Waltz Ballad—"She is so Good to the Old Folks,"	Phineas Fletcher
Serio-Comic Song—"Just Suppose,"	Ophelia Brown
Song—"Paint Me a Picture of the Old Fireside,"	Eliza Harris
Humorous Ditty—"Best Dressed Gal in Town,"	Topsy Glenn
Female Ensemble—"Honey Dat I Lub So Well,"	Cotton Pickers
Finale—"Cake-Walk in the Sky,"	Company

A short finale can effectively be made of the song, "Cake-Walk in the Sky," by having the Topsys exit while the Cotton Pickers are singing, don paper crowns, pin on a large pair of paper wings each and re-enter to refrain. Others can also participate in a general cake-walk.
A feature can be made by the introduction of two or four half-dressed pickaninnies, who are also fixed up with wings. etc. They naturally would lead the cake-walk, the curtain dropping as the walkers exit singing.

PART II.—" Plantation Pastimes."

As mentioned in other programmes selections can be made from the various sections to conclude with, either " THE DARKTOWN CAKE-WALK," " WAR CORRESPONDENT" or "PLEASANT EVENING."

"CONGRESS OF ALL NATIONS." (FIRST PART.)

"CONGRESS OF ALL NATIONS."

SCENE—Handsome interior or conservatory. Representatives of all nations are seated right and left of Uncle Sam, who acts as Middleman or Interlocutor. To Uncle Sam's left will be seen a Frenchman, Spaniard, German, Chinaman and Kaffir. These are vocalists. The end men on the left—an Irishman and a Scotchman—use tambourines. To Uncle Sam's right are "John Bull" (Englishman), Russian, Turk, Esquimaux and Indian—also vocalists. The end men (Bones) are a negro and a Japanese. The orchestra is seated at back. Costumes are shown in the engraving, and a huge flag with Dewey's portrait hangs over the assemblage.

```
                          Orchestra.
          o  o  o  o   o  o  o  o  o   o  o  o  o
                        Uncle Sam.
                            o
             Englishman.  o        o  Frenchman.
             Russian.    o          o  Spaniard.
              Turk.    o              o  German.
           Esquimaux. o                o  Chinaman.
         Indian.    o                    o  Kaffir.
       Japanese.  o  }                   Ends. { o  Scotchman.
       Negro.    o   } Ends.                    { o  Irishman.
```

PROGRAMME.—PART I.

OPENING ANTHEM—"God Save America,"	ENTIRE CONGRESS
Celtic Humorosity—"The Jack Pot," . .	. . . . Pat
Serenade—"Adios Amor,"	Spanish Representative
Scotch Philosophy—"The Change will Do You Good,"	. . . Sandy
Chinese Episode—"Yung Go Wap," . . .	. Jap
Stirring Martial Song—"How a Man Can Die,"	. . John Bull
Bass Song—"Gypsy Love Song,"	Russian Representative
Barbaric Wooing Ballad—"A Cannibal King," .	Kaffir Representative
A Parisian Romance—"Grisette," . .	French Representative
Negro Love Ballad—"I Want My Hannah,"	Sambo

Any of the finales can be used.

A good finale to this first part would also be a medley of popular and patriotic songs. (See Directory.) At the climax all rise and wave small American flags. "Goddess of Liberty" can enter from L. or R. with large flag and stand C. Colored fire will enhance this tableau. All nations salute as curtain descends.

PART II.—"International Fete."

Appropriate numbers can be culled from all the sections to make up a suitable programme for this part. A number of original tableaux and interpolations can also be added. For a concluding number either of the SHADOWGRAPHS or "ILL-TREATED TROVATORE" can effectively be used.

"SHAKESPEARIAN CARNIVAL." (FIRST PART.)

" SHAKESPEARIAN CARNIVAL."

All characters assume the costumes and peculiarities of Shakespeare's characters. The middle man represents " Falstaff." The singers are costumed as " Hamlet," "Othello," " Macbeth," "Henry the Fourth," "Shylock," "Two Gentlemen of Verona," "Richard the Third," etc. The end men are the " Dromios" and " King's Jesters." The young amateur can gain correct ideas of these costumes from the engravings in the illustrated editions of Shakespeare. Scene represents the market-place of an ancient town.

Orchestra.
o o o o o o o o o o o

Middle man—Falstaff.
o
Othello.   o   o   Richard the Third.
Henry the Fourth.   o   o   Hamlet.
Shylock   o   o   Two Gentlemen
Macbeth.   o   o   of Verona.
King's Jester.   o⎫   o   King's Jester.
Dromio.   o ⎬ Ends—Bones.   Ends—Tambos. ⎬ o
                                          o   Dromio.

CAST.
(Here substitute real names.)

Falstaff . . . . Sam Kirwin
Othello . . . . Ed. Kemble
Shylock . . . . Jos. O'Hare
Hamlet . . . . Fred Donor
Henry the Fourth . . . . Howard Espey
Richard the Third . . . . Billee Young
Macbeth . . . . Jas. Warren
Two Gentlemen of Verona . . . . Brothers Putnam
Jesters—(Bones) Eddie Shayne . . . . (Tambo) Bobbie Webb
Dromios—(Bones) Charlie Case . . . . (Tambo) Silas Wright

PROGRAMME.—PART I.

THE WITMARK OVERTURE . . . . CIRCLE

SYNOPSIS:—1, Curtain Raiser; 2, Introductory—Bones and Tambos; 3, Opening Ensemble; 4, Anvil Chorus (Trovatore); 5, Waltz Song, "Mary"; 6, Drinking Song; 7, "My Dainty Cigarette"; 8, Sleighing Chorus; 9, Whistling and Humming Interlude; 10, Coon Refrain; 11, Finale.

Ballad—" Song of the Helmet," . . . . Macbeth
Comic Ditty—" In Dear Old London," . . . . Jester Shayne
Song—" Since That Day," . . . . Shylock
Humorosity—" The Touch of a Woman's Hand," . . . . Dromio Wright
Duet—" Think Once Again before We Part," . . . . Two Gentlemen of Verona
End Song—" The Birds They Sang So Sweetly," . . . . Jester Webb
Solo—" Forevermore," . . . . Othello
Ethiopian Effusion—" I'm Dreaming of You, Baby," . . . . Dromio Case

Finale—The Burlesque Operatic Scene,

ILL-TREATED TROVATORE.

NOTE.—In order to introduce this properly, a short front scene must be introduced so as to set the stage after clearing away the platforms. Have the sextette of singers introduce aria from " Lucia," or " Cavaleria Rusticana," or a series of vocal medleys, then open the scene to " Ill-Treated Trovatore."

CAST.

Maurice, the imprisoned lover.
Lenora.
The Count.
The Sentry.
Servant.

Opera-struck ruffians by rest of Company.

PART II.—Selected Novelties.

To be selected from the various sections, as per previous programmes, or, as is often the case, the olio can be given by outside entertainers, either amateur or professional.
Conclude with " THE WAR CORRESPONDENTS," or any other after-piece, sketch, etc., that is most adaptable.

Section U.

FOR THE LADIES.

GREAT care has been taken in compiling material suitable for the lady amateurs, also to include suggestions of great importance for them. The matter of "blacking up" is one of annoyance if not properly undertaken by the novice. It would be best for the ladies to be entirely dressed with the exception of the *waists*—and have some one person appointed (professional preferred)* to blacken the features of the entire circle. This will enable them to have unsoiled hands to complete their dressing. Where parties prefer to "blacken up" themselves, some valuable suggestions relative to this can be found in the article called "How to Black Up," in Section I. A very important item is the selecting of material, such as the coon songs, ballads, ensembles, jokes, anecdotes and recitations. The conundrums are especially adapted for lady amateurs, as they go with a better snap and vim than extended stories.

The speeches, monologues and poems are also an important item for the comic element of a minstrel performance, the monologues and stump-speeches being especially good for the "olio." A choice collection is arranged for ladies, who can use their own judgment in selecting the subjects and topics, trying, of course, to present a variety that should be somewhat different from the other "end men" use.

This discourse to the ladies could be extended to untold lengths, but in doing so it would cause repetition. As space is too valuable for this, "Miss Minstrel" is especially referred to Sections I., II. and III., although it will be a *minstrel education* for her to read every section of this work. Don't overlook the "*Don'ts!*" in Section III.

The following has been carefully compiled, and specially arranged for the ladies. (As these gags are also related by gentlemen, a number of words and terms used by them can be modified by the ladies at their own discretion, they remembering, however, that it is essential to preserve the point of each story.)

SECTION VI.

"Eating and Drinking."
"War Cries of our Soldiers."
"Piano Playing."
"Peculiar Wants."

---

* Lady interlocutors and stage managers will find important instructions for the middle man and stage manager in Section III. that are just right for them; allowing, of course, for a few changes and modifications which they can readily make to suit their own purposes.

"Letters in Post-office."
"Where they Ought to Go."
"Ship is Like a Woman."
"Two Black Boot-blacks."
"How to Pronounce Tomatoes."
"Gambler's Wife."
"Coincidences of Married Life."
"Girls—Girls—Girls."
"All About Cards."
"Planting Flowers."
"About Umbrellas"
"Literary Curiosities."
"Reciting at a Party."

SECTION VII.

"The Mouse."
"Little Girl's Composition on Eggs."
"Mary's Lamb" (in Boston.)
"Squibs and Poems."
"Conundrums."
"Musical Instruments."
"Maud Muller at the Matinee."

SECTION VIII.

"THE DARKTOWN CAKE WALK" contains a number of characters for ladies, and is adaptable where ladies and gentlemen both take part.

"THE TELEPHONE" can be performed by ladies, the two end men appearing as telephone girls, and slight changes could be made in the dialogue, omitting "segars" and substituting "bonnets" or "candy"; in fact, represent it from a feminine point of view, still retaining the "Brother in England" idea.

"OUR GIRLS AT SCHOOL" is written expressly for ladies, and all characters are assigned to females.

SECTION IX.

"THE WAR CORRESPONDENT" contains a female character which can be played by a lady in a mixed performance. "A Pleasant Evening" affords chances to introduce several *extra ladies* at beginning to ask for "rooms" and be assigned to them. There is also a good part for lady in a mixed performance of this skit by ladies and gentlemen.

"IL TROVATORE" contains a female part, *Lenora*, which can be played and sung by a lady in a mixed performance.

SECTION X.

"SHADOW PANTOMIMES." Ladies can participate in a mixed performance of these pantomimes, as there are numerous female characters in them.

END GAGS AND CROSS-FIRES.

THE TWO BLACK BOOT-BLACKS.

(To be recited without hesitation.)

One day a black boot-black sat in the chair of another black boot-black, to have his boots blacked by the black boot-black. The black boot-black started to black the black boots of the black boot-black, and when he had one boot blacked of the black boot-black, the black boot-black who had his boot blacked by his fellow black boot-black said: "I merely sat in your chair for a joke." This enraged the black boot-black who had blacked the one boot of the black boot-black; and a few words passed between them. The black boot-black, who had his black boot blacked by the black boot-black, booted the black boot-black, with the very boot the black boot-black had blacked. The other black boot-black then blacked the black boot-black's eye and the black boot-black, who had his black boots blacked by the other black boot-black, just looked black, and this is the blackest lie that ever happened.

PECULIAR WANTS.

END—Have you seen our new paper? It's called the "Weekly Scandalizer." In politics, "we're on the fence." You ought to see the advertisements in the want column. No other city on earth would want such crazy things.

MIDDLE — Let me hear some of your wants.

END—(Opens paper and reads.)

Wanted—

A barber to shave the *face of the earth*.
A bed for a *tick of a clock*.
A timekeeper for a *mill race*.
A sure cure for a *pig's stye*.
A carpenter to put a roof on a *water shed*.
A charter for a *snow bank*.
Agents to handle the *spice of life*.
Some one to spin a *mountain top*.
A tonsorial artist to shampoo the *head of a river*.
A detective to unravel a *grass plot*.
A doctor to cure a *window pain*.
An audience to see a *horse fly*
A nurse maid to *rock the cradle of the deep*.
A key to a *fire lock*.
A comb for a *low head*.
A singer who can reach the *high seas*.
A man to find traces of a *lost harness*.
A lawyer to try a *watch case*.
A tailor to take the measure of a *suit for libel*.
A sign language for a *dumb waiter*.
Some use for a *dog's pants*
A pair of handcuffs for procrastination, *the thief of time*.
A hand to go with an *arm of the sea*.
A necklace for a *neck of land*.

Some buttons for a *coat of paint.*
A pump for a well *spring of information.*
A commander to take charge of a *courtship.*
A machine to thrash *wild oats.*
A harness-maker to build a harness for a *night mare.*
A thousand skippers to take charge of a *head of cheese.*
And wanted, "A girl to cook," oh! the cannibals. But here's the daisy:
" Two old maids want washing." *Turn the hose on them, quick!*

ABOUT OUR FIREMEN.

END—Our firemen are great fellows and are not afraid of anything, are they? They're not afraid of being " *roasted.*"
MIDDLE—No, sir ; where danger is thickest you'll find the noble firemen.
END—Too bad about Bill Gluckerson, wasn't it? He was a fireman and was in that boiler explosion. He was scalded to death. I wrote his epitaph.
MID—You did? What was it?
END—I put on his monument, " *To our 'steamed friend!*" Then there was Tom Ladders; he was a fireman, and when he died I wrote an epitaph for his monument. I put on it, " *Gone to his last fire.*" That was quite a severe fire we had three weeks ago, wasn't it? A musician who lived next door to us lost his violin in the fire.
MID—Did he?
END—Yes ; none of the firemen *could play on it!* Girls love a fireman, don't they?
MID—I dare say they do, for their bravery.
END—Yes, indeed, they can *spark* most any girl! Do you remember Mollie Cinders?
MID—Yes.
END—She's an old *flame* of mine.
MID—You don't say so.
END—Yes, but her father *smoked* me out. He actually turned the *hose* on me. He made it very *hot* for me. He was a great reader of novels. Are you familiar with the popular writers, past and present?
MID—Oh, yes, I'm quite a reader myself
END—What names of writers would you use to express your opinion on seeing a big fire?
MID—I really cannot mention them.
END—Why! you'd exclaim " Dickens " " Howett " " Burns !" This city ought to be reprimanded. Our firemen try to be temperance men and to shun strong drink, but this city will eventually make drunken Indians of every fireman.
MID—And why will it?
END—Because the city furnishes them with plenty of *fire water.*

ALL ABOUT DOGS.

MIDDLE—By the way, what is your brother doing at present?
END—Oh, he's doing a *corking* good business. He's working in a bottling establishment and he's *corking* bottles. He fell in love with the cruelest girl in the city. When she refused him and he said he couldn't live without her, she handed him the card of the *undertaker* she is engaged to. Wasn't that mean?
MID—Say, while I remember it, you sold me a bird dog You swindled me. I went out gunning, took that bird dog with me and he wouldn't touch a bird.
END—I forgot to tell you, you've got to *cook* the birds for him.
MID—Now, speaking of dogs—
END—How's your brother?
MID—Never mind my brother. I am about to make a present of a dog to a friend of mine, but don't know what breed or style of dog to give him.

END—That's easy ; I can tell you just the kind of dog if I know his business. There are dogs to suit all trades. For instance, a man who follows the races and gives you tips ought to have a *Pointer.* A man who is instructing a base ball team, a *Coach* dog. See how easy it is !

MID —What kind of a dog would you give a detective?
END—*Spotted Dog.*
MID—A balloonist?
END—*Skye Terrier.*
MID—A Prohibitionist?
END—A *Water Spaniel.*
MID—Butcher?
END—A *Bloodhound,* or any old sausage dog !
MID—A person who is learning to sing?
END—A *Yeller Dog.*
MID—A lazy man ?
END—A *Setter.*
MID—Colored people ?
END—*Black and Tans.*
MID—Irishman making mistakes ?
END—*Bull Dog.*
MID—Young lady who sits on her admirer's knees?
END—*Lap dog.*
MID—Dudes?
END—*Poodles and puppies.*
MID—Old colored man ?
END—*Coon dog.*
MID—Tobacco chewers?
END—*Spitz.*
MID—A dog for me and to match my nose?
END—An ugly *Pug.*

BICYCLE RIDERS' ALPHABET.

END—There's been all kinds of alphabets, but up to the present time they have ignored U's completely.
MIDDLE—U's? Whom do you mean?
END—We bike riders ! I've composed a bike riders' alphabet, and I'll just throw it at you.

A is the *Amateur* learning to ride.
B is the *Bicycle* he gets astride.
C is the *Cropper* he takes with a thud.
D is the *Ditch* where he lands in the mud.
E is the *Energy* he does display.
F is the *Fall* he gets right away.
G is the *Gearing* he talks right along.
H is the *Help* that he needs to "get on."
I is the *Injury* he will receive.
J is for *Junkman* who laughs in his sleeve.
K is for *Kicking* he does with his might.
L is the *Lamp* he forgot to light.
M is for *Mash.* Can I by you ride?
N is for *Nit* that she quickly replied.
O is for *Owe* that you owe on your bike.
P is for *Puncture.* Walk home on the pike.
Q is for *Question.* How did you do it?
R is *Remark* of the friend that "he knew it."
S is for *Scorcher* you thought to admire.
T is the *Tack* that "busted " your tire.
U is for "*Uncertainty*" on all thoroughfares.

V is the "*V*" that you pay for repairs.
W is the *Wheel* that you chop with an axe.
X is the "*Xtra*" blow when dealing the whacks.
Y is the *Youth* who advised you to "bike."
Z is the *Zip* with which his jaw you do strike.

Then you go to bed
And you lay like one dead,
And for nearly six months
"You've got wheels in your head."

ABOUT UMBRELLAS.

END—I lost a beautiful silk umbrella yesterday.
MIDDLE—Did you leave it anywhere?
END—No, the man that owned it came along and took it out of my hand. I hear that they are going to make *square* umbrellas.
MID—Umbrellas in square shape. What is that for?
END—So you won't leave them *round*. Did you ever notice how people carry umbrellas? Of course, you've heard of the handkerchief flirtation. Well, umbrellas tell the story of the people who carry them.
MID—Give me a similé.
END—For instance, if you see a man with an umbrella, and he's very careful of it, keeps his eye on it all the time; that's a sign he's just acquired it and is afraid of losing it himself. If you see a couple going along the street, and he carries the umbrella in such a way that she is thoroughly protected and *he* gets all the rain down his neck and over his new clothes; that's a sign that they are courting. They're in love!
MID—Yes?
END—And if he carries the umbrella so *she* gets soaking wet, and the umbrella covers him; why, they're *married*.
MID—Suppose it isn't his wife?
END—Then I'll bet ten dollars *it's his mother-in-law*.

GIRLS! GIRLS! GIRLS!

END—My brother has a matrimonial agency! Come around if you want to get married. He'll pick out a good wife for you.
MIDDLE—Thank you. I'm afraid he could not select a wife to suit me.
END—He's got all kinds. He can tell you just what they are and how good they are by their names.
MID—By their names only?
END—Yes, their characters and dispositions. For instance:
A good girl to have, *Sal Vation*. A disagreeable girl, *Annie Mosity*. A fighting girl, *Hittie Maginn*. A sweet girl, *Carrie Mel*. A very pleasant girl, *Jennie Rosity*.
MID—How about a stylish girl?
END—Why, *Ella Gant*. A musical girl, *Sarah Nade*. A lively girl, *Annie Mation*. A clear case of girl, *E. Lucy Dale*. A seedy girl, *Cora Ander*. A clinging girl, *Jessie Mine*. A serene girl, *Mollie Fy*.
MID—A warlike girl?
END—*Millie Tary!*
MID—The best girl of all?
END—Your own girl, of course.
MID—I've got you; a great big fat girl?
END—(Laughs.) *Ella Phant*.

RECITING AT THE PARTY.

BONES—Didn't I see you at the party last night?

MIDDLE—I was very much in evidence. Did you hear me recite and did you hear the applause?

BONES—No; I heard them inquiring after some overcoats and umbrellas.

MID—Ah, sir! I covered myself with glory.

BONES—That's better than that old bed-quilt that you've been wearing so long. What did you recite anyway?

MID—Oh, several choice morceaux.

BONES—*More so?* You looked *how-come-you-so* when I saw you under the table.

MID—I recited "Sheridan s Ride," and then that poem so dear to the heart of the children, "The Boy Stood on the Burning Deck." (*Rises dramatically and begins.*)

> The boy stood on the burning deck
> Whence all but him had fled.

BONES—Sit down; you make me sick. That's a back number. Next time you recite it, get up like this (*rises grotesquely*) and here's the up-to-date version of it.

> "The boy stood in the farmer's field,
> And ate with great dispatch
> Of all the sturdy vine did yield
> Within that melon patch.
> Yes, beautiful and bright he stood,
> With colic yet unknown;
> Yet soon the hills and dusky wood
> Did echo back his groan.
> He still ate on—he would not go
> Without just one more bite,
> Although he felt queer pangs below
> His waist-band growing tight.
> Then came a groan like thunder sound—
> The boy—oh, where is he?
> Look there, upon the torn-up ground
> His squirming form you see.
> Into his bed they laid him quick,
> This howling colicky lad,
> And though he suffered good and thick—
> *He was walloped by his dad.*

THE GAMBLER'S LIFE.

MIDDLE—Do you know John Euchre?

END—Do you mean John Euchre, the gambler?

MID—Yes; the poor fellow died yesterday, and I want you to compose something appropriate. Take your time about it.

END—I can give it to you right now. I don't have to study it over. Let's see—John Euchre, gambler. Here you are: A gambler's life is easily explained. First, he tries to *go it alone.* He's a *trump* if he's on the square. He *cuts a good deal* with a *pack* of friends and often *calls* on everybody to *raise* money, principally from his *ante*, or *sees* his uncle. He's often at the *clubs*, wears *diamonds* and plays for *hearts*. Finally he *lays down his hand* and allows a *spade* to turn him down in the *flush* of life. If he has been *straight* he *wins* the *game*, though it may be his last *shuffle.* He's got to *cash in his chips*, for the *bluff* is over and he's *euchred* at last.

THE WAR CRIES OF OUR SOLDIERS.

END—The war is over and we have proven that we are a great nation. Our soldiers would rather fight than eat. Why, we had gallant boys of all trades and occupations in the army. The bone and sinew of our land—carpenters, bakers, shoemakers and all mechanics—dropped their tools and forsook their workshops to go and fight for Uncle Sam. You ought to have heard how the different mechanics would shout a war-cry peculiar to their occupations. The colonels would say: "Attention, carpenters," or "Shoemakers to the front," or "Forward, bakers, to the battle." Then you'd hear the war cries of the different trades, what they'd shout as they went for the foe.

MIDDLE—What would the carpenters shout?

END—Go for them with a cold chisel, *shave 'em* and *nail 'em !*

MID—Tailors?

END—Go and baste 'em, boys, baste 'em. *Rip 'em right and left.*

MID—Blacksmiths?

END—Let them have it *red-hot* and *hammer the life out of them.*

MID—Barbers?

END—Barbers! Now for a good brush and a close shave, *lather 'em,* boys, *lather 'em.*

MID—Lawyers?

END—*Skin 'em, skin 'em.*

MID—Bakers?

END—Dough (Do) 'em up quick and bake 'em to a crisp. They *knead* it !

MID—Bill Posters? ·

END—Stick 'em on a wall !

MID—Doctors?

END—Charge them, *charge them*; make 'em stick their tongues out !

MID—Shoemakers?

END—Welt 'em, boys, peg away at 'em. Wax the life out of 'em. Don't let a *sole* escape.

MID—Suppose that old maids were in the army, which war-cry would suit them?

END—Let us at them ! Let us at them *before they escape !*

PLANTING FLOWERS.

END—Come and see me some day. I've got a ·hot-house. I'm raising flowers, but I don't use seed ; I just plant any old thing and up it comes in the shape of flowers or weeds. I plant anything.

MIDDLE—I'll take you at your word. If you plant a calf, what will spring up?

END—A *cows-lip.*

MID—A dancer?

END—*Columbine.*

MID—A poetess?

END—*Blue bell.*

MID—A watch?

END—*Thyme.*

MID—A crowd?

END—Why, *rushes.*

MID—A puppy?

END—*Dog rose.*

MID—Suppose you plant a bee?

END—*Honeysuckles ;* that's easy .

MID—A churn?

END—*Butter cups* A lover—why, *heart's ease.* Plant a boy, you get *bachelor's buttons.* A girl, *ladies' ribbons!*

MID—A fox?

END—Why, *foxglove*, of course.

MID—A baby?

END—*Mignonette.* Your toes, *capers.* A copper cent, *penny royal.* A sea fish, *crab-apple.*

MID—Suppose you planted me, what would come up?

END—Drunken sailor, full of *blossoms.*

MID—Suppose you planted yourself, what would spring up?

END—*Daisies ;* you bet I always throw bouquets at myself,

PIANO PLAYING.

MIDDLE—Passing your house the other night, I heard some one playing the piano.

END—Oh, yes, we all play the piano. We're all fond of music at our house. I love music I could live on music. That is, with a good dinner in addition. I love all the popular songs: "She made pretzels in Pennsyltucky," "Way down on the Swanee For Ever," "Don't you remember the Locksmith, Ben Bolt," and "Only One Girl Making Tea." Oh, I love music !

MID—But you've got the titles of the songs badly mixed. You must be fond of harmony.

END—Yes; *hominy* and molasses.

MID—Do you play the piano well?

END—I'm just an ordinary player. A plunketty plunk kind of a pianist.

MID—I love the piano, as I am a great pianist myself.

END—You don't tell me.

MID—I've been complimented by the great Gottschalk.

END—Oh, you've *got* to use *chalk* have you? So you play billiards?

MID—No, no ; the piano. The great Paderewski came out of his way to compliment me.

END—You must be wonderful.

MID—I possess a peculiar gift. For instance. I may not be able to hear a sound of the piano, yet, if I can see the fingers of the player running over the keyboard, I can tell exactly the tune he or she is playing.

END—What's that? Do you mean to say that if I had a piano in front of me, and you couldn't hear a note, you could tell which tune I'm playing?

MID—Yes; if I can see your fingers, I needn't hear the instrument, be it imaginary or real, to know the exact tune you are playing.

END—I don't believe it. I'll wager you an oyster supper you can't do it.

MID—What kind of an oyster supper?

END—Six large oysters for ten cents.

MID—Make it oysters for everybody.

END—All right; oysters for everybody, one a piece. Now, then, you'll tell me what I'm playing.

MID—Where's your piano?

END—You said an imaginary piano !

MID—All right, if I said so ; go ahead and I'll tell you what you are playing

END—(Begins in pantomime an imitation of fixing piano stool and fingers in.-aginary key board daintily.) Watch this plunk hand. (Works left hand rapidly as if playing.) There, what was that?

MID—That was very simple. That is a sonata in B flat by Giacomo Botossinni. (End looks astonished at audience and circle.)

END—Yes, that's it. Now I'll give you a hard one. (Very grotesque movements under the piano, punching keys, then cross-hand movements until climax.) There ! What was that?

MID—I'm so glad you played that for me. It's an old song I haven't heard for ten years, called "Under the Willows She's Sleeping." (End very astonished, rolls eyes, gazes around, ad lib.)

END—Yes. (Gasps.) That's it. Now I'll give you some opera. (Very funny movements, jumping up and down in seat. Both hands far apart and wind up exhausted.) What's that?

MID—The easiest thing you've yet played. That's "Home, Sweet Home," with variations.

END—(Very astonished.) Yes, that's it. Say, that's a trick. I can do it myself. Bet you some more oysters. Go on and play and I'll tell you what you're playing.

MID—(Winks to group.) All right; you'll tell me what I'm playing. will you ? Now watch me. (Makes a dash with hands and humming sound with lips.)

END—That piano wants tuning. What are you doing ? Twisting pretzels? Got a fit?

MID—(Concludes.) What was I playing?
END—That's easy. That's "Home, Sweet Home on a Vacation."
MID—With variations! (Winks.) Yes, that's it. Now watch me. (Wild movements and sound with lips as of up and down scale, cross hands.) Now! What was I playing?
END—I'm glad you played that for me. It's an old song I haven't heard for twenty years. "Under the Pillows They're Creeping."
MID—You mean "Under the Willows She's Sleeping." (Winks.) You're right; that's it.
END—I can tell it every time. Play some more.
MID—Now comes the test. Watch me. (Rises, plays wildly in the air. Right and left like a maniac, all alarmed, shouts three times at intervals, and each time louder.) What am I playing now? (End is laughing.)
END—(After third time.) *You're playing the fool. Sit down!*

ALL ABOUT CARDS.

END – When you are playing cards, you don't realize what every card means, do you?
MIDDLE—I did not know that cards had any significance beyond their merit in the game or their face value.
END—Of course not; because you never think of these things. Now, let me tell you about the cards : England's best card is the *Queen*. Uncle Sam has just turned down a *King*, a Spanish one. The Policeman's best card is a *club*. The politician's best card is a *knave*.
MID—How about a society actress' card?
END—*Diamonds!* Have them stolen.
MID—The grave-digger's best card?
END—*Spades.*
MID—Lover's best cards?
END—*Hearts!*
MID—A waiter's best card?
END—*The tray.*
MID—How about a photographer's best cards?
END—*Face* cards of course. Wives give bad husbands the *deuce*. Fox hunters want *the whole pack*. Barbers get the *edges*. Dancers get the *shuffle*. Rejected lovers get the *cut*. Parents of triplets get *three of a kind*. Merchants get the *deal*. Actors get the *play*, but butchers always get the *steaks*.
MID—I'll remember all that.
END—And if you play, get a chimney sweep and a cornet player for partners.
MID—Why?
END—The chimney sweep will always follow *soot*, and a cornet player will *trumpet*.

THE RIVAL SAFE AGENTS.

MIDDLE—I understand you went to the ball game yesterday afternoon. You told me you wanted to go to your mother-in-law's funeral.
END—I did want to, but she isn't dead yet.
MID—I would like you to be a canvassing agent for our firm. We need a bright young man to "talk up" our safes, the best in the world.
END—Are you in the safe business? So am I. There isn't a safe made that can beat ours, so don't talk about safes around here.
MID—Gentlemen, (to circle.) This young man is articulating through his chapeau. I'll just relate an incident of our safes, and you can judge of their merits. Last Saturday before we locked the safe door, a small dog, unobserved, strayed into it and lying down, went to sleep. We closed the safe door and left the office. During the night a terrific fire broke out. The building, as you remember, was totally destroyed. For twenty hours the fire raged and the safe lay in the midst

of the flames. We finally took it out, battered and almost burned up, you may say, and opened the door. And what do you think? That poor little dog crawled out of it alive, gave a glad bark and wagged its tail. The dog was saved in spite of the terrific heat around and about him. This proves that our safes can stand a red-hot condition and yet its cool interior will protect life and valuables. Now, sir, (to end man) never talk about safes again. Go hide your diminished head. (Laughs, and all join in his mirth.)

END—Something like that happened to us. We left the safe door open, and a rooster coming along got into it, and the clerk shut the door and locked the combination, and went home. That night a tremendous fire broke out. The flames roared and roared for twenty-four hours around that safe. We thought it was melted. After the fire we took it out red-hot. Yes, sir, the safe was red-hot We opened it with crow-bars, and when the door was opened, what do you think?

MID—I know just what you are going to say (laughs.) The door was opened and the little rooster stepped out, flapped his wings and crowed. (Laughs, and all join in the mirth.)

END—No, sir. There lay the little rooster in one corner of the safe, *frozen stiff.*

A SHIP IS LIKE A WOMAN.

END—Did you know that I was one of the very first volunteers that went off to Cuba?

MIDDLE—Army or Navy?

END—Navy. I didn't want any of that army beef.

MID—Were you on a gun-boat or a man-of-war?

END—I was on a woman of war!

MID—You mean man-of-war.

END—I mean *woman of war.* Now, suppose you saw a vessel approaching, decorated with flags, how would you express admiration?

MID—I should say *she* was a magnificent craft.

END—There you are. How can a *she* be a *he*? Therefore it must be a woman of war. Now a ship is just like a woman, for she has *bows* and a *waist.* It takes a *man to manage her* A ship is like a woman, for it *brings news from abroad.* She always makes up to a *pier.* She runs after a *smack*, she's ridiculous when in company of small *buoys*. She's sometimes in company with a *man-of-war.* And last of all, a woman is like a ship because the *rigging* costs more than the *hull.*

HOW TO PRONOUNCE TOMATOES.

END—Say, you're smart. You know everything, or rather you think you do. You've always got your nose into everybody's affairs. Now, let me ask you a question.

MIDDLE—Certainly ; I'll reply if I can. What is your question?

END—How do you pronounce T-O-M-A-T-O-E-S? (Spells.)

MID—Why tomatoes, of course.

END—You don't know much about it. Now I sat at a dinner table and everybody asked for them but pronounced it differently. I'll relate it to you in poetry, and please pay attention to the accent on the word in dispute. Here she goes :

Some people pass you
Mashed potatoes,
And then ask if you
Like *to-ma-toes.*

And who, when dining,
Make no barters.
Say : "Are you fond of
Raw *to-mar-ters?"*

And some who dine where
There some hate is,
Say: "Oh! do take some
Stewed *tum-mate-is.*"

And some who dine where
There no lettuce is,
Often ask for:
"More *tu-mettuce-is!*"

And some who no more
Than a mummy knows,
Pass their plates for:
"Some more *tummy-toes.*"

Now, you see, you don't know much about tomatoes; so I can't expect you to *ketchup.* In the Bowery it's: "*Say! Pass dem Toe Mats!*"

WHERE THEY OUGHT TO GO.

END—I'm in a great business at last. You know that everybody wants to go to a watering place, sea shore, resort, mountains or elsewhere, for recreation or a vacation. So I'm the party that sends them where they want to go. I pick out places for them according to who they are, what they are or may be hereafter.

MIDDLE—I don't quite catch your meaning.

END—Everybody according to his trade or condition in life must have a place suitable to it. Don't you catch on? Now ask me where certain people ought to go and I'll tell you without hesitating, for I've made it a study.

MID—Very well. Where should poultry dealers spend their vacations?

END—*Egg Harbor!* That's easy!

MID—Bike riders?

END—*Wheeling!*

MID—Surgeons?

END—*Lansing!*

MID—Cowards?

END—*Cape Fear!* You're a cinch for me.

MID—People who bet, but never win?

END—*Luzon!* (Lose on.)

MID—Gluttons?

END—*Samoa!* (Some more.)

MID—Dudes?

END—*Scilly Islands!*

MID—Lovers who eat almonds on a wager?

END—*Philippine Islands!*

MID—Those fond of singing birds?

END—*Canary Islands!* Oh! you can't get me off my perch.

MID—Segar smokers?

END—*Havana!*

MID—Thirsty people?

END—*Brandywine River and Buttermilk Falls!*

MID—Colored people?

END *Cooney Island!*

MID—School masters?

END—*Long Branch!*

MID—Crying babies?

END—*Lapland!*

MID—Hungry people?

END—*Sandwich Islands!*

MID—Old Maids?

END—(Laughs.) The Isle of *Man!* And they can't get there quick enough!

EATING AND DRINKING.

END—I was eating my dinner to-day and a very funny idea came to me. I couldn't help but laugh at it. (Laughs heartily). When you hear it you'll laugh to.

MIDDLE—Well, what is it?

END—I was wondering what it is that separates the food from the liquid when a person is eating and drinking at the same time.

MID—That's easily explained. It's very simple, indeed. You must understand that right here (pointing to throat) in the esophagus.

END—In the *what a gus?*

MID—Esophagus, or thorax; the upper part of the throat in which are two tubes.

END—Two wash tubs?

MID—(Annoyed)—Two little tubes or pipes.

END—Oh, I see; two tubs in the gas pipes.

MID—Two pipes, and at the apex of these pipes—

END—Oh, I see, 8 pecks, 2 bushels of pipes.

MID—(Earnestly and interested)—At the summit, just where it enters the eppiglotis, is a little valve or clapper. It's action is automatic. Now, when a person is eating, the little clapper falls over and closes the drinking tube, and when a person is drinking the little clapper falls over the way and closes the eating pipe, and vice versa. (Shows action with hands while describing a valve closing, etc.)

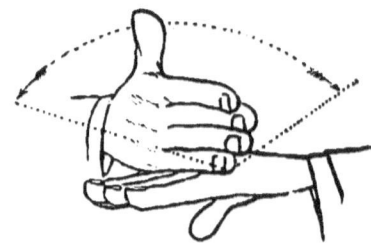

END—That's simple. Now let me see if I could explain that to somebody. Right here in the *horax* are two *gas pipes*, with the *apple dumpling* on the *eight pecks*. Then there's a little clapper full of *rheumatics*. When the little clapper falls over, it closes the *restaurant*.

MID—(Explains). The eating tube.

END—And when a person is eating, the little clapper falls over and shuts up the *drinking saloon!*

MID—Closes the drinking pipe.

END—(Laughs, as with hands, he imitates the little clapper, moving R. and L. like a flapper.)

MID—What are you laughing at?

END—I'm laughing at that little clapper.

MID—What about the little clapper?

END—I'm laughing to think what a busy time that little clapper will have when you're *eating mush and milk!* (Quick action of hand as you reach climax of speech and laughing.)

ALL ABOUT CATS.

END—There's something that puzzles me. Why does a cat, falling, always alight on its feet?

MID—Now a cat always falls upon its feet because the claws—

END—Now look here. No *claws* in the constitution about it. Drop the cat. How do you know it's always light on its feet?

MID—Let me explain. Now a cat—
END—Well, whose cat are you talking about and where is it, in your yard or on the fence?
MID—I say when a cat falls—
END—I'm not talking about cat falls or cat fish. So don't get your *back up* like a cat. If you can't explain it, just say so and don't meow about it all night. (Angry) Shut up, don't talk back to me. If you don't know why a cat walks easy along the fence and you can't hear it coming along, why, say so. But don't show your ignorance.
MID—Oh, that's your question, is it? Well, a cat walks softly and unheard because its paws are a sort of cushion, soft as velvet, which contract as the feline approaches cautiously, and it treads upon these cushions of the paw, especially if approaching its prey.
END—Oh, bosh! That isn't what makes it walk soft.
MID—What is it then?
END—*Rats !*

LETTERS IN THE POST OFFICE.

END—I thought I saw you out at the baseball game. They've got a new pitcher. His name is *Dice ;* but they found Dice hard to *rattle.*
MID—What is your brother doing at present?
END—Getting rich by collecting hush money from every family in town.
MID—Hush money!
END—Yes; he manufactures *soothing syrup.* All of our family are smart. If they wanted to find out anything they'd come to us If anything was lost they'd always come to our house to find it. We know everything and everybody. Did you know that everybody resembles a letter in the post office? Everybody— men, women and children—are letters, especially the ladies.
MID—What kind of a letter is a married lady?
END—She's a letter that has *reached its destination.*
MID—What kind of a letter is a young lady?
END—She's a letter that *hasn't been sent yet.*
MID—What kind of letters are babies?
END—They're merely *little postal cards.*
MID—What kind of a letter is a fat lady?
END—She's *overweight* and *collect postage.*
MID—What kind of a letter is an undertaker?
END—He has charge of the *dead letters* only.
MID—What kind of letters are old maids?
END—Letters that have been overlooked in the *General Delivery.*

LITERARY CURIOSITIES.

CROSS-FIRE.

BONES—I saw a thing to-day that proves how smart women are when they wish to be. This woman ran to the depot and was just five minutes late. What did she do? She turned around and grabbed her dress and *caught the train.*
TAMBO—Have you heard the new march—The Baby Coach March?
MIDDLE—No; how does it go?
TAMBO—*On wheels!* Say! Do you believe in the present war tax?
MID—Certainly. The Government needs the tax. There's a tax on every-thing.
TAMBO—You're right. When I put on my shoes this morning I had to *stamp my feet.*
BONES—You're so smart, I'm going to let you know how smart I am. I can tell you just how much water runs over Niagara Falls to the quart.
MID—You can? Well, how much water goes over Niagara Falls to the quart?

BONES—Two pints to the quart—always.
TAMBO—Say, did you know Bill Blue?
MID—I've heard of him.
TAMBO—He's a poet and don't know it. You know Bill Blue is an engineer, out West, on a freight train, and his pet engine is number two. One night he had an accident. One of the flues in the boiler of his pet engine blew out and he was stalled, blocking the main line. He reported the matter to the division superintendent, unwittingly as follows :

> Engine Two blew out a flue,
> What'll I do?—Bill Blue.

Then he sat down to await instructions. This is what came over the wires from the superintendent's office twenty minutes later :

> Bill Blue : You plug that flue
> In Engine Two, and pull her through
> In time to get out of the way of twenty-two,
> Or I'll send you to Kalamazoo,
> Doo, Doo ! my huckleberry, Doo.

MID—That's nice for railroad poetry, and a curiosity in the way of literature.
BONES—Hold on ! If you want curiosities in poetry, let me tell you what I have seen.

> I've seen the *rope-walk* down the lane,
> The *sheep-run* in the vale :
> I've seen the *dog-watch* on the ship,
> The *cow-slip* in the dale :
> I've seen the *sea-foam* at the mouth,
> The *horse-fly* in the air ;
> I know the *bul-warks* on the deck,
> And the *fire-works* many a scare ;
> I've seen *a-bun-dance* on the plate.
> A *lamp-light* on the floor :
> I've seen the *cat-fish* in the sea,
> And a *hat-stand* by the door ;
> I've seen the *mill-race* in the glen,
> The *heart-burn* in the breast ;
> I've seen a *door-step* on the street,
> And a *watch-spring* in my vest.

HOW I LOVE HER.

A SHORT "END" MONOLOGUE.

You've often heard the expression, "I love you." That's all very well, but *how* do you love her? *when* do you love her? and *how much* do you love her? I admit that I'm crazy, but there are others as foolish as I am. When a young man is in love, his mind is turned to poetry. This is a sure sign that you are getting daffy. But I'll tell you *when* I love her and *how much* I love her Now, please don't laugh at me. If there are any other love-struck people in the audience, besides myself, I hope they'll go out while I recite this :

> Oh, I love her when it's morning, and I love her when it's noon,
> I love her in the evening, 'neath the radiance of the moon;
> I love her when she's singing, and I love her when she sleeps;
> I love her when she's laughing, and I love her when she weeps;
> I love her when she's driving and I love her when she walks,
> I love her when she's silent, and I love her when she talks;
> I love her every attitude, I love her lightest whims,
> I love her when she's biking, and I love her when she swims;
> I love her when she's romping with her merry girlish mates,
> I love her when she's dancing, and I love her while she skates;
> I love her when she's eating, and I love her when she drinks,
> I love her when she's sneezing, and I love her when she winks;
> I love her after onions 'round her lips do linger yet,
> For then her love is *stronger than any love I've met.*

SYNONYMOUS.

CROSS-FIRE.

MIDDLE—I saw you engaged in a row yesterday. It was disgraceful! Don't you think so?

BONES—Yes; I had a fuss with a fellow and he threw an egg at me. It splashed all over my face and clothes, and, oh! it wasn't an up-to-date egg! It was *passe!* It was a *disgraceful egg.*

MID—It doesn't make any difference; if he struck you, you should return *good* for *evil.*

BONES—I did; I threw an egg at him.

MID—I mean return *good* for *evil.*

BONES—So I did; the egg I threw at him was a *good* egg.

TAMBO—Say! You know a great deal. Now, what is the difference between *also* and *likewise?*

MID—There is no difference; they are synonymous terms.

TAMBO—*Sell-on-y-mous tunes?*

MID—Webster defines synonymous as meaning one and the same thing.

BONES—What's Webster got to do with it? He's too fresh saying what's right and what's wrong If I see him, I'll just tell him what I think of him.

MID—Worcester says the same thing.

TAMBO—Worcester's all right; he makes Worcester sauce out of sight. He's a *sell-on-a-mous* sauce maker!

MID—You don't understand; *also* means *likewise* and *likewise* means *also.*

TAMBO—No, it does not! Now, I'll prove it You know Hummel, the lawyer?

MID—Certainly.

TAMBO—Well, he's a gentleman and *also* a lawyer—*likewise* honest.

MID—Yes.

TAMBO—You are *also* a lawyer?

MID—Yes.

TAMBO—But you're not *likewise!*

BONES—(Interrupting.)—Sell-on-y-mous means one and the same thing, does it?

MID—Yes.

BONES—What's a one-dollar bill?

MID—A one dollar bill, of course.

BONES—What's another one-dollar bill?

MID—*Synonymous!*

TAMBO—What's two things alike?

MID—*Synonymous.*

BONES—What's a pair of twins?

MID—(Laughs)—*Synonymous.*

BONES AND TAMBO—What's one elephant and another elephant and what's one clothes-pin and another clothes-pin?

MID—Silence! You are a pair of fools.

BONES AND TAMBO—(Pointing at MID)—*Synonymous!*

MUSICAL INSTRUMENTS.

CROSS-FIRE.

MIDDLE—Gentlemen, do you love music?

BONES—I could eat music!

TAMBO—I could live on music!

MID—I am pleased to note the fact, for it shows an appreciation of harmony.

BONES—We can tell you all about musical instruments. Did you know there were musical instruments for everybody? Men, women and children in all occupations?

MID—I certainly did not.

TAMBO—It shows you don't know much about music.

MID—Then tell me the suitable musical instruments for everybody.   Which instrument should a fisherman play upon?

BONES—The *bass-oon* and *cast-a-net.*

MID—An old maid?

TAMBO—The *man-do-lin.*

MID—A man with a cold in his head?

BONES—The *guitar.*   (Catarrh.)

MID—An undertaker?

BONES—The *bones.*

MID—A burglar?

BONES—The *lute.*   (Loot.)

MID—Cats on a wall?

TAMBO—*Tom Tom.*

MID—Keeper of a poor hotel?

BONES—That's easy.   A *vile-inn.*   (Violin.)

MID—A prize fighter?

TAMBO - A music *box.*

MID—Which music is appropriate for the President?

BONES—He likes a *march*—the *fourth of March.*

MID—Which is a good song for a barber?

TAMBO—*Oh, comb, oh, comb with me!*

MID—Niagara hackman?

BONES—"With all thy *falls,* I love thee still."

MID—Which is a good song for a tramp caught in the rain?

TAMBO—"*Wet* till the clouds go by."

MID—Good song for *me* at my boarding house?

BOTH—"*When you ain't got no money, well, you needn't come 'round :*"

REMARKABLE BRAVERY.

CROSS-FIRE.

MIDDLE—I understand you attended the banquet the other night.   Did you enjoy yourself?   Did you *take* well?

BONES—You bet I did; I got three spoons, four napkin-rings and a sugar-bowl.   I would have *swiped more* if I'd had a chance.

TAMBO—(Interrupting, to Middleman.) - Say!   Does your sister use face powder?

MID—She uses a *little* powder, I think.

TAMBO—A *little?*   She puts it on so thick that she ought to join the plasterers' union.   Oh!   *what* a face she has—and wrinkles!   Ugh!   They are good for the flies to hide in.

MID—I hope you will not criticise my sister's features.

BONES—Her feet!   Oh!   (Laughs.)   She'd be awful tall if there wasn't so *much* of her on the ground.   Feet!   Oh!   They are like a couple of trunks.

TAMBO—I guess she must leave her feet outside of the room when she retires at night, doesn't she?

MID—You wouldn't believe she wears number twos?

BONES—You mean *twenty-twos!*

TAMBO—*Two hundred and twenty-twos!*

MID—Now, there is a brave and noble girl.   Let me relate an incident.   The other night a burglar entered the house and began, dark lantern in hand, to search—

BONES—For her feet?   Why, he couldn't help *falling* over them.

MID—(Annoyed.)—No!   No!   While the burglar was searching, my sister heard him.

TAMBO—He stepped on her feet, and next day she felt it.

MID—Oh, listen! She heard the burglar—what did she do?
BOTH—*Stepped on him* and he died!
MID—No; she didn't scream nor betray timidity, but ran out—
BOTH—*With those feet?*
MID—(Angry.)—Yes, yes.
TAMBO—I don't see how she could run.
BONES—May be somebody *carried her feet in a wheelbarrow* and she followed them
MID—No! I tell you! I repeat she ran—
BOTH—And tumbled over them.
MID—No, sir! She ran to the corner and found a policeman—
BONES—Fast asleep on her feet?
MID—(Very angry)—No!
TAMBO—Then he was inside one of her shoes?
MID—No! She found the policeman, brought him back to the house—
BOTH—*And he arrested her feet!*
MID—(Rises in anger)—Shut up!
BONES—Shut up, yourself! They weren't *your* feet, were they?
TAMBO—Shut up your sister's *Trilbys!*
MID—(Excited.)—The policeman came to the house and arrested the burglar. That's what I call *bravery!*
TAMBO—Get out! *Any* girl in this town could do *that.*
BONES—Certainly they could if they had the *chance*, but they couldn't *get* the chance.
TAMBO—No; she'd *never* get a chance.
MID—Why not?
BOTH—She *couldn't find a policeman.*

STUPIDITY AND SOLDIERS.

CROSS-FIRE.

MIDDLE—What were you doing to-day capering in the middle of the street like a lunatic?
BONES—Trying to dodge a cross-eyed girl who was on a bike.
TAMBO—Say! How did you like the shot you got to-day?
MID—What do you mean?
TAMBO—(Talking to Bones.) He tried to be fresh and he says to a young lady passing by: "Sissy, does your mother know you're out!" The girl says: "Oh, yes! And she gave me a penny to buy a monkey. *Are you for sale?*" (Laughs.)
BONES—Speaking of money. You know how mean he is (Referring to Mid). Well, he swallowed an old-fashioned copper cent by mistake (laughs), and the doctor made him cough up *two dollars.*
TAMBO—Show you how smart he thinks he is. (Meaning Mid.) I met him at the depot and he was chuckling to himself. I says: What pleases you? He says: I've got the best of the railroad company this time. I've bought a return ticket and I'm not going to use it.
MID—(Angry.) Oh, gentlemen, I'm not so stupid as all that!
BONES—You're worse! He's so mean that he never goes to a barber to have his hair cut. He waits until winter time and sticks his head into a bucket of water and lets his hair freeze stiff; then he *breaks it off.*
TAMBO—Then he got a job in a dry goods store as clerk. A lady came in and made him take down seventy bolts of silks and satins. Then she says: I don't think I'll purchase anything; I was merely *looking* for a friend. He says: If you think your friend is *in the other bolts* I'll take them down, too. But he's a chump!
BONES—I've got to tell this one on him. He was eating his dinner at the hotel and the waiter placed a finger-bowl beside him. He looked at it, picked it up and drank half of its contents. Then he turned to me and says: *That's the thinnest lemonade I ever tasted.*

MID—(Pleadingly.) Oh, gentlemen ! Please do not hold me up to ridicule in this manner.

TAMBO—Oh ! You frozen piece of pie ! He went to the butcher's and asked him for ten cents worth of liver ; and he says : Don't give me any *liver with bones in it.* (Laughs.) He ought to work in a livery stable !

BONES—And he wanted to enlist in the army. The officer says : Which branch of the service do you prefer? Army or Navy? He says : Both. Officer says : Which regiment? He says : Put me in the Seventh regiment. I've got a brother in the Sixth regiment and *I want to be near him.*

MID—(Stamping foot.) All this is nonsense ! Now tell me who makes the best soldiers for Uncle Sam ?

TAMBO—Auburn haired soldiers, for they are always *Reddy.*

BONES—Pawnbrokers make the best soldiers. They can send *Three Balls* to the enemy. No, sir; Nigger soldiers are the best of all.

MID—Why ?

BONES—They are *fast colors* and *never run.*

COUNTERFEIT MONEY.

END—I'm the most unfortunate man you ever saw. I get into all kinds of trouble. I saw a friend of mine fall off a car and roll in the mud. I went to him and got a stick and commenced rubbing the mud off him, when along came a policeman and arrested me.

MIDDLE—What for ?

END—Merely *scraping an acquaintance.* While I was in court I saw a remarkable case; a deaf and dumb man was brought in, and the judge made a remarkable cure right there.

MID—What was it ?

END—He gave the deaf man a *hearing.* Then a pickpocket was brought in, charged with picking pockets in a crowd. The judge fined him fifteen dollars. The pickpocket said : "Judge, all the money I've got with me is a ten-dollar bill." The judge says: "All right ! Give me the ten dollars." Then the judge say to the cop: "Officer, turn this man loose in the crowd and let him get me the other five dollars." As I was leaving court, I noticed a ten-dollar bill lying on the sidewalk. I stooped to pick it up, but it looked like a counterfeit bill, so I passed on.

MID—And the bill turned out to be a good one, of course ?

END—No ; but I was arrested before I had gone a dozen steps further.

MID—Arrested ! What for ?

END—For *passing* counterfeit money.

A CYCLONE STORY.

END—I went to a party last night, and we had a great cake-walk. Do you remember when cake-walks were done for the first time on the stage?

MIDDLE—No, I do not. Do you know?

END—Yes ; cake-walks were done for the first time on the stage in "Uncle Tom's Cabin," when Eliza crossed the river on the *ice-cakes of ice.* I came near being a *cake* myself a few weeks ago. I was caught in a *hurry-up-cane.*

MID—A hurricane—a *cyclone.*

END—You bet I was a *sick coon* after it struck me. It made me see the color of the wind.

MID—The color of the wind ?

END—Yes; it was *blew.* When the cyclone struck our town it changed the whole map. You remember the main street, don't you ?

MID—Yes; it ran north and south.

END—Well, it's east and west and all twisted up and down. Oh, how it blew ! It blew the paint off of all the houses.

MID—You don't say so.
END—Blew the knot-holes out of the fence.
MID—Terrible tempest!
END—Yes ; it blew the cellar out from under the Court House. It blew the sun back three hours.
MID—You don't say so !
END—Do you remember Johnny Fitz Hugh? He had the catarrh in his nose?
MID —Yes ! (All are excited.)
END—It *blew his nose!* He hadn't blown it in three years. Oh ! it was an awful cyclone. It blew all the fishes out of the river, then it blew them back again. Blew open a safe, and *blew in all the money!* Do you remember Fitz Hugh's dog? A little, tall, lean kioodle dog? Well, it was running down the street with its mouth wide open and the wind *blew the dog inside out* and he ran the other way.

ALL ABOUT LAW.

END—I was coming up to the city in a railroad train, and I noticed a very loving couple seated ahead of me, and the young lady's mother sat in the seat ahead of them. Suddenly we came to a long, dark tunnel and when we emerged the young lady looked indignant and angry. Her mother leaned over and said to her: "Don't make such a display of temper ! Did he *dare kiss you* while we were in that dark tunnel? The girl says: "*No ; he didn't!* The coward !" Now, if I'd been in his place, she wouldn't have said that about me. I saw you one day last week with a lot of books under your arm. What are you, a book agent?
MIDDLE—No, sir. Those books were law books. I'm practising *at the bar.*
END—Tell me which one you practise at, and I'll go with you. They *won't trust me* at any of the bars up my way.
MID—(Angrily.)—I mean to tell you that I am a lawyer, a *criminal lawyer.* Some day you may need my services, or I shall be the lawyer to cross-examine you.
END—I don't care. I'm seldom out of jail anyway.
MID—I've long wanted to put you under oath and question you, the same as I would were I in the Court House and had you on the witness stand.
END—Well, I've got no time to be questioned. I might *give myself away.*
MID— Dignified.)—I dare say ! Gentlemen ! (To circle.) I'll cross-examine this fellow and show you how easily I befog and tangle up a witness with as little gray matter under the skull as this representation of *nothing* has in his cerebellum ! Look at me, you miscreant ! You *mustard seed* in a vast, fathomless sea of nothing.
END—Hold on ! I'll punch your jaw if you call me a *mustard plaster.* I know I'm *hot stuff,* but don't call me that.
MID—Silence ! What is your business?
END—I'm a tin roofer. I've worked at it *off and on,* but I've worked at it steady the past twelve years.
MID—How long, *off and on,* have you worked at it?
END —Thirty-three years.
MID—How old are you?
END—Thirty-three years old.
MID— Then you've been a tin roofer from birth ?
END—No; of course I haven't.
MID—Then why do you say you've worked at the trade thirty-three years— and you are only thirty-three years old? Come ! Answer the Court.
END—You asked me how long *on* and *off* I worked at it. I have worked at it *off and on* for thirty-three years. Fifteen years *on* and eighteen years *off.* Fifteen and eighteen are thirty-three ! What kind of a lawyer are you, anyway? *Smoke up!*
MID—I'll *smoke you up* before I'm through with you. You remember seeing Farmer Jones struck by Farmer Benson?

END—I do. I was the principal witness. I was the whole case.
MID—How far were you from Benson when he struck Jones?
END—Oh! I can tell that easy enough.
MID—(Enthusiastically.)—I've got you where I want you. Remember that you are under oath. How far were you from Benson when he struck Jones? The lawyer has *got you at last !* Ha! ha!
END—(Thoughtfully.)—Three yards, two feet and four inches and a half!
MID—Why are you so particular about the distance to the half inch?
END—Because I thought some *fool of a thick-headed lawyer* would ask me!

GLADIATOR.

END—Courting is nice, isn't it?
MIDDLE—Yes, sir. Love's young dream is the Elysian fields through which we hand in hand wander in dreamland, beside purling brooks and—
END—Break away! Don't get foolish too quick. We know you're crazy, but don't tell everybody. There's one thing certain—the girls are diplomatic and no relation to George Washington.
MID—What do you mean?
END—I mean to say that they'll get you *on a string* if they can   When I was first courting I had proof of it. I called on her and went into the dark parlor and she jumped up, ran into my arms, and said: "Oh! Charley, I'm so glad you called." I says to her: "My name is not Charley; my name is *George.*" She said : "*Excuse me,* I thought this was Wednesday night." She got her dates mixed. I guess I got in on Charley's night; but it just goes to show how they *string us* along.
MID—Ah, sir, woman is Heaven's best gift to man.
END—Yes; and she's often got to chase him to make him take the gift. But man is brave and can stand all the taffy and give her lots in return. It makes him feel like a *glad*iator—happy! jolly!
MID—(Patronizingly.)—Do you know the meaning of *gladiator?*
END—Certainly I do. Do you suppose I came here to show my ignorance as you do?
MID—Then define the word gladiator.
END—I don't have to *find* it; I've *got it.*
MID—Well, what is it? Come.
END—I know what it is all right.
MID—Well, give us the definition.
END—Gladiator is about a happy man. He goes to sea on a ship. He has his wife and his wife's mother with him. They are on deck looking at the foamy billows. Suddenly a huge wave dashes over the ship and sweeps away the man's mother-in-law. He yells for help as he sees her in the water. Just then a big, ravenous shark appears, opens its jaws, swallows the happy man's mother-in-law—
MID—Well?
END—(Dryly)—He's *glad he ate her!*

AUTOMOBILE.

END—Say, do you know Briggs? Well, he and his family are living in a house-boat. He rented an old canal-boat and they pole it along the bank. Briggs wrote me that all they needed to make it seem like real canal life was an old, spavined, knock-kneed, flea-bitten mule—and he wants you to come up.
MIDDLE—That is a very ambiguous invitation.
END—It's a big boat. Oh, I must tell you about my mother-in-law. She fell in a well.
MID—You don't say so.

END—And the well was so deep that I didn't hear the splash for two weeks afterwards. Some day I must take you out riding in my *auto-mo-bill-eye*.

MID—You ignoramus! Go and study up proper pronunciations before you display such lamentable ignorance in the company of scholars.

END—What's the matter with you? Been eating boarding house hash again?

MID—*Auto-mo-bill-eye!* (Laughs.) The word is derived from the French—*auto-mo-beel*

END—(Imitates Middle's voice)—*Auto-mo-beel!* You can go to Mobile or New Orleans, if you want to. I don't think anybody knows how to pronounce the word.

MID—Nonsense! Do you think that *everyone* is as dense as you are?

END—I stick to my assertion! You can pronounce the name of the new horseless wagon any way you like and be correct. I can prove it for five dollars.

MID—Well, it's worth five dollars to have you make a fool of yourself. It's a bet. Go ahead and prove that each and every pronunciation of that word is correct.

END—I'll give it to you in poetry, so that you can see that *I'm right and you're wrong*. Listen!

Faster than ever rode Budd Doble,
Speeding along in his *auto-mo-bel*.

And he went along so nobbily,
In his brand new *auto-mobbily*.

There he rode for many a mile
In his dashing *auto-mo-bile*.

He had no need to cry "whoa, Bill!"
Riding in his *auto-mo-bill*.

Thus he went across the lea
In his swift *auto-mo-blee*.

Faster sped each whirling wheel
Of his flying *auto-mo-beel*.

So, do not pick me up for a fool,
About this new-fangled *auto-mo-bool*.

It's cost you five to hear me say
It might be called *auto-mo-blay*.

You bet I'm right—you hear me *sneeze*,
Pronounce it any way you please,
For on to your five I'm going to *freeze*.

A THRILLING STORY.

END—Did you know that I was one of those long-haired poets and writers? I'm worse than Laura Jean Libbey! I have great powers of description.

MIDDLE—Then you will become a successful writer.

END—You bet your life I will. I write from actual occurrences. Listen! (Rises and recites.) 'Twas a fearful night; the Storm-king, out of humor, let loose the howling wind and pelting rain, and clothed the earth with darkness as dense and impenetrable as an Egyptian sepulchre. All instinctive life was hushed, save the tempest bird, whose shrill screams mingled with the crashing blast and made it more terrible in its mighty frenzy.' 'Twas dark as midnight; the trees moaning and sighing piteously, were rudely tossed about, and ever and anon huge masses of mutilated timber fell to the ground. Before an open window stood a beautiful girl; her glossy ringlets waved like streamers in the passing wind; her exquisite form, which bore the impress of nobleness innate, was splendidly erect; and her flashing eyes, full of excited lustre, shone brighter still through the impenetrable darkness. Proudly she stood there, defying the tempest in its wrath. See her rosy lips separate like the leaflet of the morning rose, and with one tremendous effort she screams out at the top of her voice. (Imitates woman's voice.) *Jim, if you don't let go that pig's tail, ma will thrash you like thunder!*

NEWSPAPER REPORTER.

END—I'm a newspaper reporter now. I had a job working for the railroad, but I gave it up. I was brakeman in a baggage room!

MIDDLE—What are the duties of a brakesman in a baggage room?

END—Breaking trunks! After I had smashed everything in sight, I went to reporting for newspapers.

MID—Are you florid or pacific in your style of writing?

END—No; *I hoist 'em with a derrick*. I'll give you a sample of how I reported a sensational occurrence for our paper. Open your large ears and drink in the following peroration: (Gradually becomes agitated.) "Yesterday was an inspiring one in our town. Fleecy clouds floated athwart a sky of amethyst. The lake was glorious in green, blue, purple and deep violet tints. The sweep of the gull was majestic. The wind that blew across the velvety lawns in the parks was exhilarating, and one standing at the edge of the clear, cool water at evening saw, if he looked toward the roseate West, a sky line that was magnificently broken and a color scheme that surpassed the most extravagant dream of the artist. Suddenly, as if the swift lightning had permeated a blackberry bush, came the cry of *Fire!* Huge tongues of the firey element shot into the agitated firmament, and the conflagration became general. I rushed into the debris of the flaming domicile and through the volumes of blinding smoke and embers, I brought them out and cried: *"Saved! saved! saved!"*

MID—What?

END—Two little *potato-bugs*, one in each hand.

THE SAILOR'S LETTER.

END—You know old Mrs. Sassafras! Well, she's very ignorant; she can't read or talk United States worth a cent. Her son, John Sassafras, went as a sailor on one of our war ships cruising in foreign waters, and he wrote her this letter, telling her about a storm: " We have been driven in the Bay of Fundy by a pampoosa right in the teeth. It blowed great guns and it carried away the bowsprit; a heavy sea washed overboard the binnacle and the companion. The captain lost his quadrant and could not take an observation for fifteen days. At last we arrived safe at Halifax." The old woman couldn't read, so she got me to read it over to her several times. Then she began to cry: "Oh, my poor son, poor John Sassafras!" I says: "What's the matter? He's not lost!" She says: "Thank goodness he's safe, but he has been driven into the *Bay of Biscuits* by a *bamboozle* right in the teeth. It blowed *great cannons* and it carried away the *pulpit;* a heavy sea washed overboard the *bicycle of the constitution*, the captain lost his *indigestion* and couldn't get any *salvation oil* for fifteen days. At last they arrived at *Hallelujah*."

HE SPOKE TO ME AT THE GRAVE.

END—I went to Saratoga last summer, and one of the most beautiful women I ever saw stopped at the same hotel with her invalid husband. I s'pose he came there to get well, but he didn't, for in a week or so he died. So I told my friend Brown that I was going in to win the widow. Brown is the freshest duck you ever saw.

MIDDLE—I've heard of him; a most nervy, bare-faced fellow.

END—I told him I was going to try to win her, and he says: "I'm going to try to win her myself." I was bound to get ahead of him, so the minute she returned from the funeral I didn't lose a moment. I rushed into her presence and took her hand. I knelt at her feet and said: "Madam, excuse this seeming haste, but I cannot help it. I love you sincerely, and have loved you while your poor invalid husband was dying. I could not wait a moment, but I know that right after a funeral seems so hasty, but I love you, and here I offer you my hand and heart " "I am so sorry, but you are too late; *your friend Brown spoke to me at the grave!*"

HE DIED LYING.

MID—When does a young lady go into the lumber business? When she *pines* for her sweetheart, who is a *spruce* young man with *ebony* face, and of whom she thinks a great deal. Now don't say that this is a *chestnut*.

MIDDLE—While I remember it, I wish to call you to account. You told certain people that I was a famous liar.

END—No; I didn't say that. I never made use of such an expression. I said you were an *infamous* liar. Speaking of liars, how's your father? There is the greatest old liar that ever lived.

MID—Don't dare to call my father a falsifier !

END—He's not a falsifier, he's just a plain old liar. He'd rather lie than eat. He'd lie all the time

MID—Don't speak of him in that manner ; he's dead.

END—You don't say so. What was the complaint?

MID—*There was no complaint.*

END—*Everybody was satisfied, I s'pose.* Where did he die?

MID—He died in the house

END—Did he die standing up?

MID—Certainly not. He died *lying !*

END—*He kept it up to the last didn't he ?*

THE RESTAURANT AND CUSTARD PIE.

END—They have the brightest waiters in this city I ever saw. They know just what you mean when you order Now. I went into a restaurant and called for a lobster. The waiter brought me a picture of (some local crank). A man once called me a lobster. I took him into a restaurant and made him *eat his words*. There is a restaurant in the city where they have all kinds of signs on the walls. For instance, one sign reads : *Remember, Heaven sees Everything*, and a sign next to it reads : *Keep your eyes on your umbrella.* Then there's one, *Try our mince pies*, and under it, *Be prepared to die.* When you get a plate of hash, you can see a placard staring you in the face, *Have faith in me;* or, if you break an egg that's antiquated, you'll see a sign on the wall, *Honor thy father and thy mother.* That's all right if you're a chicken. And when you get a glass of milk you read a placard that seems to be about the milk, for it says : *Shall we gather at the river?* Then there's one that reads : *Honesty is the best policy.* They've got that one stuck up over the cashier's desk. But there was an accident there the other day A countryman came in and ordered custard pie. The colored waiter brought it to him, and the jay says : *Where's the lid that goes on top of it ?* The waiter told him they never put a top crust on custard pie.

MIDDLE—It was never intended for the upper crust.

END—Of course not. That's why you never get any of it When the old coon told the countryman that, the jay scooped out a handful of the custard and threw it at the old colored waiter's head, and there it stuck. (Laughs.) What a sight he was ! The landlord rushed in and seeing the waiter, he yelled out : "'Rastus ! get out of the dining room. *Don't go 'round here with all your brains knocked out !* ''

ANIMALS GOING TO THE CIRCUS.

END—Are you fond of the circus, and do you like to see your ancestors, the monkeys, climbing around and having fun? There was a circus out our way last week, and all the animals thought they'd like to go and see the other animals with the circus. So the frog. the duck, the lamb and the pole cat, commonly called the skunk, started to visit the show They were anxious to get in, so they hopped and waddled and trotted to the circus. The first animal they met was the door-tender. He says : *"Tickets or money! No deadheads here !"* Well, the frog had a *greenback* and passed right in.

MIDDLE—That was good for the frog.

END—Hopping good. The duck had a *bill* and followed the frog. The lamb had *four quarters* and followed the duck. But the unfortunate skunk was left outside. He had only a *scent*. Naturally he turned away feeling pretty blue.

MID—I don't blame him!

END—As he was slowly going back over the hill, he met a hoop snake rolling along at a lively rate toward the show. The skunk greeted him, but the snake did not stop. ''Don't interrupt me,'' he cried, over his shoulder; ''I've got to do a *turn*, and I'm a little late.'' And he rolled along. At the top of the hill the skunk noticed another old friend approaching. It was the sardine. ''Hullo!'' cried the sardine; ''what's the matter?'' So the skunk told him. ''I can guess how you feel about it.'' said the sardine sympathetically. '' I belong to the *smelt* family myself. But, say, old fellow, you come right back and go in with me. I've got a *box*.''

MID.—That was lucky!

END—Yes; so when they got into the tent they found it crowded. The sardine couldn't use the *box*, but they all went and sat on the elephant's *trunk*, and gave three cheers and a *tiger*, and I'm not *lion*.

FIXING THE PANTS.

END—I got an invitation to go to a party, but I didn't have a pair of pants suitable. So, I went and bought a pair, and found, when I got home, that they were two inches too long for me. I says to my mother : '' Mother, I bought a pair of pants, and they are two inches too long for me. Will you cut off two inches and sew up the bottoms?'' She says: ''I'd like to, but really I'm too busy, and can't spare a moment.'' So I went to my sister Arabella, and I says : ' Bella, I bought a pair of pants and they're two inches too long for me; will you cut them and sew them up?'' She says: ''Don't bother me with your pants, I'm busy; besides, I expect Charley to-night, so I haven't got time.'' Then I went to the servant girl, Bridget, and I says to her: '' I've bought a pair of pants two inches too long for me. Will you cut off two inches, and baste 'em up for me!'' She says: ''No! emphatically, no! Get out of the kitchen! I haven't got time to bother with you or your pants!'' So, I took them to a tailor, had two inches cut off and the bottoms sewed up. I brought them home and threw them over the back of a chair, and went out to get shaved. My mother came in and saw the pants. She says: '' That poor boy wants to go to the party; I'll fix his pants.'' She cut off two inches and went out. My sister came in, she saw the pants and she says : '' I guess I'll have time to fix 'em before Charley calls,'' and she cut two inches off the pants and went out. The servant girl came in with a pair of shears, and she says: '' I guess I'll oblige him and fix his pants for him.'' She cut two inches off the bottoms.

MIDDLE—You didn't go to the party?

END—Yes, I did.

MID—You didn't wear those pants?

END—Yes ; I *wore them for a belt*.

YACHTING TERMS.

MIDDLE—I dearly love a yachting trip, but, as I am not a sailor, I do not know anything of the yachting terms or understand the nautical jargon of the salt water folks.

END—I thought you'd understand any kind of a *jag on;* but you're talking to an old yachtsman when you're talking to me. I love the sea. I can't sleep unless buckets of salt water are splashed against my window, just to lull me to sleep.

MID—Then you are a sailor?

END—I was rocked in the cradle of the deep by Davy Jones. I'll give you all the pointers you need about yachts.

MID—But the expressions and their meanings?

END—Plain as the nose on your face, and that's pretty plain. For instance, when they *weigh the anchor*, they put it *on the scales*, and you can see for yourself how much it *weighs*, and they can't cheat you. You must always remember that there are three kinds of yachts—first class, second class and steerage. For instance, *water line* means where the *temperance line* is drawn. *Load line* is when the sailors get a *jag* on board! *Time allowance*—that's when you buy your yacht on instalments. Sex of vessels : all yachts and ships are called she, except *mail* steamers ; don't forget that! Can buoy means a young sailor who *rushes the can*. *Lead line* is a line drawn with a *lead* pencil. *Wind-lass*—that's a sailor's *sweetheart*. *Starboard*—that means a *star boarder* on a yacht. *Port* means any old port in a storm or any old port wine that's lying around loose. *Capsize*—the caps for yachtsmen vary in sizes. They wear bigger ones in the morning, of course. *Avast heaving*—that means, *stop being seasick. Captain's quarters*—All the *25-cent pieces* he can lay his hands on.

THE RIVAL POETS.

END—You seem to be a very busy man now-a-days. I can never find you home when I call.

MIDDLE—I am extremely busy. I am writing poetry, essays and storyettes for a young ladies' magazine.

END—You don't tell me. I never knew that you were a poet. (Teasing him.) I thought you'd make a better oyster-opener or driver of a wagon, or something like that. So, you're a poet, are you?

MID—Yes, and I take great delight in my work because I am successful.

END—I'm something of a poet myself. I'm a *peculiar* poet. I can't start a poem, but I'm great in putting on the finishing touches, *the varnish, as it were.* I shine it up!

MID—I see; you are not much in *promulgating the theme*, but you are excellent in concluding the *rhythmic effusion.*

END—(Looks at him in astonishment.) You've changed your boarding house again, haven't you? Now to show you what kind of a poet I am, you just begin a few stanzas and I'll put the finishing touches to it.

MID—In other words, I am the *alpha* and you are the *omega.*

END—Yes, I'm after the *old nigger* this time. Start your muse.

MID—Very well; I'll begin a stanza and you are to finish it. (Romantically recites.)

> Throughout the woods
> The little birds,
> The sweetest music thrills
> It is the time all nature turns—

END—(Interrupting.) *To Carter's Liver Pills !*

Now, isn't that sweet and appropriate? Go ahead ! You've got me hungry now.

MID—Oh! that's awful! (Disgusted.)—Carter's Liver Pills.

END—They're awful, but it rhymes with thrills, and hills and ills. Give me some more; my poetic brain is working.

MID—Here's another: (Enthusiastically.)

> The farmer's boy now gladly comes
> With all his merry tunes,
> He sits down quick, beside the maid—

END—(As before) *And rips his pantaloons !*

You can't loose me. See how quick I got the rhyme for you?

MID—Your poetry will never do. It would not please the ladies. Now, I'll

show you the style of poetry the ladies admire.   This is my own composition.
(Points out toward audience dramatically.)

> See the little cloudlet,
>   Over the little wavelet,
> Like a tiny leaflet
>   *Dawn-cing o'er the sea.*

END—*Dawn-cing* o'er the sea! You ought to have seen your mouth.   It looked as if it had dropped out of its place.   (Imitates him)

> See the little cloudlet,
>   Over the little wavelet,
> Oh, somebody ought to hit
>   You with a ten-inch gimlet.
> You ought to go down in the yardlet,
>   To the pumplet,
> And soak your big fat headlet,
>   *Dawn-cing* o'er the sea !

You make me tired and weary.
MID—Here is something I think real sweet and pretty.   (Recites again.)

> I know a maiden young and fair,
>   With heart as light as feather ;
> With garlands in her nut-brown hair,
>   Tripping through the heather.

END—You ought to go out in the street and let a trolley car run over you.
The idea of a girl with nothing but garlands in her hair, tripping through the
heather.   Why, the poor girl would catch cold tramping around in the wet grass.
Here, I'll show you how you ought to recite that :

> I know a maiden young and fair,
>   Her shoes were made of leather,
> She fell down stairs and broke her hair,
>   And the air was full of weather.

MID—I don't like your poetry.
END—Well, I don't like yours.   Somebody ought to go out and get a nice
warm custard pie and push it up against your face.   "Tripping through the
heather !"   You're a nice plum, you are.
MID—I'll try you again.   Listen to this.   (Recites.)

> She thought of the flowers and stars above
> And then she thought of the power of love.

Now, isn't that very, very pretty?
END—You make me sick !   Here's what she ought to say :

> She thought of Mike
>   Who was often beside her,
> And then she turned, and
>   Stepped on a spider.

See ! that's natural.   The spider is liable to be there, and she could step on it.
The public wants natural poetry.   Things that are liable to happen, not the crazy,
mushy things you've been writing.   You ought to be arrested !   You're worse than
a cigarette crank !
MID—Here !   This is positively the last poem that I'll recite to you, for it is
casting pearls before swine.
End—*I haven't got any pearls to cast before you,* or I would.   But go on !
MID—

> Down in the Meadows
> A maiden fair
> Was braiding her wealth,
> Of golden hair.

END—Not a bit like it. I'll give you that. Listen :

> Down in the kitchen
> A maiden fair
> Out of the hash
> Was picking her hair.

(End overjoyed at his success and Middle thoroughly disgusted and speechless.)

CRYING GAG.

MIDDLE—I was just thinking of the time I sang at a party, and the song is one I shall never forget. It carries me back to dear old England.

END—Carries you back ! I guess that's the *only way you'll ever get back*. It's cheaper than paying your fare.

MID—Here it is. (Takes out ballad, sheet music.) Now, very few people know how to render a ballad, but I flatter myself that *I* can. This is called " Sweetheart, why did you leave me? "

END—I see you put the emphasis on *why* did you leave me. You place the *adverb* before the *avoirdupois*.

MID—Now listen ! I'll read you the poem and sing the chorus. (Begins to beat time with one hand.) Oh-o-o-o.

END—You have a touch of the *hydrophobia*, haven't you?

MID—That's how it begins. Oh-o-o-o.

END—I know you *owe* everybody, but go on.

MID—You see it is carried over into *the next bar*.

END—You *owe* the next bar, too, do you? Well, show me some bar you *don't owe*.

MID—(Reads)—Oh-o-o sweetheart, *why* did you leave me? Tell me, was it fault of mine?

END—He wants to know if it's his fault that he owes every bar.

MID—(Annoyed, but resumes reading.)—Oh! 'tis the first time you have grieved me; you always were so good and kee-ind.

END—Good and " kee-ind ! "

MID—(Reads)—Do you recall when last we parted ?

END—Do I ? Well, I thought you'd never get home.

MID—(Reading)—You were so full of joy and bliss.

END—Oh ! but you had a *load of joy and bliss on board*. (Laughs.) Where was that we parted? Corner of Freeze to Death and Chilly Avenues, wasn't it? You went one way, I went three different ways.

MID—(Angry)—I'm reading you the song.

END—I'm telling you how we parted.

MID—I don't wish to hear it. (Reads.) You were so true and gentle-hearted. I never thought (begins to sob) 'twould come to this.

END—Come to what?

MID—(Sobs)—I never thought 'twould come to this. (Weeps and sobs, then repeats *I never thought 'twould come to this*. End begins to sob and cry also. Both are now crying.)

MID—Oh, 'tis the wail of a saddened heart.

END—It sounds more like the *exhaust of a bath tub*.

MID—(Sobs)—You don't know how this touches me. (Weeping.)

END—I don't care as long as *you don't touch me*.

MID—(To Company)—Would you like to hear the chorus? (They all nod yes.) (To end.) Would *you* like to hear the chorus?

END—I'll stay if the rest do ! (All the weeping and sobbing is done according to judgment of both Middle and End.)

MID—It is in seven flats. (Wails.)

END—That sounds *a little flat* to me.

MID—(Half sings or wails)—Sweetheart ! Sweetheart ! I'm singing through the lattice.

END—It sounds as if you were singing *through your nose.*
MID—This song is sung to the accompaniment of the crickets.
END—Poor little crickets. It's tough on them.
MID—Sweetheart !
END—(Sobs)—Are there *two* of 'em?
MID—No. It is slurred !
END—The second sweetheart is *slurred*, poor thing. (Sobs.)
MID—(Sings)—Some day you will return to me. Oh! I can't sing it.
(Breaks down in sobs.)
END—Whistle it !
MID—Oh ! I can't see a note.
END—You never can *when they're due.* But go on; make me weep.
MID—(Sings)—'Twill free my heart from every—there's an accidental.
(Looks at music.)
END—Tear it off ! (Wipes eyes with 'kerchief.)
MID—Oh ! I can't finish it. (Weeps.)
END—I'm so glad. (Weeps.) You've got a nice voice and you read a song
so pathetically. Your voice is *fishy* and *scaly* like, but it's good. I was a good
singer before I got married. (Weeps) Oh! I'm so happy I wish I were dead.
MID—You married late in life. (Sobs.)
END.—(Sobs)—*I wish I'd made it later.*
MID—Whom did you marry ?
END—Widow Jones. Hank Jones' widow.
MID—Did he leave any real estate?
END—Yes ; *he left the earth.*
MID—I mean, did he leave anything?
END—(Crying)—What ?
MID—Did he leave anything?
END—Yes ; *I married what he left !*

N. B.—This is what is called a "Crying Gag," and judgment is required to
not overdo the sobs and weeping, gradually working up to a good crying finish.

MODERN DEFINITIONS OF COMMERCIAL TERMS.

END—Are you a man of business?
MIDDLE—No, sir; I am a gentleman of leisure. I'm living on my income.
END—I guess you haven't got long to live, have you ? Now, let me give you
a pointer about banking affairs, a sort of up-to-date definition of commercial
terms.
MID—What is a bankrupt?
END—A man who gives everything to his lawyer so that his creditors will
get it.
Assignee is the chap who has the *deal* and gives himself four aces.
A bank is a place where people put their money, so it will be handy when
other folks want it
A depositor is a man who don't know how to spend his money, and *gets the
cashier to show him.*
President is the big fat man who promises to boss the job and afterwards
sub-lets it.
A director is one of those that *accepts a trust* that don't involve either the use
of his eyes or ears.
Cashier is often a man who undertakes to support a wife, six children and a
brown stone front, *on thirty dollars a month and be honest.*
Collaterals are certain pieces of paper as good as gold and payable on the
first day of April.
Assets usually consist of five chairs and an old stove; to these may be added
a spittoon, if the *bust* ain't been a bad one.

Liabilities are usually a big *blind* that the assets won't *see* nor *raise* at any time.

A Note—"A promise to do an impossible thing at an impossible time."

MID—Suppose, in business, a man robs you of twenty dollars, what is he?

END—He's a thief, a mean, paltry thief.

MID—Suppose he robs the bank of half a million dollars?

END—Oh! *He's only a defaulter and a tourist.*

THE BOY STOOD ON THE BURNING ROOF.

END—I went to a party the other night and I heard a great recitation by Monahan, the Irishman that works in the lumber yard.

MIDDLE—What was the name of the recitation?

END—The Boy Stood on the Burning Roof.

MID—You've got it wrong, I know the recitation very well. It begins thus:

> The boy stood on the burning deck,
>   Whence all but him had fled.
> The flames that lit the battle wreck,
>   Shone brightly o'er his head.

END—Oh, cheese it! Not a bit like it. Yours is the old way. It won't do now-a-days. They want it up-to-date, with new ideas.

MID—Nonsense; that poem cannot be improved upon.

END—That's all you know about it. You ought to hear Monahan recite it, with his Irish brogue and the way he used his hands.

MID—Go ahead, recite it for us.

END—I'll show you how Monahan walked, talked and looked.

(Gets up and limps to C. and recites in Irish dialect, accompanying with grotesque gyrations and grimaces.)

> The boy stood on the burning roof,
>   Whence all but him had fled,
> The building being quite fireproof,
>   With flames was painted red.
>
> Huge tongues of flame in fiendish joy
>   Kept darting out like mad,
> And began to lick that noble boy,
>   As if they were his dad.
>
> "Jump!" yelled the horror stricken crowd,
>   "Jump, bubby, from the ridge."
> "I can't!" he dancing shrieked aloud,
>   *"This ain't no Brooklyn Bridge."*
>
> The firemen tried in sad despair
>   That gallant boy to soak,
> But alas, no stream could reach him there;
>   *And he began to smoke!*
>
> Then came a voice of thunder sound,
>   From one cool man below:
> "I'll save ye, boy, unless you're broiled—
>   Jump! when I say, to go!"
>
> Then snatching up a hose, he aimed
>   A mighty stream on high;
> *"Jump on that water!"* he exclaimed,
>   "And *grab it tight* or die!"
>
> Hurroo! With one terrific scream;
>   Out jumped that little kid,
> He grabbed that solid stream of water,
>   *And safely to the ground he slid.*

(Returns to seat.)

A VEGETABLE STORY.

END—I worked for a farmer and fell in love with his daughter. Her name was *Marjerum Pickles*, and her father was an *Old Seed Cucumber*. I had charge of the vegetables and I'd make love to his daughter as I worked in the garden, she was a vegetable girl. She had *carroty* hair, *reddish* cheeks, *turnip nose and eyes like onions*, and they'd always *leek*. I suppose you know the names of all vegetables, so I'll use their names to tell you my story. I was working one day, taking my *thyme* when along came *Sweet Marjoram* with such a *sage* look on her face that I said "Oh" seven times. I was about to *put eight o's* when I saw she had a bottle. She said it was *Pa's nip*, so I couldn't *cabbage* it. Just then *Old Pickles* came over the fence. It was of barbed wire and it tore his clothes badly, which made him *rue barb* fences after that. I saw he was mad for the bunch of *spinach* on his chin was agitated by the breeze. I says *lettuce* have *peas, beans* it's you! He says: "No; you can't *string beans* around here. I'll cut down your *celery*, you lazy *cauliflower*." My anger began to *sprout*. I threw a *tomato* at him, but it fell on his *corn*. Then he was *beet*. He found out that I was some *pumpkins* for I pickled that *cucumber* quick. I've been the *dandy lion* ever since. and now I'll *squash* my story.

HOLD YOUR HEAD UP.

END—I went to see my young lady the other night and her father came in. He says, "Who are you?" I told him I was a newspaper man and was going to start a paper. He says: "It looks so, you began to make your visits *weekly*. Then it grew to be *tri-weekly* and now it's *daily*, with a *Sunday supplement*." I told him after marriage we might have an *extra*. But there was no use starting a newspaper in that town. The old maids would go around and tell all the news before I could print it. When I proposed to this young lady I couldn't say a word. I got a sort of stage fright. I fell on my knees and couldn't think of anything. Just then her father came in and *helped me out*.
MIDDLE—For a fellow who pretends to be smart, you have a peculiar way in walking. You carry your head down. Why don't you walk with your head upright as I do!
END—I hang my head down and your head always stands up!
MID—Certainly, (laughs) your head hangs down.
END—Have you ever been through a field of wheat when its ripe? Some of the heads stand up and some hang down!
MID—Well, what of it?
END—The heads that stand up are empty. There's nothing in them.

THE SEGAR TRICK.

MIDDLE—I attended a reception last evening and I saw a clever thing. I think I can reproduce it. It is an optical illusion. (Produces two segars from vest and holds them up to view.) How many segars do I hold in my hand?
END—Two!
MID—You are wrong; I have three! I'll prove it. Here's one, and here's two! Two and one are three. See! It's a simple trick in addition and an optical illusion. (Is about to return segars to vest and laughing over his cleverness.)
END—Wait a minute. Do that again, will you? (Coaxes Mid. to show the trick again, which he does by pointing to one segar, then to the other, then adding them.)
MID—Here's one, here's two. Two and one are three. (Laughs.) Three segars. Very clever, very clever!
END—Let me see if I could do that.

MID—Oh, no! you're not clever enough. (End coaxes him to allow him the use of the segars.)

END—If it was too clever, you couldn't do it. (Holds up segars.) Here's one, here's two. Two and one are three (Laughs.)

MID—That's it. Give me the segars!

END—Let me do it again? (Counts as before.) Here's one, here's two. Two and one are three. Very clever, very clever! (To other End man.) Have a segar? (End man takes it.) I'll keep this one. (Puts remaining segar in his vest pocket and returns to seat.)

MID—Here, here! Where's my segar?

END—(Laughs.) You smoke the *third* one!

COINCIDENCES OF MARRIED LIFE.

Can be related alternately after overture, by 2 or 4 men

FIRST END.—There are some very strange coincidences in married life; something strange in the names of wives selected by business men. Now for instance; you remember Mr. Smith, the furniture dealer? Well, what do you think is his wife's name?

MIDDLE.—What is the name of the furniture dealer's wife?

FIRST END.—*Sofy* (sofa).

SECOND END.—You know Muldoon, the liquor dealer? Well, what do you suppose her name is?

MID.—What is the name of the liquor dealer's wife?

SECOND END.—*Ginny*.

THIRD END.—Say, you ought to hear what the fish dealer calls his wife!

MID.—What does he call her?

FIRST END.—*Nettie*.

FOURTH END.—Say, you know Johnson, the letter-carrier? Well, what do you think he calls his wife?

MID.—What does he call his wife?

FOURTH END.—*Carrie*.

FIRST END.—Say, (laughs) you know that man from Chicago? Well, he calls his wife *Trilby*. (Points to his feet.)

SECOND END.—And there's (name) the tonsorial artist! What do you think he calls his wife?

MID—What does he call her?

SECOND END.—*Barbera*.

THIRD END.—You know Mr. Courthouse, the lawyer? What a coincidence in his wife's name!

MID.—What does he call his wife?

THIRD END.—*Lize*.

FOURTH END.—And there's Jackson, the farmer. What do you suppose he calls his wife?

MID.—What is her name?

FOURTH END.—*Tilly*.

FIRST END.—Oh, I nearly forgot. (Laughs.) There's Simpson, the dentist.

MID—What does he call his wife?

FIRST END.—*Tootsey*.

SECOND END.—(Laughs) I came near forgetting about (mention his name). You know his wife is very fat. What do you suppose he calls her?

MID.—What does he call his wife?

SECOND END.—*Leaner*. (Lena.)

THIRD END.—Can you tell me an appropriate name for a shoemaker's wife?

MID.—I can't say that I can?

THIRD END.—*Peggy*.

FOURTH END.—Now, what would you call an auctioneer's wife?

MID.—Don't know!

FOURTH END.—*Bid-dy*.

COURTING AND THE NEW METHOD OF WEIGHING.

END.—I don't like my girl's little brother. He's a villain. He put a tack on the chair the other evening. And the *business end* of the tack was up. Well, I sat down and I jumped about ten feet. Now, if there's anything that will make a man rise quick in this world—it's a tack. And that boy laughed and laughed at me. Well, it *wasn't my place to laugh*, so I had to grin. We sit on the sofa and call each other pet names. She calls me *lovey-oh-lovey* and I call her *dovey*. Her right name is Livery Stables, but I don't call her that. Her people are all *high strung*. Her father was hung. All her folks belong to a base ball club. She used to *catch me* and ask me in the house and her big brother would *pitch me* out. Then I'd make a *home run* and stay there. Whenever I wanted to get her out, I'd go under the window and shout *fire*. She'd look out and say *Where's fire?* and I'd put my hand on my heart and say *Right here*. Her mother got on to my racket, for one night she threw a bucket of water all over me and *put the fire out.* Say, do you think (local town) is a healthy place? I do. Now, a friend of mine said to-day that when he first came here he weighed 86 pounds. Now he weighs 201 pounds. Must be a healthy place. Now when I first came here I only weighed 6 pounds ! Look at me now !

MIDDLE.—That's wonderful.

END.—Not so wonderful; I was *born here*. Speaking of weight, come down to the fish dock and see me *weigh the stuff;* then come over to the slaughter-house. I'm in great demand. I don't think this city could get along without me.'

MID.—Have you charge of the scales?

END.—No ! It's a new method. (Explaining.) They drive the cattle past me and I say those oxen *weigh eleven hundred pounds.* Those calves *weigh three hundred and six pounds,* those hogs *six hundred pounds,* those sheep *one thousand pounds,* and it's always accurate

MID.—You guess at it.

END.—No—No—right every time. It's a gift I have. I can tell the *weight* of anything. Tell how long you *wait* for her on the corner.

MID.—You can tell the weight of anything? I'll try you (To circle.) Gentlemen, I was weighed to-day and you know my weight. (Rises.) Come, sir ! How much do I weigh?

END.—Come down where I can see your feet. (Looks him over.) You—you weigh exactly 172 pounds and an ounce.

MID.—That's my weight to a fraction. This is wonderful. How do you do this? How can you do it?

END.—That's nothing? I'm weighing *hogs* every day !

(Middle man sits, disgusted.)

MUSICAL INSTRUMENTS.

END.—Come down and see me. I'm working in a music store. I'm head clerk. If a fly gets on the window, it's my duty to brush him off, and I chase dirt with a broom. When they are short of shavings they use me for shavings to pack boxes. Do you know that I can tell just what kind of a musical instrument a man wants the minute he comes into the store. If I know his occupation, I know just what musical instrument will suit him.

MIDDLE.—Do you mean to say that a man's business should have anything to do in selecting a musical instrument?

END.—Yes—and I'll bet you an overcoat—*something you need*—that I can prove that all occupations need certain musical instruments.

MID.—Very well; I'll try you. What would be a suitable instrument for a *letter carrier?*

END.—Letter carrier—*Bag pipes.*

MID.—What should a doctor play on ?

END.—Nose doctor—catarrh (*guitar*) and an ear doctor, the *drum.*

MID.—Musical instrument for free masons?
END.—*Cymbals.* (symbols.)
MID.—For bank cashiers and escaped swindlers?
END.—*Gong.* (Gone.)
MID.—A man that keeps a bad hotel?
END.—A *vile inn.* (violin.)
MID.—Good instrument for a pawnbroker?
END.—*Jew's harp.*
MID.—Good one for a politician?
END.—Any kind of a *wind organ.*
MID.—Good musical instrument for a mother-in-law?
END.—The *jaw bone.*
MID.—For ball players?
END.—The *double base.* (bass.)
MID.—Now what is a good instrument for two young lovers?
END.—*Mouth harmonicas!* Yum, yum, yum!

THINGS ARE VERY MIXED.

CROSS-FIRE.

BONES.—Peculiar thing I saw in a cemetery. A woman had buried *seven* husbands there, and to be economical she had one tombstone for the whole lot; she had a hand chiselled on it pointing upwards; I suppose in the direction she thought they had gone. An old gambler came along and wrote under the hand *seven up.* Speaking of gambling, did you ever hear the A B C of poker?
MID.—I don't quite comprehend
BONES.—The *A B C of poker*—an alphabet composed expressly for people who play poker. I'll recite it for you.
MID.—I'm all ears.
BONES.—Anybody can see that you're a donkey without *you* telling us. Now listen:

THE POKER ALPHABET.

A is the *ante*, B is the *bluff;*
C is the *cash* which is vulgarly *stuff;*
D is the *draw* a momentous event;
E is for *elevate*, takes your last cent;
F is the fun you have when you win;
G is the *gillie* who loses his tin;
H is the hand that is dealt to you *pat*:
I stands for *in*, an important thing that;
J is the *jack pot*, whose praises we sing;
K is the *kitty*, vivacious thing;
L is the loser, he's always around;
M is the money which does not abound;
N is the *noodle* that plays up *two pair;*
O is the *opener* laying his snare;
P is for poker, our national game;
Q stands for *quit*, but you don't all the same;
R is for *raise*, and it often sounds hard;
S is the *squeezer* that's marked on the card;
T is the time that you waste when you deal;
U is your *uncle* to whom you appeal;
V was the *come in*, you know the cost;
W is the *widow* who wins what you lost;
X is the sum that you bet upon *trips;*
Y is the youngster who *collared* the chips;
Z is the zeal with which one will expend
Time, money and gaslight to *do up* a friend.

TAMBO—Poker is all guess work, it's palmistry; trying to read other peoples' hands. I wish I could read my hand and find out who I am.
MID—Find out who you are? Why, don't you know?
TAMBO—No; I belong to the most mixed-up family you ever heard tell of.

I'm so mixed up that I'll commit suicide if I don't soon find out who I am and where I am.

MID—Tell me of your troubles; perhaps I can solve the problem for you.

TAMBO—It's all through marriage. I married a widow who had a grown-up daughter. My father visited our house very often, fell in love with my step-daughter and married her. So my father became my son-in-law. and my step-daughter, my mother, because she was my father's wife, and sh was also my mother-in-law. Soon afterwards my wife had a son; he was my father's brother-in-law and my uncle, for he was the brother of my step-mother. My father's wife, who was my step-daughter, had also a son ; he was, of course, my brother and in the meantime my grandchild, for he was the son of my daughter. My wife was my grandmother, because she was my mother's mother. I was my wife's husband and grand-child at the same time. (Begins crying.)

MID—Well, who are you?

TAMBO—I am my own grandfather.

WHAT LOVE WILL DO.

END—I attended a party last night, and a married man next to me got himself disliked. Some one passed him the tongue and he says: *No thanks; I get plenty of that at home.* Say, did you hear about it? My mother-in-law committed suicide. She left the gas turned on all night and in the morning she was defunct

MIDDLE—That's too bad.

END—I should say it was. *See the gas bill I'll have to pay.*

MID—I did not know that you were married.

END—I'm just beginning to realize it myself.

MID—Marriage, Sir, is like a beautiful dream.

END—That's right; you go into it with your *eyes shut.* But oh ! *how you wake up afterwards.*

MID—You shouldn't complain ; none but the brave deserve the fair.

END—It takes mighty brave men to get along with them after you deserve them. A man never gets through with dressmaker's bills and millinery. You don't see any more "Jerseys" worn now do you? That was purely an American invention.

MID—I beg to differ; they were made and worn abroad.

END—No, sir; the map of the United States was the first to wear a *New Jersey.* Are you married?

MID—No, but I expect soon to be.

END—Who would have you, I'd like to know?

MID—Ah ! I have several chances, but the girl I want for a wife must possess certain qualities. She must be sensible and not vain. She must be a help-mate in every sense of the word. I want a young lady for a wife who will go down in her mother's kitchen and knead bread !

END—(Laughs.) You bet your life, if she marries you, *she'll need bread.*

MID—No, sir ; for a good wife, I'd live on bread and water, and (enthusiastically) if we love each other, we'll both live on bread and water.

END—Correct again ! She'll have to furnish the bread, and you'll manage to get a *pail of water now and then.*

TWO NOBLE HEROES.

END—I see you are wearing a lot of medals on your coat. You're not Sousa or a hero from Manila, are you?

MIDDLE—No sir ! but I am a famous life-saver.

END—A life saver?

MID—If you have not heard the story I'll tell it to you. I chanced to be down at the sea-shore last summer.

END—You chanced to be there? Sneaked down, did you, in a freight car?
MID—(Annoyed.) Oh, no! As I said before, I chanced to be there. and while
strolling on the beach I saw a yachting party quite a distance out. Suddenly a treacherous squall swept in from the sea. The yacht was instantly
capsized. I heard a woman scream as the vessel careened and they were cast
into the sea. What did I do?
END—*You stole the boat.*
MID—(Vexed.) Nonsense! I instantly plunged into the water; swam out
with the over-hand stroke, for which I am famous, and reached one of the
ladies and brought her safe to the shore. I plunged in again and swam out
once more.
END—With the same *underhanded stroke* that you touch with?
MID—(Not noticing him.) I swam thus: (Illustrates the motion and becomes
excited and dramatic.) I reached another lady and brought her safe to the
beach. Then, sir, I plunged in again—(everybody excited) swam out to what
I supposed was another drowning woman. I reached out and grasped—what?
A lady's switch! But I brought it ashore and presented it to the woman who
had lost it.
END—And you call yourself a life-saver? You're not a hero nor a life-saver.
MID—What am I?
END—You're a *hair restorer.*

THE NEW HOTEL.

RULES AND REGULATIONS

END—If you're ever hungry and sleepy, come down to my new hotel. I'll treat
you all right.
MID—So you've opened a hotel, have you? Are you doing well?
END—As well as could be expected   I have a set of rules and regulations, or I
could never run it at all. Would you like to hear them?
MID—I certainly would.
END—Here they are: (reads from paper.)

ATTENTION, BOARDERS, STRANGERS AND GUESTS.

Board, 50 cents per square foot ; meals extra.
Breakfast at five, Dinner at six and Supper at seven.
Guests are requested not to speak to the *dumb waiter.*
Guests wishing to *get up* without being called, can have *self* raising flour
for Supper or a pint of yeast to *rise* earlier.
Not responsible for diamonds, bicycles or trunks left under the pillows. *Leave
them with the landlord.*
The hotel is convenient to all cemeteries. Hearses to hire at 25 cents a day.
Guests wishing to do a little driving will find a *hammer and nails* in the
closet.
If the room gets too warm open the window and *see the fire escape.*
If you're fond of athletics and like good jumping, *lift the mattress and see the
bed spring.*
Baseballists desiring a little practice will find *a pitcher on the stand.*
If the lamp goes out, *take a feather out of the pillow ;* that's light enough for
any room.
Any one troubled with night-mare will find *a halter on the bed-post.*
Don't worry about paying your bill ; the house *is supported by its foundations.*
We do not ring a bell for breakfast, we *wring* a towel or let the *napkin ring.*
If you find anything valuable in the soup, please return it to the landlord, so
he can *use it again.*
Eggs, two cents for two ; each, *if hatched, one cent extra.*

If you wish to see gaudy insects fluttering in your room to remind you of summer, get some bread and butter.

It is the *grub* that makes the *butter-fly*.

Rooms, with or without floors, walls or ceiling.

At the table if you wish the milk, don't yell *pass the cow;* somebody will *take you for a calf.*

If you are from (local town), blow out the gas. You don't know any better.

A DIFFICULT PROBLEM.

END—I was working on the farm last summer and a dude came up to me and wanted to be funny. He says: " Boy ! bring me a ' milk shake ' quick."

MIDDLE—What did you do?

END—I brought him the churn ! That was a milk shake   Are you married ?

MID—No, sir; and don't intend to be.   Marriage, sir, is just like a lottery.

END—Oh, I don't know ; you don't have to *keep the lottery ticket.* I don't think I'll get married either.   My young lady and I are out.   I had a tandem and she wouldn't ride on the front seat.

MID—Why not ?

END—She said it looked *too forward.*   How funny life turns out ; it's full of " *izes.*"

MID—Full of "*izes ?* "   I don't quite understand you.

END—Then I'll "illustrasize" it for you.   At twenty a man theor*izes;* at forty he philosoph*izes;* at sixty he real*izes ;* also, at twenty he scrutin*izes* all the girls ; at twenty-two he idol*izes* some other fellow's sister ; at twenty-six he jeopard*izes* his neck by staying out late; at twenty-seven he paral*izes* himself if he has the price.   So, you see, life is full of '*izes.*'   Are you good at figures and problems?

MID—Yes ; I am counted quite clever.

END—Take out your paper and pencil and figure this out for me.   (Middle with pencil and card.) Now then, a man of thirty-five years old marries a girl of five.

MID—*Five years old ?   Nonsense !*

END—Put it down.   A man of thirty-five marries a girl of five.   He is now *five* times as old as his wife.

MID—Yes ; seven times five are thirty-five.

END—They live together five years; now he is forty and she is ten years old, and he's only *four* times as old as his wife.

MID—Ten times four are forty; go on !

END—They live together five years longer.   Now he's forty-five and she's fifteen.   Now he's only *three* times as old as his wife.

MID—Yes, sir.   Go on; you've got me interested.

END—They live together fifteen years longer; put that down.   Now he is sixty years old and his wife is thirty years of age.   Now he's only *twice* as old as his wife.

MID—(Anxiously.)—Yes, yes; go on !   He's now only *twice as old* as his wife.

END—Now figure it all up and tell me *how long they have got to live together until they're both of the same age ?*

(Middle completely floored and End triumphantly laughs and looks at audience.)

BON VOYAGE.

END – What business are you in?   I saw you taking a lot of old tin cans into a grocery store.

MID—I'm in the *canning business*—canning pears, peaches and tomatoes.

END—Is that so?   I'm in the wholesale dry goods business.   So you're in the canning business, are you?   What do you do with such a whole lot of pears and peaches?

MID—Well, we eat what we *can*, and what we can't eat we *can*. (Laughs at his witty retort.)

END—(Thoughtfully.)—Eat what you can, and what you can't eat you *can!* Just like my business.

MID—How?

END—We *sell* an order when we can *sell* it and when we can't *sell* it, why, we *can-cel* it. (Laughs derisively.) Eat what you can, and what you can't eat you *can!* You're a *can-can* kind of a chump, you are.

MID—I heard that you went to Europe last summer. Did you have a *bon voyage?* (Strong French accent.)

END—The *bummest* you ever saw.

MID—I mean was it exhilarating?

END—No! I went *in the steerage*.

MID—You don't quite comprehend me. Did you have a *bon voyage?*

END—I tell you it was very *bum* all the way over.

MID—"*Bon voyage*" means a good trip, a splendid voyage. Friends will stand on the wharf and as you sail away they will wish you a *bon voyage*.

END—That's what you mean, is it? Well, I never want to see such a trip again. The first day out, it was splendid. Everybody was on deck. The ladies swapping magazines ; the men swapping cigars and chews of tobacco. It was a happy family, and all were on the best of terms. But the third day ! (Makes a motion with hands and a grimace of pain shows on face.) The third day ! The ship turned a somersault. Oh, but it was rough and stormy ! All the passengers would come upon deck and look at one another kind of suspicious like. They didn't trust one another or care to be friendly. It seemed that if they knew anything about one another, they'd *throw it up* right away. I was down in my cell—

MID—Not cell, state-room.

END—Yes ; I'm getting the tips mixed. I was very sick. I was just able to crawl on deck and holler "New York" and "Europe" in a subdued manner. Talk about your *bum* voyage. It was worse than that. Everybody was sick. The captain and even all the sailors were sick. I felt sorry for one poor sailor. Oh ! he was the sickest sick sailor on the ship, and I felt sorry for him on this *bum* voyage.

MID—(Correctingly.)—How do you know he was the sickest man on the ship?

END—Because the captain ordered him to go forward and *heave up the anchor !*

Section UII.

MONOLOGUES.

In this section will be found many novel monologues, etc., yet the monologuist is not confined to them, as the gags and cross-fires in Section VI. contain many bright anecdotes and squibs which can be made to become part and parcel of an original monologue. By recalling a number of these short happenings, the story-teller will be able to construct any number of monologues upon varied subjects. The inventive entertainer can easily arrange some original patter that will consistently lead from one subject to another, and as monologuists have a wide license in the selecting of their topics or *chatter* he will find abundant material in Sections VI. and VII. for his use.

ARE WOMEN MORE BEAUTIFUL THAN MEN?

A MONOLOGUE.

I have been asked to come here before this assemblage of graduates, learned people, bond holders and the sheriff, who is concealed somewhere in the building, to take up a knotty problem. I know that I shall get myself disliked by the men and I shall be hated by the women, but the truth is mighty and must prevail, and my maiden name is Truth. The subject is, "Are women more beautiful than men?" I want you to take a good look at me and then ask such a silly question; yet, it is a question agitating many minds and must be sifted at once. Are women more beautiful than men? Do men stand admiring themselves or combing their hair for hours at a time? Rubbing rouge on their faces; salve on their lips? Penciling their eyebrows and blackening their eyelashes; do they? I've seen them black each others eyes, but that was done when they didn't expect it. Do men lace themselves so tight that they can't sit down? They get tight, I'll admit, and can't stand up, or get up, but that's not through lacing. Its through fullness, that has been accumulated in several places. You ask, "Is man more beautiful than woman!" Go to the menagerie; look around you! The lioness is a very plain-looking animal. Look at the Lion. A noble-looking fellow, with a mane and a superior look in his face. Take a look at the Peacock's wife. A plain ordinary looking affair; but he, the gentleman, the Peacock! Isn't he a beauty? Isn't he a dream? Talk of loveliness! Then look at the bird of Paradise, gorgeous plumage and lovely feathers on his head. He's a *he* too! His wife looks like thirty cents. Then look at the majestic Rooster in the barn yard! What a display of beautiful manhood and elegance. What does the hen look like? She's a sight! She's going around in a wrapper, scratching here and there, and talking; back-biting her neighbors. She looks up to her husband as a superior being, and she knows he is. She's thankful she's alive, for she's too homely to die. Look at the gentlemen Ostrich! See him strutting about. eating nails, horseshoes and scrap iron. There is a vision of manly beauty, and his wife, a little sawed-off, measly-looking bird, with hardly enough feathers to make a bustle. Nothing could be more handsome than a beautiful man! *Are you looking at Me!!* I have taken the animals as an illustration and a proof.

Now we come to the next generation of animals—man! Nobody wants to descend from monkeys, but sometimes we can't help that which our ancestors do, or were. I am not here to go back into my family tree and find out who cut up monkey-shines in it.

We hear the gabbling of this one or that one, saying that woman, the beautiful creature, chooses her mate. And that often she marries a homely man! In olden times man stole his wife. He'd dash right in, grab whoever he could and away he went. Now-a-days he wishes somebody would rush in and steal her from him, but they won't. There's where times have not improved. I said primitive man stole his wife; later on he bought her. He's given horses, sheep or furs to her parents, and thus bought her. Of course he was buncoed ; just as he is now-a-days. She didn't care about his looks as long as he had money and was soft and easy. In fact, what we call now-a-days "a good thing." In the present century woman often buys a husband. All she gets in return is a title, a broken-down, moth-eaten bargain-counter duke or an earl. This shows that man is still the handsomest creature, or why would they go across the ocean after him and give him all that good American money—just to get his name? There is no doubt that woman is very beautiful, artificially or accidentally, and they are called the "fair sex" because they are always fair in dealing with the men, if the men are out of their reach. Their fancy colored silks, satins, false hair, manufactured cheeks and per-oxide of hydrogen, blond tresses, of course, give them additional charm, but we do not need these deceptions to increase our beauty. We do not sail under false colors. You see us *just as we are.* Our beauty speaks for itself, and we are the real dairy butter and *not oleo-margerine.* Are woman handsomer than men? Ask this question of one another and look around you—upon the natural beauty of the speaker and the gentlemen here assembled. An old English law states that any woman with false hair, false color on cheeks, defective eyesight, or in any way passing herself off as a beauty and natural looking woman ; and luring a poor man into marriage, why, it was a crime and the marriage was null and void. A fine law, a good law, but if that law was in force in this city, what a lot of old maids would be looking for work ! (Exits.)

GOATS.

A MONOLOGUE.

I see that another wonderful medical discovery has been made which will give long life to the human race. Ages ago they sought for the elixir of life, so man could live for ever. Just think of a man who is about seventy taking the new discovery and he becoming a school boy at once. Cheating the undertaker and everybody who expects him to croak. Think of a giddy old maid of sixty, gulping down the elixir and sailing in, capturing all the men from the grass widows and young flirts This time the elixir of life has been discovered in goats, and in Chicago. The goat has a strong constitution and never dies; therefore, he is the very one to prolong life in the human race. Wherever goats are abundant, you will see eternal life and life blooming around you. This has been successfully tried in Chicago and it worked all right. They always *work* you all right in Chicago. This goat lymph or "Life cells" as is called, is a great thing for mankind. One dose of it will make a man *butt* his mother-in-law down stairs and eat up all the old tomato cans and posters off the wall, especially if they advertise a burlesque show. Any father can be harnessed to a little wagon and used as a "goat" to amuse children of a younger age. It has been tried and proven to be the real thing in Chicago. But the experimenters, with commendable caution, first made up their minds to carry out the process known as ' trying it on the dog." A canine of fourteen years was made the recipient of these "Life cells" through the medium of hyperdermic injections. And lo! his doggish age was transformed into the liveliness of the frolicsome puppy. He capered. He barked joyously. He chased his own tail in wild abandon. He chewed up all the rugs and old boots in reach with a keen appetite. And the disciples of science were satisfied that at length they had discovered a sure method to forestall the approach of age and turn tottering senility into the pulsing glow of youth. Several human beings have been inoculated with this wonderful lymph, and confident hopes are entertained that they will presently show themselves as responsive to its influence as the dog. If this proves to be the case, life insurance companies may go out of business and the doctors can pull in their shingles. Nobody will grow old or die. All that will be necessary to insure perpetual youth will be the ownership of a healthy goat, warranted not to butt.

It is indeed a thrilling thought, and there will always be an explanation hereafter of any erratic conduct on the part of Chicago's citizens. If any of their number should be arraigned before a Magistrate for too much hilarity he can repel the charge of intoxication with scorn. It will merely be a case of *too much goat.*

FLIRTATION AND ITS CONSEQUENCES.

A SHORT MONOLOGUE PREFACE.

I have just a few words to say about flirting. Girls don't do it! Better remain old maids all your lives than flirt with strangers. Now, with me it's different. You needn't treat me as a stranger; I'll be a brother to you all. I've had over fifty girls tell me they'd be a sister to me, so I can get even by being a brother to some of you. But remember you can't wear any of this (pointing to self) brother's clothes; he hasn't too many of 'em himself. Here is a little poem on flirting. Mark well the consequences.

Man sees maid; no word said.
She drops glove; he's in love.
Hands to her, "Thank you, sir."
She says that. He lifts hat.
They soon talk; then take walk.
They have cream, love's young dream.
Out with moon, how they spoon!
"Will you wed?" She nods head.
They are tied. Life they've tried.
Don't like it, just one bit.
Knot's untied. 'Way they glide!

WHAT IS A KISS?

A MONOLOGUE.

I spent the summer at a watering place. I had charge of it; that is to say, I had to keep it filled with water so the horses and cows could drink out of it. My! but it was warm. I had to keep my mouth full of cracked ice to keep my teeth from melting. It was so hot that ice cream began to fry and boil the minute it was frozen. I never saw such hot weather. I guess the thermometer must have been sixty degrees below (principal tree). But for all that I enjoyed myself courting. I can't help it; I'm so susceptible. Girls tell me I'm soft, but I don't believe it. I've got a confiding nature, and if they fool me I'm not to blame. But there I'd sit and court and we'd hold hands. What is nicer than to see a couple going along the street, he having her by the hand? He takes her by the hand; and if he's married, when he gets home, he takes her *by the neck.* As I said before, we'd court and I'd stay late. I would have stayed later but I was afraid her father *would kick.* Her father called me a soda water man; that is the first time I ever knew I looked like a squirt. He once threatened to turn the gas off; that would just suit me. We didn't need any light, for they say love is blind. To prove that love is blind or isn't blind, I was passing the parlor floor, where a young man was courting her sister, and it was quite dark in there I heard her say: "Oh George! you haven't been shaved to-day." How did she know he hadn't been shaved?

I distinctly heard them kiss each other. It sounded like a cow drawing her foot out of the mud. It must have loosened all her back teeth. But what is a kiss? Don't you know? A kiss is an application of two heads and four lips; they create a spark of electricity, which generates a blaze of love and a flame of admiration and a "hot time" in your heart; which burns with the fires of Cupid. What is ove? Love is an *itching* of the heart, and you can't *scratch* it out.

STUMP SPEECHES.

WOMAN'S TONGUE.

THIS CAN ALSO BE USED FOR A MONOLOGUE.

Fellow citizens, sceptics, Cubans and Filipinos:—I have been called upon to address this assemblage, and I may as well commence—by beginning. Now, we hear of strikes every now and then, but strikes are no new things. Cain's strike was a bad thing for both Abel and Cain. A blacksmith once *struck* "while the iron was hot" and people have been talking about it ever since. George Washington went on a *strike* in 1776, and he won it without any arbitration. No man ever succeeded in a strike against his mother-in-law, or striking for pie. Having begun with strikes, I'll now strike into my subject. My dear hearers, there's nothing destroys so many lives, as death. Some people are killed by accident, and some in battle ; some are lost at sea and some are devoured by wild beasts ; but, my hearers, it is a solemn truth, that nothing kills so many as *death*. Aye, death has been at work ever since sin entered the world, and has destroyed millions on millions of the human family. Lots of people died this year who never *died before*. In view of all this and hotel fires, I have pasted the following hotel regulations in my boarding house : Guests jumping from fifth-story windows will be charged extra. In the office of the hotel is a large fire-proof safe ; the proprietor will not be liable for any guest who does not deposit himself in it for the night. Fire-pumps, served in the rooms, charged extra. But that is neither here nor there. I started in to address this assemblage on the crisis and expansion of territory, on imperialism and the board of strategy in general. To show you the memory and rapidity of the American people, I will relate the following: A Delaware farmer sent his ten-year old boy to the spring after a pitcher of water. The boy hid the pitcher near the spring and went away to the West and grew up with the country. Fifteen years later he sold a thousand long-horned steers and started for his old home. Stopping at the spring he found the pitcher just as he had left it when he went away mad. He filled it, and walking beneath the parental roof like the prodigal from Squedunk said : "Father, here is the pitcher of water." "Thanks, my son," said the thirsty ancestor, "you always were a quick boy to go on an errand."

Now, always remember that woman's tongue is her sword, and she never lets it rust in the scabbard. What does man want? All he can get. What does a woman want? All she *can't* get. Once a Boston woman, tall, thin, with false curls and sour visage, sat in a restaurant and beside her sat her husband, a meek, demure-looking man. Presently a man at another table roared out: "Waiter ! fetch the vinegar bottle." Then the little man turned to his wife and said: "Dovey, somebody wants you." Now see the difference. A man in New York was arrested for trying to set his wife on fire. That's the meanest way a man can take to make it warm for his wife. Another young lady who was being treated to ice cream for the first time, was asked by her young man how she liked it. She says : "It tastes very good, but I always prefer my pudding hot " She was from (local town near by.) Now the meanest way a girl can treat a young man is to refuse his offer of marriage, writing it to him on a postal card. It shows she does not care *two cents* for him. A girl who was locked in her sweetheart's arms for nearly two hours says it wasn't her fault. She says *he forgot the combination*. But that is neither here nor there. This is the age of cheapness and economy. For ten cents a man can get his shirt washed or a drink of whiskey. That accounts for so many dirty shirts worn in this town. But I want to say right here, that this is the age of progress, invention. "go-ahead—ac-tive-ness," electricity and mechanism. You can do anything. You can stop Niagara Falls with a few planks, you can dip up the Atlantic with a teaspoon, you can hold yourself out at arm's length, you may flit from star to star or from Pole to Pole. From North Pole to barber pole, from satellite to Israelite. You may lasso a comet or ride bareback on a melting rain-bow, you may harness a wild tornado or capture a blizzard in a pill box, you can pull down the sun and squeeze the moon into a potato bag, you can put out the fires of Mount Vesuvius with a cup of water, but you'll never put a stop to woman's tongue! (Strikes table with umbrella and exits).

THE MOUSE.

STUMP SPEECH FOR LADIES.

Ladies! I again exclaim, ladies! Your attention, please, as I am speaking to *you* only, and not *that* which is seated beside you. The men are not in this, and I am not addressing them either. They are too insignificant to be noticed by me. I won't even address them as men, but I'll call them, *it* or *that* or *those*, and you'll know what I mean. I came here to advocate your cause, to speak on woman's *rights*; for she has been *left* too often. I want you ladies to insist on your rights. If you are married, grab it by the hair, pound it's head on the floor, walk on it's neck until it shouts as did Spain: "I surrender!" Be masters, be your own conquerors and hold the insect called "man" in the chains of obedience. Let him know that we are the real people, and he is but a yellow dog under the band wagon. Let us look around and see what has been accomplished? What have we done for ourselves? Have we *done* man sufficiently? Of what use is he? Can anyone tell me what he was created for? Where does he come in? Of course somebody has got to pay our board. Somebody has got to pay for our new dresses, bonnets, jewelry, ice cream, candy, suppers, theatres and excursions. That is why man was put upon this earth. All evils have their uses, all animals, no matter how venomous are here for a purpose. Man was placed here for a rug for us to wipe our feet upon. Will you tell me of what use it is besides this? (Pause.) Speak out! What are you afraid of? If you lose the fellow you've got here to night, you can get a dozen more to-morrow! The idiots are waiting to be gathered up! To see the important airs assumed by a man is enough to give a progressive woman a fit, or a spasm, or the chills and fever. He thinks we're crazy after him, the fool! He allows us to sit on his lap until his limbs are dead from his knees down. Then later, after he has coaxed us to marry him and we sit on his lap he says: "Oh, Gertrude, you are so heavy." Couldn't you slap his face? I could. And when he's courting us, hear the lies he tells us, and we, like *chumps*, believe every word There is where we are weak. Sisters, we have got to shake this ungrateful monster called man. You can get along without it, if you'll only try. It doesn't cut any ice. It tries to blame everything on us After it is married to us and it stays out late and we reprimand it about it, with a poker or a flat iron, it says it's our fault that it stays out late. That when he was courting us and he'd start to go home, we'd say: "Don't go yet; you've got plenty of time," and we'd hold him at the front door. Of course it's a base fabrication. I never held anyone there. When he wanted to go, I'd sit on him quick, and he couldn't go. Did you ever hear such a petty larceny excuse in all your life? I*f* taught him to stay out late. And now that he's married, he can't break himself of the habit. Girls, break his head with a nice fat rolling-pin. And hit him on top of his thinking place. Don't be afraid to hit him hard. You'll look sweet dressed in black, and maybe you'll get his life insurance, too.

But I am here to better your condition, to elevate you, to obtain for you your rights. You have as many rights as a man. Be sure you get your rights; forcibly if you must, but get them any way. The cunning wretches take mighty good care that we take their names; nobody else would, I guess. We take their names! It ought to be reversed. They ought to take our names, for sometimes everything a man has got is *in his wife's name.* Are you going to stand his tyranny? Are you going to be under man's foot all your lives? Assert yourselves! As you are going home to night, and he like a viper, whispers in your ear: "Will you have some ice cream, dear?" Turn on him! Let indignation flash from your eyes, and hiss at him: "No! I can buy my *own* ice cream." But will you do it? Will you rebuke him? Those girls in the audience who will rebuke him thus, please stand up! (Pause, then louder.) I say, those who will not have ice cream from any man, stand up! That'll do; sit down. Nobody stood up. You're afraid to lose a good thing, you're afraid the poor, mushy, soft fool at your side would leave you. You couldn't club him away. He's a leech, a sticking-plaster, a necessary evil in the ice cream line. I stand here, bold and defiant, and like Ajax defying the lightning. I hurl my abuse at the men. Here I stand like the rock of Gibraltar. Not ten millions of hated men could make me move from my position. Like dirt under my feet, I spurn them; bid them come on! I'll show you what one brave woman can do. One brave woman whom man can never intimidate, one brave woman—(suddenly screams.)—Oh, a mouse, a mouse! (Gathers up skirts and dashes off stage yelling : Police! Help me! Can show part of funny pantalettes in hurried exit).

MARK ANTHONY'S ORATION.

HUMOROUS SPEECH.

Friends, Romans, Countrymen ! Lend me your ears. I will return them next Saturday. I come to bury Caesar because the times are hard and his folks can't afford to hire an undertaker. The evil that men do lives after them, in the shape of progeny, who reap the benefit of their life insurance. Brutus has told you Caesar was ambitious. What does Brutus know about it? It is none of his funeral. Would that it were. Here under leave of you I come to make a speech at Caesar's funeral. He was my friend, faithful and just to me. He loaned me $5 once, when I was in a pinch and signed my petition for a post office. But Brutus says he was ambitious. Brutus should wipe off his chin. Caesar hath brought many captives home to Rome, who broke rock on the streets, until their ransoms did the general coffers fill. When the poor hath cried Caesar hath wept, because it didn't cost him anything, and it made him solid with the gang. Ambition should be made of sterner stuff, yet Brutus says he was ambitious. Brutus is a liar, and I can prove it. You all did see that on the Bowery I thrice presented him with a kingly crown, which he did thrice refuse, because it did not fit him quite. Was this ambition? Yet Brutus says he was ambitious. Brutus is not only the biggest liar in the country, but he is a horse thief of the deepest dye. If you have any tears prepare to shed them now. You all do know this ulster. I remember the first time Caesar put it on ; it was on a summer's evening in his tent, with the thermometer registering 90 in the shade. But it was an ulster to be proud of and cost him $7 at (local clothing store) sign of the red flag The old man wanted $40 for it, but finally came down to $7 because it was Caesar. Was this ambition? If Brutus says it was he's a greater liar than Aguinaldo. Look ! In this place, ran Cassius' dagger through. Through this place, the son-of-a-gun of a Brutus stabbed ; and when he drew his cursed steel away, mark how the blood of Caesar followed it. I came not, friends, to steal away your hearts. I'm not the thief Brutus is. He has a monopoly on all that canned beef business, and if he had his deserts, he would be in the penitentiary, and don't you forget it, for life ! Kind friends, sweet friends ! I do not wish to stir you up to such a flood of mutiny, nor do I want you to go back on Brutus, David Hill, Grover Cleveland, Tom Platt or any of the senators. I merely want you to step on Brutus' neck and keep your feet on it for a week. As it looks like rain the pall bearers will place the coffin in the "Bier" wagon and will proceed to bury Caesar in (local cheap hotel.) (*Points off and exits*).

HOW ADAM AND EVE TURNED WHITE.

A DARKEY'S SERMON TO HIS CONGREGATION.

To be delivered in a slow-loud tremulous voice.

My beloved sistern and breddering. I'm a man what reads a great deal, and I'm going to 'splain to you how Adam and Eve turned white, for dey was originally black as you am, or I am. Well, it 'pears dat de Lawd, after he done made Adam and Eve, sot'em in de Garden ob Edem, dat de Lawd he tol' em bofe dat dar was a sartin tree dar and dat dey musn't eat none of eet's fruit. Dis tree, it 'pears to me, if I don't disremember, eet bared a *kind* 'er apple. You know same as me, dat a woman 's a powerful curus pusson. She allus like to be a-peekin' and a pryin' into something or other—no matter whether it consarns her or not. Ole Miss Eve—dat dar was ole man Adam's wife—she warnt to be stopped from nothin'. 'Twant long afore she knowed dat de Lawd didn't want her to meddle wif dem apples dat she went and made a pie and sort er bobbecued some of the Lawd's apples. She did this, for truth. 'Twant no yarn dat some of de mean white folks have brung agin ole Miss Eve. She sartinly did get de Lawd's apples. When dat ole woman don got 'em, sure enough, de Lawd he war monstrous mad. He put all de blame on ole Adam, 'cause de Lawd he sorter think dat ole man Adam oughter have took better care of ole Miss Eve dan to 'low her to bobbecue de Lawd's apples. When de pair of 'em had done eat de apples dey crope off and hid in de bushes. Dey war so scared of de Lawd, dat scared ain't no name for de business. Dey war so scared dat dey turned deef and den dey turned white Dey neber did 'zactly git over their scare. Dey did git to hearin' ag'in, but their skins never did get colored no more, and dat am how de white man come here. He's white because of de meanness of ole man Adam and ole Miss Eve. But let me go on wif my history. When de Lawd done found out dat dese ole pussons had done eat some of his apples, he war monstrous mad. He yell out: "Yo' Adam!" but 'pears Mr. Adam he didn't hear. Den de Lawd ses, ses he: "Adam, why yo' eat my apples, sah? Is you so deef you can't hear nuffin', or is you gone foolish, sah? You go right away and bring Miss Eve here, sah; gyarments or no gyarments!"

My friends, you mought say dat ar war powerful bad manners of de Lawd. But den de Lawd ain't agawine to be fooled with. When He's plum mad he don't spar' no one. Bime-by up crope ole Miss Eve walkin' sorter behind ole man Adam, and kind of giggling and peeking over de ole man's shoulder. When dey done come up to de Lawd, de Lawd he ses, ses he: "You's both a par of no count triflin niggers. You done stole my apples, and you's fixin' to git my chickens next. Git outer dis garden bofe of you, and never come back here no more for nuthin', not even for your gyarments. Git out from here quick." Den de Lawd showed 'em de gate, and give de ole debil de job ter watch dat gate, to see dat neider Miss Eve nor Mr. Adam come in dar no more. And Miss Eve, she was forced to sit in de bushes outside dat gate, 'twell Mr. Adam, he done made 'em some new gyarments. And while Mr. Adam, he sewed, Miss Eve she sang dat good ole hymn: "I Loves to steal awhile."

And dat, my friends, am de trufe of de trouble what ole man Adam had wif de Lawd, and de history of how de white man come here. Bofe Miss Eve and Mr. Adam dey war so scared dat dey never got back their color no more. Some of their young'uns war black and some war white, most same as you often see an ole white hen with a hull gang of chickens, some white and some black. Don't fool with de Lawd, my friends, else he'll scare you so bad dat you'll be arunnin' around looking foolish, jest same as de mean white trash.

CONUNDRUMS.

In telling these the End man asks the question, the Middle man responds: "I do not know," and repeats the question, which is answered by the End man. (Example):

END—"If your sister fell in a well, why couldn't you rescue her?"

MIDDLE—"I don't know. If my sister fell in a well, *why* couldn't I rescue her?"

END—"Because you could not be her brother and *a-ssist her too.*"

What reptile is up in arithmetic?
The *adder.*

When is the army like a tuck in a lady's skirt?
When it is *hemmed in.*

Why should a man never be trusted for a hat?
Because he is then *over head and ears in debt.*

When is an old maid like a segar?
When you have no *match* for it.

When is a loaf of bread inhabited?
When there's *Indian* meal in it.

When does a man impose on himself?
When he *taxes* his memory.

What word is pronounced wrong by the best scholars?
Wrong of course.

Why are old maids the most charming of all people?
Because they are *matchless.*

Why is the polka like bitter beer?
Because there are so many *hops* in it.

Why is an angry man like a camel?
Because he's got his *back up.*

Why is the letter "P" like a sympathizing friend?
Because it's the *first* in pity, but the *last* in help.

Why is the sofa your father is sitting upon like most railway stock?
Because it is *below pa.* (Par.)

What's the hardest thing to *beat?*
A hard boiled egg.

Why are apples the enemies of pears?
Because it was an apple that drove a *pair* out of the Garden of *Eden.*

Why did Eve swear when Adam asked to kiss her?
Because she replied, I don't care *A-dam* if I do.

If Satan should lose his tail where would he find another?
Where they *re-tail bad spirits.*

Why was Noah the first base ball player?
Because he sent the dove "*out on the fly.*"

Why was it useless to take the dogs into the Ark at the time of the flood?
Because they had *barks* of their own.

What paper has the largest circulation in the world?
Paper of tobacco!
Who is the editor?
Anybody that *chews*!

When does a farmer double a sheep without hurting it?
When he *folds it.*

When is a shoemaker like a doctor?
When he is *heeling*.

Why is a butcher's cart like his boots?
Because he carries his *calves* there.

When are potatoes used for mending clothes?
When they are put in *patches.*

Why are lawyers like fishes?
Because they are fond of *de-bate.*

Why are troubles like babies?
Because they grow bigger by nursing.

How can you make people acknowledge their corn?
Tread on their *toes.*

Why is a minister like a locomotive?
Because we look out for him *when the bell rings.*

Why should a bachelor never be a president of the United States?
Because he doesn't believe in *union.*

How can you avoid drowning?
Always keep your head *above* water.

Why is a new-born baby like a cow's tail?
Because it was never *seen before.*

What is a mother-in-law?
She is the person who attends to the *pickles* and *preserves* the family sweet-meats and matrimonial *jars.*

Which islands are good to eat?
The Sandwich Islands.

What would be the most suitable watch for a farmer?
An eighteen *carrot silver turnip.*

Why do the ladies hate parrots?
Because they want to do *all the talking themselves.*

What is the funniest burglary on record?
Bursting into a laugh.

Why does a duck go under water?
For *divers* reasons.

What ought a steamboat captain give to a big rascal?
Give him a *wide berth.*

Why are some of the bills in Congress counterfeits ?
Because they have such difficulty in *passing* them.

How can you cheat the enemy in battle ?
Charge them with cavalry which *they never get.*

If two fat men fall out of a third story window, what kind of a vegetable can you raise?
Two large *squashes.*

What will make a pensive husband ?
An *ex*pen*sive wife.*

What is always ready but never wanted ?
Old maids.

Why is a palm tree like an almanac?
Because it furnishes *dates.*

How does a ghost enter a room that is locked ?
He uses a *skeleton key.*

When is a whip most likely to break ?
When it is *cracked.*

Why is the fair sex in winter suspected of a tendency to homicide?
Because they are fond of *sleighing.*

Why is a henpecked husband like an opera hat ?
Because he's *big* when he gets out, but *shuts up* when he gets home.

What's the difference between a novel and a painted damsel ?
One is read because it is interesting, the other is interesting because it is *red.*

When a man falls out of window what does he fall against?
He falls *against* his will.

Why is an author the most peculiar of animals ?
Because the *tale* comes out of his head.

Why do ladies make bad telegraph operators?
Because you can't prevent them from having the *last word.*

Why is a chair-maker very much disliked ?
Because people get *down* on his works.

Why do old maids make the best euchre players ?
Because they are used to *going alone.*

What's the earliest Spring?
Jumping out of bed at one o'clock in the morning.

When is a ship at sea not on the water?
When she is *on fire.*

What can a man have in his pocket when it's empty?
A big hole.

Who are the acrobats in every household?
The *pitcher* and the *tumbler.*

What length ought a lady's petticoat be?
A little above *two feet.*

In what three countries are most books bound?
Morocco, Turkey and *Russia.*

What ladies light up well at night?
Those with *lantern jaws.*

When are soldiers like good flannels?
When they don't *shrink.*

Why is an old coat like an iron kettle?
Because it represents *hard ware.* (Wear.)

What's the difference between a mischievous mouse and a charming young lady?
One harms the *cheese* and the other charms the *hes.*

If I were to take an axe and knock your teeth down your throat, why would you forgive me for it?
Because it was *a.xe-i-dental.*

Why are bachelors like criminals?
Because they hate to go to *court.*

Why is a solar eclipse like a woman beating her boy?
Because it is a *hiding of the son.* (Sun.)

Why is a lady without any friends unable to smoke if she wanted to?
Because she hasn't got any *to-bac-k her.*

Why is a pawnbroker like a confirmed drunkard?
Because he takes the *pledge,* but cannot always keep it.

Why is a hog the most extraordinary animal in creation?
Because you first kill him and then you *cure* him.

Why did Adam bite the apple?
Because he had *no knife* to cut it with.

Why are ladies like bells?
Because you never find out their metal until you give them a *ring.*

Why is a muff like a fool?
Because it holds a lady's hand *without squeezing* it.

Why is an overloaded gun like an office-holder?
Because it *kicks* awfully when it is *discharged.*

Which is the quickest way to destroy weeds?
Marry a widow.

Why is it dangerous to walk in the woods in early spring?
Because the trees are *shooting.*

What mechanic outlives all others?
The shoemaker, for he is *everlasting.*

Why are blacksmiths never satisfied with their pay?
Because they are always *striking* for wages.

When is a man thinner than a shingle?
When he's a *shaving.*

Why are good husbands like dough?
Because the ladies *knead* them.

When are soldiers covered with tar?
When they engage in a *pitch* battle.

Which is the greatest organ in the world?
The organ of speech in a woman, for it is an organ *without stops.*

What is it that has a mouth and never speaks, has a bed and never sleeps?
A river.

When did Adam first use a walking stick?
When Eve presented him with a *cane.* (Cain.)

Why are good resolutions like fainting ladies?
Because they want *carrying out.*

With what colors would you paint a storm at sea?
The waves *rose* and the winds *blew.*

Which lady is never dry?
The lady with a *cataract* in her eye, a *creek* in her back; forty *springs* in her skirt; *high tied* shoes; *swimming* in tears; with a single (*n*)*otion* in her mind and a big *water fall* on her head.

What dress should a lady have to keep the rest of her wardrobe clean?
A lawn dress. (Laundress.)

Why is a keg of beer like a shoe?
Because it must be *tapped* before it is *soled.*

Why is a confirmed drunkard like a vain young lady?
Because neither is satisfied with moderate use of the *glass.*

Why is man with a bad cold like a chest?
Because he is a *coffer.* (Cougher)

Why is a philanthropist like a good old horse?
Because he stops at the sound of *woe.*

Why are crows the noisiest birds we know of?
Because they "*carry on*" so over a dead animal.

Which is the largest jewel in the world?
The *Emerald* Isle.

Why are policemen always gloomy and sad?
Because they look *blue.*

Why are printers very great drinkers?
Because they are always "*setting 'em up again.*"

Why do ladies have to get new dresses so often?
Because they are *worn out* as soon as they get them.

What animal is most to be pitied?
A turtle; because it's always in a *hard case.*

Why is a doctor like an auctioneer?
Because the articles he handles are continually *going, going, going.*

Why is a dog biting his tail like a good economist?
Because he *makes both ends meet.*

Why are auctioneers the strongest men?
Because they can *knock down* a house at a single blow.

Why is a bankrupt like a clock?
Because he must either *stop* or go on *tick*.

When is a ship like a manufacturer of wines?
When she's making *Port*.

When can iron be made into sausages?
When its *Pig-iron*

What part of a ship is like a farmer?
The *Tiller*.

When does a man sneeze three times?
When he can't help it.

What is the first thing a young lady looks for in church?
The Hymns (hims).

Why is Ireland like a bottle of wine ready for sale?
Because it has got a *Cork* in it.

When is iron like a bank note?
When it is *forged*.

What day in the year is a command to go ahead?
March 4th (Forth.)

Why are chimney-sweeps satisfied with their business?
Because it *soots* them.

In what ship have the greatest number of men been wrecked?
*Court*ship.

When is a tired man like a thief?
When he needs *a resting*.

What is the difference between a fisherman and a truant schoolboy?
One bates his *hook* and the other hates his *book*

When does a bullet resemble a sheep?
When it *grazes*.

What's the best thing *out* for real comfort?
An aching tooth.

What is the greatest case of cannibalism on record?
When a *rash* man ate a *rasher*.

Why is a fountain like the Prince of Wales?
Because one is *thrown* in the air and the other is heir to the *throne*.

Spell mouse-trap with three letters?
C-A-T.

Who sounded the first bell?
Cain when he hit *A bel*.

SQUIBS, ETC.

FUNNY BITS TO BE ADDED TO MONOLOGUES OR SPEECHES.

For economy's sake I went into partnership with a friend. We had a room together. He bought a stove and I paid a mason to make a hole in the wall. We finally fell out and dissolved partnership. He took what belonged to him and I took what belonged to me. He took the stove and left me *the hole in the wall.*

I was walking with my sweetheart, and passing a clothing store, I saw suits advertised for $10 apiece. I says: "Look, darling! Suits for $10 apiece." She says: "Is it a wedding suit?" "No," I replied, "it's a business suit." Well, she replied: "I meant business."

"Man wants but little here below," and he generally gets it where I am boarding at present.

Out West, when they marry a couple, the Justice of the Peace doesn't waste time with a lot of silly questions. He just says: "Arise! Grab hands! Hitched!" Hands over six dollars to the Court, and you're murdered for life!

Some people say that dark-haired women marry first. I differ with them. It's the *light-headed ones.*

There is about as much satisfaction kissing through a telephone as there is eating soup with a fork. I like electricity fresh from the battery.

A scientific writer says that kissing is delightful because the jaws are so full of nerves. After a man gets married, he sort of wishes nature hadn't put so many nerves into the jaws.

There is a woman in Philadelphia who thinks so much of her husband that she commences *warming* him the moment he comes into the house.

Take my advice. Marry for love and not for money. That's the way to fill the Poor House

A drunkard lying on the sidewalk being discovered by a policeman said he was studying astronomy because he was thirsty. He said he was looking for the *Dipper.*

A LITTLE GIRL'S COMPOSITION ON EGGS.

A RECITATION IN CHILD TALK.

Thair is a good menny kinds ov aigs. Mi pa sez ime a bad aig, but momma sez yu can't most always beleve what pa sez, an' i think this is a good chance for me tu oba mi muther, az the Sundy skule teecher sez little gurls must du. Mebbe i am a bad aig, but mi pa is a ole rewster, fur Tommie Jones, that's mi bo, sez he is, an idle beleve Tommie if i dide fur it. It's mity funny how gurls beleves whot the boys sez. Wimmin duzent beleve that wa ennyhow, all ov them don't after tha air marryd, fur i here momma expressin her douts tu pa verry frequent indede When aigs gits old tha carry a offul smel with them whairever tha go an tha go a long wais in most familys. Evvery kind ov fowl lais aigs. Jo, that's mi bruther, sed the fowels the base bal players nox don't, but i say tha du, fur i here the boys tawkin all the time about givin thother side "guse aigs," an' if the fowels don't la' em, what duz, ide like tu no? Mebbe the bats, but whuevver heard ov bat's aigs? Bats fit like uther burds, but a bat ain't a burd an' don't la' aigs A guse aig iz the largest domestik aig an' a duk aig iz grene onto the shel. Hen aigs iz nice tu fri, an hatch little chickens out ov, an oysterich aig iz az big az a gallon buckit, bu it don't hav a ball onto it an hoops. Al fethered animals iz hatched out ov aigs excep' allygaters an' tertuls an, thoas kind ov trash. Mi sisterz bo woar allygaiter butes thother nite, an when i ast him whot he pade fur them he blusht red an' sed he didn't remember. I wunder if he pade fur them a tall. I gess he's a bag aig. I here pa sa he's going to crak his shel if he don't sta way an' let mi sister aloan.

POEMS.

TO BEGIN OR INTRODUCE IN GAG.

"Ouch, Lucy !" I howled,
"You love me no more.
You've never wore pins
In your belt before."

Although athletic girls are strong
And run and jump and row ;
A girl who never trained at all
Can draw a six-foot beau.

Once more the cranks are filled with glee,
Their hearts with joy are aflame.
Where'er you fly, you'll hear the cry,
"The (local) ball club have won a game."

The stories of the kissing bug
Aroused in her no fears,
For she a maiden lady was
Of forty some odd years.

'Twixt a blonde and brunette I've a call
To declare upon whom choice would fall,
But between you and me,
I've no choice—for you see
I'm in love—bless their hearts—with them all.

Kate Karney on a summer's day
Went out in the meadow to rake the hay ;
She wasn't afraid of the bumble bee,
For her bloomers were tied below the knee.

Husband comes home at night,
Gets a kiss—that's all right ;
Playful wife on his knee,
Gayly chatting, waiting tea.
Sudden start, and a stare.
On his coat she sees a hair;
Hair is red—hers is black—
Regular row, for talking back.
Husband goes out, mad as a bull.
When he comes back, he's " boiling full."

A little bag—a pair of skates—
Hole in the ice—Golden gates.

When the pug dog sits in Edith's chair,
Oh, don't I wish that I was *there* ;
When her fingers pat his head,
Oh, don't I wish 'twere mine *instead* ;
When her arms his neck imprison,
Don't I wish my neck were *his'n*,
But, when she kisses that pug dog's nose,
Oh, don't I wish that mine were *those*.

MAUD MULLER AT THE MATINEE.

A RECITATION ON "HATS."

Maud Muller on a winter's day
Went forth unto the matinee.

With twinkling eyes and rougish smile
She *sauntered* down the centre aisle.

She *sauntered* down, and then she sat
Beneath the biggest kind of hat.

I *sauntered* down the aisle and sat
Behind her continent of hat.

Then, with her hattish hemisphere,
Maud sweetly raked the atmosphere.

I, being five feet three, sat there
And gazed upon Maud Muller's hair.

The people all around agreed
The play was very fine indeed.

Maud's hat with sweet excitement swayed
With what the players said and played.

In its wild bobbing here and there
I read joy, pleasure, grief, despair.

When Maud's hat trembled in affright,
I knew the villain was in sight.

And when it wobbled through the air,
I knew the funny man was there.

And when that hat with tremblings bobbed,
Methought the hero-lady sobbed.

At last I 'rose and went my way
From out that weary matinee.

Out to the street I made my way
And paused a bit to sigh and say:

"Of all sad words on earth, I ween,
The saddest are these. 'I might have seen ·"

And I pitied those men, who, like me, sat
Right behind that woman's hat.

HAMLET ON THE HASH HOUSE.

To eat or not to eat, that's the question.
Whether 'tis better on the whole to suffer
The slurs and slaps of rambustuous waiters
Or to take arms against the set of trollops,
And, by shooting, end them? To dine, to sup—
No more; and by a fast, to say we end
The insults and the thousand usual shocks
Who dine are heir to, 'tis a consummation
Devoutly to be wished. To eat, to dine;
To sup, perchance to shoot—aye, there's the rub!
For by that shot what officers may come
And drag us to the station house,
Must give us pause. There's the respect
That compels compliance with the law;
For who would bear the fare, the bolts and bars
Life in the Tombs in Murderers' Row,
The loss of liberty, the law's delay,
The infamy of prison, and the lies
Made up by rascally reporters,
When he himself might his quietus make

By simply starving? Who would farther bear
The sneers and snubs of a slugging scamp,
But that the dread of something more than words—
The trifler returns—puzzles the will,
And makes us rather bear our hungry lot
Than fly to chop-rooms that we know not of !

MARY'S LAMB ; IN BOSTON.

AS RECITED BY A FOUR-YEAR-OLD BOSTON GIRL.

Mary was the proprietress of a diminutive incipient sheep,
Whose outer covering was as devoid of coloring as congealed atmospheric
    vapor,
And to all localities to which Mary perambulated
The young Southdown was sure to follow.
It tagged to the dispensary of learning
    One diurnal section of time,
Which was contrary to all precedent
And excited the cachination of the Seminary attendants,
When they perceived the presence of the young mutton at the establishment
    of instruction.
Consequently the precepter expelled him from the interior ;
But he continued to remain in the immediate vicinity
And continued in the neighborhood without fretfulness,
Until Mary once more became visible.

(N. B —The reciter of the above puts on a pair of spectacles and imitates a
precocious youngster of either sex, but very wise and intelligent for its years.)

Section UTTT.

A REPORTER'S DESCRIPTION OF A SOCIETY CAKE-WALK.

REPRODUCED HERE AS A SUGGESTION FOR COSTUMES, PLACING OF JUDGES, ETC.

"Jack," said the little girl in the bright green gown with peacock feathers in her hat; "Jack, they're going to start. Now don't forget to take my hand when we get in front of the judges." "Trust me," returned Jack, a long young man in a frock coat, flaring collar and a heart-besprinkled shirt front. "The judge who sits in the middle 'll come right down if you give him one of those melting looks of yours." The girl in the green dress and peacock feathers was one of a long line of strangely costumed feminine figures. The long young man in a frock coat was one of another long line of similarly attired beings of the male persuasion. The two lines were parallel arrangements of every color under heaven, and both lines wound about the large dining-room in the rear of the dancing floor at Manheim. The time was last evening. The occasion was the long-talked-of "cake-walk." Three hundred persons occupied chairs about the walls and in the balconies of the ball room, and beat time to the music of "Lucinda's Serenade," and watched and waited for the big doors at the end of the room to open and disclose the walkers. Then the doors did open and the double line of walkers came up the room. The girl in red, with a small parasol, brought down the house with a *passeul* that would have done credit to Letty Lind. Her partner realized that he was stepping on a red-hot iron plate kept polishing the floor with red gaitered feet. A tall young woman, in a costume smacking of Spanish sympathies, executed a catch step that made a pair of very pretty slippers fairly twinkle. The gentleman who had the honor to be her escort jammed his pan-cake hat on his "guaranteed AI black curled head," and suddenly developed an immense fondness for walking on his knees. Another black lady in snow white duck suit, devoted herself with manifest enjoyment to a promenade back and forth near the spectators, while inviting her escort to take her arm one moment and the next flaunting his advances. Another sprightly walker in a gown of alternate lemon and green panels, cast languishing glances at the men she passed, and made her partner despair with her continuous flirtations. Then on the arm of a slender gentleman, who seemed to take great relish in his role, came a small girl in green and yellow and orange, and pink and salmon and blue, and violet and red and lemon, and violet and cerise and lilac, and all other colors, except black and white. This young woman gave a combination Carmencita and Pitti Sing, of Mikado fame, and was evidently very proud of a much beflounced and beflowered underskirt, and everyone seemed just as interested in her performance as she was herself. But, for a matter of fact, there was no one on the floor in whom the spectators didn't seem to be interested. The gentleman with the punch bowl diamond threw its search-light rays over on a hundred faces, and in every one saw a friend and from whom everyone got an encore. The man with a canvas coat and top hat of white recognized some one he knew in every quarter of the room. The very elegant and tall "cullud" Adonis in tight black and white checkered trousers, with white spats and a cut-away coat was kept busy replying to the remarks with which amiable critics assailed him. The stoutest man who preserved his gravity and also, much to everyone's surprise, the integrity of his

THE DARKTOWN SOCIETY CAKE-WALK—"THE AUSPICIOUS OPENING."

exceedingly close-fitting garments, despite his gymnastic exercises, was bombarded with queries as to how he did it. A willowy girl in a floating gown, which gave everyone the impression of a mantle of lilacs, found herself and her partner singled out again and again for a round of applause. And best of all seemed to be that everyone knew every one else and also called them for the most part by their first name, and freely offered of that large share of advice which those out of the game are so generous with when addressing those who are in the game.

'Round and 'round the room the sixteen couples in the walk proceeded, 'round to the stage where the three judges were seated on a raised dais, and again facing the gallery at the end of the room, whence bouquets and salvos of handclapping greeted them. Only the presence of so many sober-minded persons and the fact that the lights were out of reach prevented a razor fight—the invariable ending of a cake-walk. But, as it was, the affair resulted in a peaceable division of one half of the splendid edifice of frosted lady cake, and the presentation of the decorated half to the winners ; while a pair of giant chickens were triumphantly borne off by the winners of second prize, and a handsome beribboned razor by the winners of the third prize.

THE DARKTOWN SOCIETY CAKE-WALK.

CAST :

PERRY WINKLE, The Floor Manager and Drum Major.
AMINADAB JOHNSON,
SKUSE CRABAPPLE,
MARSHMELLOW MUNSEY, } Representatives of Society.
SHAMPOO ORNDORFF,
CHIROPODIST PENCE,
LAVALETTE HENDERSON.
ZEMUEL BEASLEY, a Society Tough.
BAKESHOP, a Pastry Cook.
MISS ANODYNE SELTZER, the Leader of the "Set."
MISS REBECCA RABBITFOOT, Beasley's Gal (*best to be played by a Comedian*).
MISS OLEANDER MASSET,
MISS LULU BATWING, } "Buds."
MISS MAZY SPIVINS,
MISS CENTIPEDE KIPLING,

Cake-Walkers, Society Buds, Judges, Blue Bloods, etc., by rest of Company.

SCENE—*Handsome Interior, Fancy Chamber, Full Stage. Aminadab Johnson and Skuse Crabapple discovered surrounded by a group of colored society folks, male and female. The dudes and ladies are dressed in the most extravagant costumes, of very showy colors and patterns. All affect very "society" manners in talk and deportment. Johnson and Crabapple come down stage.*

JOHNSON.
This will be the cream event of the season, and no one but the blue-blooded four hundred of Darktown will be allowed on the floor.

CRAB.
Nobody that works for a living can be admitted to our exclusive circles.

JOHNSON.
No, indeed ! The opaque and colored exotics cannot mingle with the sub-strata of miscellaneous humanity.

Aminadab Johnson.   Skuse Crabapple.

THE DARKTOWN SOCIETY CAKE-WALK—" BLACK CLOUDS APPEAR."

CRAB.

Well, I should exhale breezes from my lungs through my nostrils.

MISS ANODYNE.

Tell me, gentlemen! Is that very ordinary colored person called Rebecca Rabbitfoot coming to this resplendency?

JOHNSON.

Not on her parsimonious. If she or her admirer ventures in here, they'll meet with some violent opposition.

(*Enter* PERRY WINKLE, *the Master of Ceremonies and Drum Major, L. 1 E. He is a very important personage, very airy and as if the entire affair depended upon him. Everybody greets him pleasantly and all shake hands.*)

PERRY.

I'm glad to see you all. I don't s'pose there's a razor in the crowd!

Miss Anodyne.

ALL.

No, indeedy! This is society!

PERRY.

That's right! You don't need razors where there's good breeding. (*All bow.*) And you don't need razors where I am. I'm as good as a regiment of razors. I don't like to throw bouquets at myself, but when it comes to close quarters and fighting, you know me! I've got Injun blood in me, and you know what that means!

JOHNSON.

Yes, indeed! You've got the name of being a very warm member, when it comes to slashing with a sharp blade.

CRAB.

You certainly wears a wreath of roses.

PERRY (*with pride*).

You ain't a-flattering me one bit. I knows all my qualities and my record tells for itself! When I steps in the middle of the floor, it means "give me room," and when I produce my battle-ax it means "desolation and funerals." (*All applaud.*)

Perry Winkle

JOHNSON.

As floor manager, you've got charge of this cake-walk.

PERRY.

I own everyone, body and soul.

CRAB.

We look to you that no one mingles with our set during the festivities. This is *recherche* in the extreme, and the ladies are under your protection.

PERRY (*bows*).

The ladies have a protector in me. I love them all!

(*Enter* REBECCA RABBITFOOT *and* ZEMUEL BEASLEY. REBECCA *is a fat, uncouth wench, and* BEASLEY *a tough specimen of a barber. He is smoking a long segar and acts very impudently. They enter L. 1. E., strut to centre. Everybody falls back R. and L. in surprise.*)

BEASLEY (*to Rebecca*).

We're just in time, and if anybody brings the cake home it's going to be you and me. (*Each pointing to self. Funny pose for both.*)

JOHNSON (*to Perry*).

You'd better go over and inform them that this is a strictly private affair.

PERRY (*weakening*).

I guess they know that without me telling them. Just don't notice 'em and they'll get insulted and go out.

CRAB.

They'll have to be put out.

PERRY (*assuming dignity*).

Well, go over and put 'em both out. Tell 'em I said so.

Beasley and Rebecca.

CRAB.

But you're floor manager!

PERRY.

I know, but I resign my position right now.

JOHNSON.

You're not afraid, are you?

PERRY (*half nervously.*)

Afraid? You know my record! Do you want to start in with a couple of corpses on the floor? You can't walk on a floor all covered with blood, can you?

JOHNSON.

Ah! You're afraid!

MISS ANODYNE.

I think the presence of very ordinary negroes is most disastrous to my sensitive diaphragm. (REBECCA *becomes angry.*)

REBECCA.

Don't you call me nigger. Don't you call me nigger with a *sanitorium* diagram.

Miss Spivins.

(*She makes a dash at the crowd, but BEASLEY holds her back. The ladies scream and run to PERRY for protection. PERRY tries to hide behind the crowd of ladies himself in great fear. REBECCA is very furious, shouting: "Let me go! Let me at them!" She jumps up and down wildly, but is held back by BEASLEY. Finally everything is quieted down*).

BEASLEY.

This lady has been insulted in here, and I demand an apology.

Munsey.

Pence.

Miss Masset.

PERRY.

Go ahead ! Somebody apologize to him.

BEASLEY.

I'm going to get an apology or I'll kill every nigger in here.

REBECCA.

And I'll kill every wench in the room !

(*Another furious fit of jumping, and she is held back by* BEASLEY. *Everybody is terrified again!*)

Miss Batwing.

PERRY.

Henderson.

Hold on ! Hold on ! We apologize, we apologize !

BEASLEY.

All right. We accept your *humiliation !*

REBECCA.

The Filipinos have surrendered and the American Army is victorious ! Labor downs capital this time.

BEASLEY.

We will allow you to mingle with us !

REBECCA.

Yes, we don't despise you because you're ignorant. You ain't as good as *we* are, but we tolerate you. We'll tolerate you. Go on with your cake-walk. The pastry belongs to us any way !

BEASLEY.

Yes, I'll kill the judge that decides against us.

REBECCA.

Who's going to be the judges ? (*Ready to attack again.*)

PERRY.

Not me ! I'm only floor manager.

JOHNSON.

Not me. I'm only a society bud !

BEASLEY.

You'll be *cut* down in the flower of your youth if you pester with us !

REBECCA.

There'll only be one nigger wench left in this room and that will be me !

PERRY (*not noticing them, to balance of company.*)

The judges are to be selected from the spectators or the audience.

Miss Kipling.

Orndorff.

BEASLEY.
I'll be the judge and the jury ; don't you forget it.

REBECCA.
And I'll be the Court House ! I've been in 'em all my life.

PERRY.
Then take your places for the Darktown Cake-Walk !

(*Whistles and music begins; everybody crowds over to L. U. E., so as to step out in couples, to compete. All through the cake-walk* PERRY *is very attentive to everybody. He capers about in front of each couple, juggles the baton and seems to order every movement. Soon as a couple concludes, he goes up to L. U. E., and motions the next couple to step out and begin.* PERRY *tries to be the central and most prominent figure throughout, mingling here and there, bowing, capering and juggling the baton. If he can do this, it adds to his importance very much*).

Miss Batwing and Mr. Henderson.

FIRST COUPLE.

(*Step out from L. U. E., cross over to R. Turn to each other and bow. Then come down R. towards the footlights. Then pause. Execute a few movements, passing before each other then back again. Then both bow to* PERRY, *who is down R.*

Then both gaily walk across stage on tips of toes towards L. 1 E., pause and bow to audience, then go up stage L, looking back over their

Mr. Munsey and Miss Spivius.

shoulders at audience. Then stand up stage. PERRY *motions another couple to step out.*)

(They step out, cross over to R. bow to each other, walk around in a circle twice. She has movements with her parasol, swinging it in a circle and up and down as he holds his hat aloft. Then they come down R. towards footlights. Here they pause, then turn and bow to PERRY. *Then the couple move around each other in a circle. He kneels, she places one foot on his knee ; he pretends to tie her shoe. Rises, bows, she courtesies and swings parasol. Then arm in arm she crosses over to L. C. Pause, bow to each other and go up stage, she swinging parasol and he waving hat aloft. Bow and finish up stage.* PERRY *motions next party to step out.*

JOHNSON *with two ladies step out followed by* CRABAPPLE. *They go arm in arm to R.* JOHNSON *swings the ladies around by tips of fingers. Then the trio come down stage R.,* CRABAPPLE *trying to join in as he follows down after them. When they are down R.* JOHNSON *turns and swings the ladies over to* CRABAPPLE *who is C. The ladies whirl around and* CRAB, *extending his arms, catches them and he has them on each arm. He whirls around and laughs at* JOHNSON *as he walks away towards L. I. E. with the ladies.* JOHNSON *a little put out following up. They pause L. C.* CRAB *whirls the ladies around and bows to each. Takes one by tips of fingers and circles around her. Then takes the other in the same way. Then puts on his hat and takes both ladies by tips of fingers and they turn their backs to audience and go up stage L. looking over their shoulders at audience and smiling.* JOHNSON *walks up afterwards in a very grotesque manner, and they all conclude up stage and bow*

FOURTH COUPLE.

A very tall man and short lady to make it grotesque. They cross over to R. C. The gentleman spins the lady around like a top, holding her by one hand. Then they walk down R., he walking in a twisting, bow-legged manner and bending over in funny shapes. Down stage they bow to PERRY and gentleman kicks over short lady's head (if he can). Bows to her, offers his arm and they walk over to L., both bending backwards as far as possible to make it appear as if they were going to topple backwards and fall, but they manage to just barely keep their feet. Pause at L. and go up stage and then finish.

Mr. Orndorff and Miss Kipling.

(*As many grotesque couples as possible can now be introduced to suit talent of the company. Then when last couple has completed their cake-walk, both* BEASLEY *and* REBECCA, *who, during above, have been very impatient now yell out : " Give us room, give us room ! " They step out in very grotesque manner to R. and dance a few steps.* BEASLEY *very agile and capering and* REBECCA *affecting a very uppish and extravagant style in her walk and conduct. They circle around each other and start down R.* BEASLEY *executes a few steps and* REBECCA *tries to imitate them At this moment a darkey with white apron, cook's cap and jacket, enters at back holding up a huge cake. All shout for joy at its appearance, and soon as* REBECCA *sees the cake she utters a whoop and yell and goes into a fit, capering and jumping. Everybody alarmed. All the men draw out razors.* BEASLEY *pulls out a large razor and rushes forward, captures the cake, and a general razor fight takes place.*)

Beasley and Rebecca in a walk of their own.

BEASLEY *smashes the cake upon* REBECCA'S *head. The bottom of the cake is covered with paper and her head comes out through the card board top. She yells and capers while the ladies up the stage faint, the men defending themselves from* BEASLEY'S *attack. On this picture a quick Curtain.*

NOTE :—*Another finish to the cake-walk would be :* All gather around RE-BECCA *when she has the fit and all bring her bottles, etc., to revive her. Then let* PERRY *ask the judges (audience): " Who is entitled to the cake ?" And the audience will confer cake upon the couple who, in its estimation, walked the most gracefully , and with novel movements. As the cake is thus presented to the winning couple, all join arm in arm and march off up the stage, looking at the audience, two by two, or, they may stand in a circle bowing, as the curtain descends, the winners being in the centre of the circle. Music playing and all cheering.*

THE WONDERFUL TELEPHONE.

A FIRST PART FINALE.—ALSO GOOD FOR AN AFTER-PIECE.

N. B.—*This sketch reads as if the events were transpiring in Philadelphia. It can be localized to suit any town or city. Have the " Brother from London " journey across the ocean, land him in New York; then, ad lib., describe his journey rapidly to your own town or city—east, west, north or south.*

IMPORTANT.—*A wire is attached in flies, L. 1 E., and crosses over to a point in R. 1 E , where it is attached by a screw-eye in the stage. On this wire—up in the flies—is attached the dummy ready to cross, descending at an angle of 45°. It is held in place by a string, which is cut or loosened at cue and sent down and across. See illustration below.*

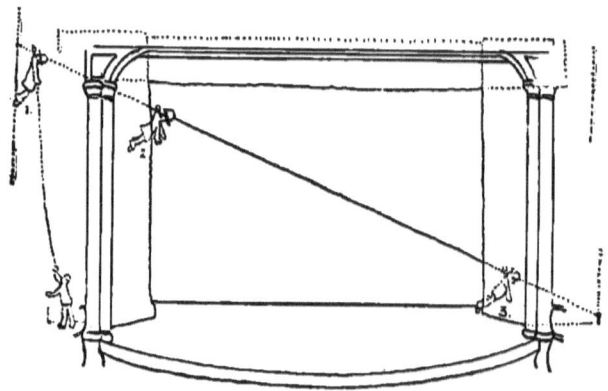

This sketch or finale can also be played by ladies, in which case change names to suit.

MIDDLE *(after last song is sung on first part).*

Gentlemen, I'm going down to the telephone office to send a message to a friend.

TAMBO.

To the telephone office? Why, I belong to the Edison Telephone.

BONES.

What a strange coincidence.   I belong to the Bell Telephone.

TAMBO.

Now, there's no use of you going down to the office.   I'll bring the office up ' here.   (*Substitute I have my office here, if 'phone is already hung on proscenium arch.*)

MIDDLE.

You'll bring (*or substitute You have*) the office up here?

TAMBO.

Yes ; I'll bring (*or, I have*) an instrument up here.   Our telephones are the best.

BONES.

Excuse me ; our telephones are the very best.

MIDDLE.

Now, we'll settle it this way. Both of you bring (*or*, *show*) your rival telephones up here and I'll test them. Whichever is the best I'll patronize in the future.

TAMBO.

All right! I'll go after mine (*Exit*), (*or*, *Here's mine, pointing to his 'phone*).

MIDDLE.

Gentlemen, we'll now see a test of the long-distance telephones, and be judges of the claims advanced by the rival agents.

(*End men bring imitation telephones from R. and L. and hang them at extreme edge of proscenium by a ring on a nail. Or, if the telephones are in place during the entire show, the end men need not go out after them, in which case the end men will use the substituted speeches.*)

TAMBO.

Now for the test—and mine is in good order.

BONES

This is the instrument. This is what's called the hear-o-phone. This is where you talk. I s'pose you can *tell a 'phone* when you see it? That's *phony* but I can't help it. Now I'll show you how it works. (*Rings.*) Hello! Hello! Chicago! Chicago! (*Pauses and rings again.*)

(*NOTE.—The ends must work as though they were at real 'phones, using their best judgment to make it seem as natural as possible.*)

Sometimes you have to wait two or three years for an answer from Chicago. (*Alarm clock or electric bell rings in entrance.*) Ah! there's the answer! (*Calling in 'phone.*) What was the matter? (*Receiver to ear, calling out as if repeating.*) St. Louis was standing on the line? Ah! yes—eh?—of course—yes—(*in 'phone*)—New York—I say, New York! (*louder*) New York—where is it? Why, it's the liveliest town of its age you ever saw. Yes—its down near Hoboken (*or mention small town near by*). Yes; now you know where it is. Yes—we're giving a show here—Who? Yes—he's here—Sam! Chairman of our committee —yes—(*To Middle*)—By the way, Sam, what is your name?

MIDDLE.

Why, Sam.

BONES (*imitating and calling in 'phone*).

Why, Sam!

MIDDLE.

No! no! no! Sam, without the why.

BONES (*in 'phone*).

Yes—Sam without the why.

MIDDLE.

No! no! Just simply Sam.

BONES (*in 'phone*),

Yes—simple Sam.

MIDDLE.

No, sir! no, sir! no, sir!

BONES (*in 'phone*).

He says he's got no nose, sir—Where?—Sherman House—$27—Oh! he'll settle that when he goes West.

MIDDLE.

What's that?

BONES (*to Middle*).

Did you stop at the Sherman House while in Chicago? They're asking about a bill you owe them of $27.

MIDDLE.

I don't owe anybody in Chicago.

BONES (*yells in 'phone*).

He says he owes everybody in Chicago!
(TAMBO'S *telephone rings, and he darts suddenly to it.*)

TAMBO.

Hello! I've got a bite! (*Comedy bus. at 'phone.*) Hello!—hello!—hello!— hel—lo! (*Louder and louder. To Middle.*) I guess I've struck a deaf and dumb asylum! *In 'phone.*) Hello! (*Bell rings.*) Ah! you're there, are you? Where have you been? (*Smiles, talks through 'phone.*) Send me five cents and I'll go out and get one too   Stand further away from the 'phone; you've been eating onions.   Yes, yes—(*laughs*)—certainly (*laughs*)—yes—I knew them when they were courting.   No! no! (*Surprised*).   You—you—don't say so!—when? This morning! (*Laughs.*)   What!   Twins?

MIDDLE.

Now, look here! I'm quite dry.   Let's go out and have a glass of beer. (*Say soda for ladies.*)

TAMBO.

You needn't go out.   I'll bring a glass of beer over our line.

MIDDLE.

Do you mean to say you can bring a glass of beer over the wires?

TAMBO.

Yes, sir; I'll show you? (*Rings bell.*) Hello! (*Outside bell replies.*) Connect me with a brewery—send over a glass of beer (*outside bell rings*), and here it is. (*Takes a glass of beer from a box attached beside the 'phone, or it is handed out slyly from side of entrance close to the 'phone, unobserved by the audience.*)

MIDDLE.

That's wonderful! (*Tambo drinks it.*) Here! I thought that was for me!

TAMBO.

'Tis for you. For you to look at! (*Replaces glass.*)

BONES.

Do you want a glass of beer? Hold on. I'll get one for you. (*Rings 'phone and bell replies.*) Connect me with (*local place*). One glass of beer for Sam. (*outside bell rings*) and here it is. (*Takes out glass of clear water.*)

MIDDLE.

Why, that's water.

BONES.

I guess they must know you at the brewery. This beer isn't brewed yet. I guess you owe a bill there too. (*Replaces glass*)

MIDDLE.

I tell you what I'd like. I remember they have some very fine segars (*ladies say candy*) at the (*local hotel or store*) in (*neighboring town*). Can you bring me a box of segars from that city?

BONES.

Certainly! Hello? (*Calls name of city several times.*) Connect me with (*local*) Hotel. (*Bell rings.*) One box of segars.

(*Bell rings, and a man with a segar box dashes out flip-flapping from R. 1 E., places box in Middle's hand and dashes out quick again R. 1 E. After he goes out both End Men jump and dance ad lib.*)

END MEN.

Goodness! We're full of electricity too!

MIDDLE.

Well, this is truly wonderful ; I wish my brother could see this.

TAMBO.

Where is your brother?

MIDDLE.

London, England.

TAMBO.

I'll fetch him over. (*Goes to and calls in 'phone.*) Hello! hello, London! I want London! I don't want much, do I? (*Bows grotesquely at 'phone.*)

MIDDLE.

To whom are you bowing?

TAMBO.

The Prince of Wales just passed by. (*Bus. at and talks in 'phone.*) I want Sam's brother—yes, Sam's brother—what? Oh! all right. I can't bring him. (*Hangs up receiver.*)

MIDDLE.

What's the matter?

TAMBO.

His time isn't up yet. They've got him at work making shoes.

MIDDLE.

My brother is not in jail, and he's not a shoemaker.

TAMBO.

No; he's only learning. Wait until I try again. (*Calls in 'phone*). I want Sam's brother. (*Repeats.*) All right (*to Middle*), I've got him, I've got him, Sam! (*Calls in 'phone.*) Take our telephone line and come over. (*To Middle.*) He says he'll come. (*Looks in 'phone.*) He's packing his trunk—there goes the same old paper collar I lent him. Now he's started.

(*Music very piano, galop. Bus. of describing the journey.*)

Now he's half way over. Oh, Sam! Sam! There's a big steamship run right over your brother (*all in alarm*), but he's all right. His cheek hit the vessel and knocked off the propeller. Now he's coming like a flash. Oh, Sam! Sam! (*cries*) prepare yourself for sad news—there's a shark after your brother! Oh, Sam! the shark has swallowed—

MIDDLE (*despairingly*).

My poor brother? (*Circle excited.*)

TAMBO.

No ; your brother has swallowed the shark.   Now he's at Sandy Hook, now
he's passing Jersey City, now he's crossing the Delaware River, now he's

*(Describe all the towns he passes through to reach your city, or rather
name them rapidly.   This is arranged for Philadelphia.)*

in *(mention your city.)*   He is turning the corner *(name street)*, and here he is !

*(Hurry, music forte, everybody excited, and a dummy with carpet-bag and
distinct costume—duster, white hat, black pants, etc.—darts down a wire from
flies L. down at an angle of 45 degrees, far into R. 1 E. where it is fastened.   All
shout as it crosses.   Soon as dummy is sent into entrance a man in exact counter-
part of dress, etc., runs out of R. 1 E. and Middle, End Men and all joyfully
greet him, shaking hands and cheering him.)*

QUICK CURTAIN.

OUR GIRLS AT SCHOOL.

CAST :

MISS DISCIPLINE, The Teacher.
BABY MOLASSES, The Victim.
SALLY FRECKLES, The Dunce.
LUCY LOCKET, A Bright Girl.
MARY GRAMMAR,
EDITH SYNTAX,
BELLE GEOMETRY,
CARRIE ALPHABET,   } The Young Lady Scholars.
RUTH ALGEBRA,
LILLIE DIVISION,
MATTIE MATHICS,

SCENE—*Plain chamber; door in flat; several benches ranged across stage R ;
Teacher's desk down L. C.; split sticks, books, bell, etc., upon her desk; a
stool R C. with Dunce's pointed cap. made of white cardboard, with the
word " Dunce " in black letters.*

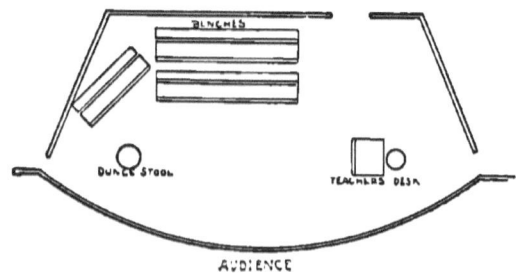

*(Teacher, who is supposed to be an eccentric old maid, with spectacles, funny
wig and old-fashioned garments, is discovered, bell in hand.)*

TEACHER.

My scholars are late this morning. I'll let them know it.

(*Rings bell violently. Girl scholars with books. A B C cards, etc., enter door in flat. All exclaim, "Good morning, Teacher." Teacher replies, "Good morning, young ladies," and they seat themselves upon the benches and begin to study.*)

TEACHER (*at desk*).

My scholars are not all here. Where is Baby Molasses and Lucy Locket?

GIRLS.

We don't know.

(*Baby, who is a fat girl, and Lucy sneak in through door in flat—run to benches and push girls away to make room and they sit down and study aloud. Teacher, rapping for silence and attention, discovers them.*)

TEACHER.

Ah! there you are. Come here, both of you. Come here, Baby Molasses, and you, Miss Lucy Locket. (*The girls indicated come down C. sniffling*) What kept you so late, Miss Locket?

LUCY.

Well, you see, teacher, I was home dreaming, and dreaming that I was going to Europe. (*Hesitates as if making up the story.*) And I dreamed that I was late and I ran to the wharf to catch the boat for Europe because I could hear the bell ringing, and—and—I woke up—and it was the school-house bell that was ringing. (*Smiles in a silly manner at her excuse.*)

TEACHER.

A very good excuse; and you, Baby Molasses. what kept you so late?

BABY.

I—I—I went down to the wharf to see her off to Europe.

TEACHER.

Go to your seats, both of you (*they go to seats*) and study your lessons! Ah! Who has seen our dunce? Who has seen Sally Freckles?

GIRLS.

Nobody.

(*Sally, the dunce, runs in through door, pushes a girl off bench and sits down. Takes a book from another one and begins to study. "Twice one is two, twice two is six, twice six is fifty-four," etc. Teacher checks her.*)

TEACHER.

Stop it! Stop it! That is not your place, Miss Freckles. Put on that dunce's cap, and stand on that pedestal until you learn your lessons.

(*Sally pouts and sniffles, but puts on dunce's cap, and stands upon the stool R. C. All the girls secretly laugh at her and she tries to reach over to slap one of them and nearly falls off the stool. Teacher raps for silence and attention.*)

TEACHER.

Now, young ladies, we will begin our studies and I want you to be very attentive.

(*Sally has a putty-blower and shows it to girls, who appear delighted. Sally blows putty at teacher—some one in entrance L. makes a sound of two blocks of wood striking each other to imitate putty striking teacher's face. Teacher yells, jumps and capers out to L.*)

TEACHER.

Oh, dear! oh, dear! My eye is put out! Who blew that putty at me? (*All the girls point at Baby.*)

GIRLS.

Baby Molasses!

BABY.

Oh, teacher, I didn't do any such thing.

TEACHER (*C.*).

Come out here. (*Baby comes to her, crying.*) Hold out your hand, Miss.

(*After a few commands, Baby crying holds out her hand. Teacher strikes her hand with split stick or ruler made to sound. Baby cries very loud and returns to seat. Girls all laugh. Sally is delighted and dancing with joy. She nearly falls off stool. Teacher goes to desk and raps for order and attention.*)

Now, young ladies, I hope we shall have order! First class in geometrical hypnotism and concatenation. What is a volcano?

GIRLS.

A mountain with a fire-place on top of it.

TEACHER.

Who said that?

GIRLS.

Baby Molasses.

TEACHER.

Come out here, Miss! (*Sobbing and crying, she comes C.*)

BABY.

Teacher, I never said a word. It was the dunce.

TEACHER.

Hold out your hand, Miss!

(*Baby is whipped as before, she returns crying to her seat to great delight of dunce and girls. Teacher checks their mirth by rapping for attention and order.*)

First class in muscular geography and elementary physique. What is a strait?

GIRLS.

It beats two pairs. That's what my brother says.

TEACHER.

Who said that?

GIRLS.

Baby Molasses!

(*Baby denies it. Is brought out again. Whipped as before and ordered back to her seat. She cries louder and louder each time. Dunce and girls enjoy the whipping.*)

Now, young ladies, first section in historical addenda and aboriginal alluvium. Who was General George Washington?

GIRLS.

First in war, first in peace, and first in the hands of a policeman!

(All rise and dance a " break," dance nearly falls off stool in doing so).

TEACHER.

Who said that George Washington was in the hands of a policeman?

GIRLS.

Baby Molasses.

(Baby begins to cry loud and denies it. But she is brought down and made to hold out her hand and is whipped as before and ordered to her seat. She cries, very much to the delight of the girls.)

TEACHER.

I never saw such a girl in all my life—always in trouble and never knows her lesson.

SALLY.

She's pretty near as smart as I am! I'm head of my class, any way.

TEACHER.

Now, young ladies, attention! Second class in coast survey and progressive weather bureau. Who discovered America? *(Girls look over books and do not reply.)* Who discovered America? *(Baby begins to cry, rises, comes down and holds out her hand.)* Why, Baby, you didn't discover America.

BABY.

Didn't I? Well, I get blamed for everything. I thought maybe I did discover America.

TEACHER.

No; you didn't discover America.

SALLY.

I know who did. Dr. Mary Walker.

TEACHER.

Young ladies, get ready for your music lesson. Fall in line as I beat time for you.

(All the girls laugh and jump for joy.)

(She gets a sheet of cardboard with burlesque music notes upon it and by this time all the girls are ranged in line ready to sing as Teacher extravagantly beats time at extreme end of line or in front of the scholars.)

Medley of popular songs or the march song, "High School Girls," with drill to terminate the final.

NOTE: *This finale can be elaborated and more questions can be asked (local if desired) at discretion of stage director.*

CURTAIN.

SUGGESTION FOR A NOVEL MUSICAL ACT.

THE WORLD FAMOUS MUSICAL ARTISTS,

PICK AND PLUNK.

In their new selections upon instruments of peculiar make, shape and sound,
appearing as the

"MUSICAL CONVICTS."

SCENE:—*Represents interior of a prison cell. The convicts amusing themselves
upon familiar instruments, performing solos on the following objects:
The bars of the cell door, tin cups, chains (bells) on the locks, tin pails, hammers and brooms.*

N. B.—The objects are those furnished to prisoners from which they evoke sweet music
while in durance vile. These instruments must be made to order as they will *not* be found in
stock everywhere.

Pick discovered sweeping his cell.

PICK.

I haven't got much longer to serve, and for good behavior I've been allowed
to enjoy myself with musical instruments of my own make. And who would
believe that this broom was a musical instrument? Yet it is.

*The broom has a horn or cornet hidden in the brush part, and the mouth-piece
is in the handle of the broom. He blows several trumpet calls or plays short solo.
At end of it Plunk enters cell. He is the comedy element in this act and has an
eccentric prison costume and make-up.*

PLUNK.

Are you selling fish?

PICK.

No, sir. Don't you know a cornet from a fish horn?

PLUNK.

Not when *you* play it.

PICK.

Who are you anyway?

PLUNK.

I'm number 7,001 ; I've got a holiday along the corridors for good conduct.

PICK.

Well, go and enjoy it, and don't bother me.

PLUNK.

You're bothering me with that old root-te-toot-toot you've got stuck in that broom! Are you a musician?

PICK.

I'm proud to say that I am ; I know every bar in music.

PLUNK.

I guess it was too many *bars* that brought you here. I'm a little on the music order myself. I can get music out of anything.

PICK.

Then a brother musician is always welcome here. I've got all sorts of musical instruments made of articles allowed prisoners. Everything you see here is capable of producing music.

PLUNK.

I must tell my brother about this. He's in this prison. He's an overseer.

PICK.

Overseer?

PLUNK.

Yes ; *overseeing* the walls to see if he can get out.

PICK (*laughs*).

What brought you to prison?

PLUNK.

I was brought here by my own *conviction.*

PICK.

Well, join in and enjoy yourself.

PLUNK.

What did you steal?

PICK.

I didn't steal anything. I was a bank cashier.

PLUNK.

Oh, I see; you didn't steal *anything,* you stole *everything.* I dare say they pinched you before you could reach Canada.

PICK.

Come, join me in sweet sounds or leave this room.

PLUNK.

Anybody who told you that this was a room meant it for a " cell."

PICK.

Take the chain and rattle it.

(*Solo on chains which are sleigh bells disguised.*)

PLUNK (*at end.*)

That's very nice. No matter how poor a convict may be in this prison he's always got a *watch* and *chain.*

PICK.

Now try these blocks of wood and see what sounds they'll produce.

(*Solo on sticks of wood, which are 8 pipe organs, thus disguised.*)

PLUNK.

You've quite a music store in here, haven't you?

PICK.

Indeed I have, Mr.—Mr.—Mr.—what's your name?

PLUNK.

Smith! And my name got me into trouble. I was down in a pool room when they made a raid on it. A cop caught me and brought me before the judge who says to me : " What were you doing in that pool room?" I says : "Attending to my business; I'm a locksmith and was making a *bolt* for the door."

PICK.

That was a good excuse.

PLUNK.

The judge didn't think so. He says : "What's your name!" I says : "Smith." Judge says : "And you're a Locksmith, are you?" I says : "Yes," "Well," says he, "we'll *lock Smith* up," and here I am.

PICK.

Try the bars on the window; let's see what you can get out of them.

PLUNK.

I wish I *could get out* of them. I wouldn't be here. If I had the measles, I'd be all right, wouldn't I?

PICK.

How would the measles help you?

PLUNK.

I'd *break* out !

(*Solo on bars of the window and cell door. These are pipophones.*)

PICK.

You are doing very well. I didn't think you knew anything about music, especially bits of steel.

PLUNK.

It was big chunks of steel that brought you here.

PICK.

Don't mention it. I feel sorry.

PLUNK.

Sorry you didn't steal the building and the sidewalk I suppose.

PICK.

Take your pick of these hammers.

(Shows eight mallet-shapped hammers. These hammers each contain a note and when the mallet is struck on a flat slab laid upon a table, it produces a note, thus forming an octave.)

PLUNK.

(Laughs.) Get your hammer. You've got everything here haven't you? I don't see what you want to leave this place for.

PICK.

Oh! Just a little change.

PLUNK.

I don't think you left any. I'll bet you stole every cent in the bank.

PICK.

Now here, I've saved every bottle I got hold of and formed a musical instrument. I call it the " Bottle-phone."

(Brings out upright frame on which are strung bottles of all kinds, tuned with water in them and suspended by wires to the cross-piece of the frame. The bottles are struck with small Xylophone hammers. Solo on bottles.)

PLUNK.

I wish they were filled with something good—but they are merely ghosts; " Departed spirits "—they do not even give a fellow a smell. *(Pick has removed frame and bottles.)* You didn't get your license did you, and you've got to close up!

PICK.

Here are a lot of rags!

(Puts down lots of rags comprising bits of pants, vests, old hats, ets. In each there is a cow bell or smaller bells. In pretending to search for certain rags, they play upon the bells by shaking the fragments of clothing.)

PLUNK.

There's something in old rags after all. These are the freshest old rags I ever saw. They're bound to "ring-in" on us every time.

PICK.

Well, that's all right. We're *doing time!* Here! Try these and blow your brains out.

PLUNK.

There's where I've got the advantage of *you. You haven't got any* to blow out.

(They take up two pails which have cornets disguised within the shape of the pails, or two feather dusters will be appropriate, and conclude the act by a stirring march ; and both exit playing, Plunk marching behind in an eccentric manner.)

Section IX.

A VERY PLEASANT EVENING.

FARCE IN ONE SCENE. ADAPTED BY FRANK DUMONT.

CAST.

*EBENEZER GREEN, a hayseed.
NAPOLEON AUGUSTUS WRENCH, an Adventurer.
COLONEL THUNDER, a retired officer.
CHARLES HOWARD, in love with Fanny.
MR. MONEYPENNY, a hotel boarder.
BOOTS, employed at the hotel.
WAITER, another attentive (?) servant.
FANNY THUNDER, the Colonel's daughter.
MRS. WAITRESS, the landlady.

PROPERTY LIST.

Bed, with mattress, sheet, short blanket and pillow.
Table with hotel register and writing materials.
Chairs.
Placard with figures " 25."
Locomotive imitations, bell and whistle, (organ pipe and bar of steel.)
Traveling satchel for Fanny.
Carpet-bag and umbrella for Green.
Loaf bread, slice of pie.
Tray with bottle and glass. •
Large watch-wallet and boots for Green.
Dark lantern and pistol for Wrench.
Horse-whip for Colonel Thunder.
Brooms, hoes, rakes, clubs, etc., for guests.
Stuffed dog with snap hook in its mouth to be fastened to a ring securely sewed to seat of Green's pants.

Costumes for " Pleasant Evening " are ordinary, every-day dresses for male and female. The comedian can wear extravagant clothing, misfit or in colors, to denote a very countrified fellow.

SCENE :—*Plain chamber ; a bed R. C. up stage. Window in flat. A fire-place R. 2 E. for Green to climb into. In some conspicuous place the figure " 25." Table down L. C. with Hotel register, pen, ink, etc. Furniture R. and L., the whole representing the best room in a country hotel. Landlady discovered arranging chairs.*

LANDLADY.

Every room in the house is taken save this one, and I had to put a bed into it. If business keeps up this way, I'll soon be able to retire and live on the interest of my money.

---

* The part of Ebenezer Green can be played as a darkey, in which case he will assume coon dialect and his name will be POMPEY JOHNSON. It can also be rendered in German dialect, and the character can be called HENNY DINKELHEIMER.

Engine whistles and bell heard outside. Use bar of steel hanging by stout cord—struck by small hammer for bell—and organ pipe for whistle.

Ah! There's the express train—and more visitors! (*Looks L. 1 E.*) I don't know where I'll place them. Oh, but I'm a very busy woman. I will have to give up my own room, number ten, but I don't care as long as I'm well paid for it.

Enter Gustavus Wrench and Fanny Thunder in traveling costume L. 1 E.

WRENCH (*to Landlady.*)

My dear madam, will you have a room prepared immediately for this lady? She is very much fatigued and wishes to retire.

LANDLADY.

Yes, sir. She can occupy No. 10, near the parlor. It is in order, and a fire burning brightly.

WRENCH.

Thank you. (*To Fanny.*) Keep up your spirits; you shall see your father to-morrow. I will put you on the first train in the morning that passes through your native village. Say nothing about our elopement to anyone. They will think you have come direct from school for a short vacation.

FANNY.

I will do as you say, and never will I be tempted to commit so foolish an act again.

LANDLADY.

This way, if you please, Miss. I will show you to your room.

Exeunt Landlady and Fanny R. 2 E.

WRENCH.

Well, I've got myself into a precious scrape, and now I've got to get out of it. I became acquainted with Fanny, old Colonel Thunder's daughter, at the young ladies' seminary at Vassar and persuaded her to elope with me. On our way here I discovered that Colonel Thunder is worth only about $5,000. It won't do for me to marry less than $30,000. She has repented and so have I ; and if I can get her safely home without her father's knowledge of what has happened I shall think myself a lucky dog. But I can't help laughing to think what that fellow will say, whose pocket I picked of this fat wallet, when he discovers his loss. Ha! ha! I told him I was a cousin of Admiral Sampson and he swallowed it all down. Now, before I leave this house, I must pick up enough to pay my expenses.

Enter landlady R 2 E.

LANDLADY.

Now, sir, if you will register your name, I will give you a room.

WRENCH.

Oh, certainly, certainly, my dear madam !

Goes up and registers his name.

LANDLADY.

I will give you the bed room I have vacant. You see we are quite full to-day.

WRENCH.

Very well ; I will go to my room immediately, if you please.

LANDLADY.

This way, sir.

Exeunt landlady and Wrench R. 1 E. Enter Colonel Thunder in a great passion L. 1 E. Walks up and down greatly agitated.

COLONEL THUNDER.

The impudent puppy, whoever he is! I wonder where I can find the landlady. The unprincipled scoundrel! Here I was going to see my daughter at school and give her an agreeable surprise when a boy handed me a note from the principal of the school, informing me that she had eloped with a stranger. I should like to catch him. Here, landlady! landlady!

Enter landlady, R. 1 E.

LANDLADY.

Here, sir, at your service.

THUNDER.

Any new arrivals, landlady?

LANDLADY.

Oh, yes, sir; quite a number.

THUNDER.

Any females?

LANDLADY.

One.

THUNDER.

Ah, ha! A gentle—no, he's not a gentleman. A man accompanied her?

LANDLADY.

Yes, sir; quite a good-looking gentleman.

THUNDER.

Bah! They are all good-looking in your eyes.

LANDLADY (*aside*).

The old grizzly bear.

THUNDER.

Madam, I must see that man immediately. Do you hear?

LANDLADY.

I have ears, sir; I suppose I can hear.

THUNDER (*shouts*).

Very well. Go and tell this *good-looking* rascal I wish to see him.

LANDLADY (*aside*).

The old Rocky Mountain buffalo! (*Exit Landlady R. 1 E.*)

THUNDER.

If this proves to be the villain I'm in search of, I'll kill him within an inch of his life. (*Enter Wrench R. 1. E.*)

WRENCH

Well, sir, your business! (*Aside.*) By Jingo, I'll bet that's Fanny's father.

THUNDER.

Ah! I've found you, have I? The destroyer of my family's peace and happiness! Where's my daughter, sir? Oh, that I should live to see this day!

WRENCH.

But, sir, allow me to explain.

THUNDER (*walking up and down*).

I shall allow you nothing, sir! I'll allow you ten minutes to live.

WRENCH (*following him.*)

But, my dear sir—

THUNDER.

Don't *but* me. You bare-face scoundrel. I'll blow your brains out, if you have any.

WRENCH.

My dear Colonel—

THUNDER.

Don't *dear* me. I'll have you hung.

WRENCH.

Allow me one word of explanation.

THUNDER (*stopping short*).

Well, proceed. I'll give you five minutes ; at the expiration of that time, sir, I'll give you—*thunder*

WRENCH (*aside*).

Now for a lie. Invention befriend me. (*Aloud.*) My dear sir, be calm until I give you the particulars of this most melancholy affair. You have no idea, sir, the injustice you do me. No, sir, I am the preserver of your daughter's honor and good name. I was seated behind your daughter and the man you seek, in the car and overheard their conversation. She had already repented of her foolish action, and was expostulating with him, entreating him to take her to her home. He refused to do so, villian that he is, when I interposed, sir, and rescued your lovely offspring from the clutches of as vile and contemptible a scoundrel as ever breathed the breath of life. I brought her here. She is now enjoying the sweet repose she so greatly needs, and to-morrow it was my intention to restore her to your arms.

THUNDER (*cooling down*).

My dear sir, how can I thank you? Will you overlook the hasty words I uttered a moment ago? I can never repay you. Ask me for anything I possess; you shall have it and welcome.

WRENCH.

Oh, my dear sir, I did but my duty. You think too much of it. There is nothing I can ask of you. But say—during the tussle the villain and I had together, I lost my pocket book, and I have every reason to think he abstracted it from my side pocket. If you could favor me with a small loan until I return to the city, I should feel that I was amply repaid.

THUNDER.

Certainly, sir, certainly! The smallest favor you could ask. (*Takes out wallet.*) How much shall I have the pleasure of loaning you?

WRENCH.

Oh, the small sum of fifty dollars will suffice for present needs.

THUNDER.

Fifty dollars! Of course. (*Gives money.*) Fifty thousand, if I had it. Now sir, may I know the name of my benefactor?

WRENCH.

Yes, sir; my name is Napoleon Gustavus Wrench, formerly a stock broker in Wall street, but, at present, Councilman from the 'Steenth Ward, New York.

THUNDER.

I am happy to form your acquaintance. It is an honor of which I feel proud. But what has become of the scoundrel who sought to injure me so deeply?

WRENCH.

From what I could learn, he intended to stop at this very house. He is disguised as a countryman. You wouldn't know him. I'll keep watch and when he arrives will inform you of the fact.

THUNDER.

Thank you. And now, let us adjourn to the next room, and take a little hot water with some sugar in it, and talk over what has happened.

WRENCH.

With all my heart. (*As they go off arm in arm, Wrench over Thunder's shoulder to audience*) How are you, fifty?   (*Exeunt R. 1 E.*)

Enter Ebenezer Green L. 1 E. with carpet-bag, etc., speaks off at wing.

GREEN.

I tell you it's a swindle and I'll have you arrested. I shan't pay it. (*To audience.*) The idea of charging a man sixteen dollars to ride a square. They may think I'm green, but I'll make some of them black and blue if they come any of their fooling over me. I wonder where the boss of this house is. I'm mighty tired and would like to go to bed.

Enter landlady R. 1 E.

LANDLADY.

I presume, sir, you wish accommodations.

GREEN.

Well, you presume about right. I do. I'd like to have a nice big room full of sophys and cheers and first-rate fire, and I want it as cheap as—well, in fact, I don't want to pay anything for it if I can get it for nothing.

LANDLADY.

I guess we won't overcharge you. Will you register your name, if you please?

GREEN.

Certainly. Anything to please a feminine gander. Write my name in this book?

LANDLADY.

Yes, sir.

GREEN. (*Enters his name with considerable flourish.*)

I guess that gal thought I couldn't write. There it is—a G and an R, two E's and an N.

LANDLADY.

Very well, sir; I'll give you this room. There is a very nice gentleman in the room next to yours.

GREEN.

I'd like to get about fifty winks before the next train comes along. I've got to be in Albany to-morrow. I've got a little business with the Legislature. Now, where's the dining-room, so I can get a sandwich?

LANDLADY.

Follow me, sir, and remember this is your room, Number 25.

GREEN.

I won't forget it's on the book. Get the sandwich, and cut the bread and meat thick as you can for five cents.

(*Exit landlady and Green R. 2 E. Enter Wrench R. 1 E.*)

WRENCH.

Well, I'm in luck. I left the Colonel sipping his hot water and sugar, as he calls it, and made a short trip through the house. I've collected two or three watches and as many pocket books, and now I must throw the victims off the scent. (*Goes up to register.*) Hello! another fresh arrival. I guess I'll change rooms with this fellow and throw all the blame on him. (*Changes number in register.*) There, old fellow; now I'll see if you have any stamps.

(*Exit R. 1 E.   Enter Charles Howard, L. 1 E.*)

HOWARD.

I've tracked the villain to this house. The landlady said the gentleman that came with the lady was in No. 25. I'll teach him better than to run off with another man's intended wife. I'll find the rascal and fight him a duel.

(*Exit Howard R. 1 E.   Enter Moneypenny L. 1 E.*)

MONEYPENNY.

No. 25, is it? I'll teach the rascal how to rob respectable people. He went into my room and took my watch. I'll send him to jail.

(*Exit R. 1 E. Enter three or four boarders together L. 1 E. talking about robbery, saying, "He's in the room, Number 25," and exit R. 1 E.*)

(*Enter Green, R. 2 E. eating loaf of bread, slice of pie in the other hand— carpet bag under his arm. Landlady follows in with tray on which is a bottle and a glass. She places it on table.*)

GREEN.

That's it! Now, don't let me be disturbed. I'll eat my lunch and then go to bed.

LANDLADY.

Very well. Good night, sir.   (*Exit L. 1 E.*)

GREEN.

Good night, Miss. That's a nice girl.

(*Puts down carpet-bag, sits at table. Bus. eating, talking, all the while. Gets up with pie in one hand and beer in the other, looks about the room, sees No. 25.*)

Hello! That gal put me in the wrong room. She said No. 24 was my room, but I don't suppose it makes any difference.

(*After eating, puts what is left in his carpet bag.*)

This will do for a lunch on the cars to-morrow. I guess I'll go to bed now.

(*Bus. taking out night-cap, night-gown, etc. Pulls off his boots, places them at foot of bed. Hangs his coat on chair near foot of the bed, etc. Places watch and pocket-book under the pillow. (This scene all rests with the comedian. Make it as funny as possible. If you can introduce good Bus. do so.) Green finally gets into bed, saying:*)

All I want now is to get about fifty winks.

(*Enter Boots, whistling; wakes up Green, who sits up in bed. Boots takes Green's boots and is about going off.*)

Here, bring back my boots.

BOOTS.

I'm only going to black them, sir.

GREEN.

But I don't want them blacked.

BOOTS.

You must have them blacked. It's the rule of the house.

GREEN.

I don't care about the rule. I want my boots.

BOOTS.

Can't help it, sir. Must obey orders.

(*Boots exits L. 1 E. whistling.*)

GREEN.

That's a nice trick. Take a man's boots away. I wonder if I'll get them again.

(*Lies down again. Enter Waiter, dancing up to bed. Takes Green's coat, throws it over his shoulder and is going off. Green starts up again.*)

Here, where are you going with my coat?

WAITER.

Going to brush it, sir.

GREEN.

I don't want it brushed !

WAITER.

Yes, but you must have it brushed. It's the rule of the house.

GREEN.

Oh ! Confound the rules. Put that coat down.

WAITER.

Can't do it, sir. You must have it brushed.

(*Waiter dances off L. 1 E.*)

GREEN.

Well, I never seen such a house as this   One takes my boots, another takes my coat. Suppose there's a fire in the middle of the night, what'll I do? I'll never get my fifty winks this way.

(*Lies down. Stage darkened a little   Wrench puts his head in L. 1 E. Then enters cautiously, with dark lantern.*)

WRENCH.

All right. I guess he's asleep. Now to see if he has any valuables. Of course he put them under his pillow.

(*Goes to bed and takes Green's watch and pocket-book from under his pillow. Green awakens and starts up.*)

GREEN.

Hello ! What do you want ?

WRENCH (*Pulls pistol on him.*)

Another word and you are a dead man.

GREEN.

(*Frightened to death. Pops his head under bed clothes, then out, then under again, etc. Feels for his watch, etc.*)
Here, where's my watch and pocket-book?

WRENCH.

If you speak above a whisper, I'll let day-light shine through you. Have you any more money?

GREEN.

No? You've got it all. I'll holler murder!

WRENCH.

If you do, I'll shoot you. Lie perfectly quiet for five minutes or I'll kill you. I shall watch you through the key-hole.
(*Backs off holding pistol at Green. Bus. of coming on every time Green puts his head out.*)

GREEN.

Oh, Lord! Oh, Lord! What'll become ot me? Boots, coat, watch and money, all gone. Rule of the house! They'll take me next. I'll never get my fifty winks.

(*Lies down again. Enter Howard L. 1 E.*)

HOWARD.

Where is the man that would make me miserable for life?

(*Goes up to bed, shakes Green.*)

I shall expect you in the morning to give me the satisfaction of a gentleman, sir, a gentleman! There's my card!

(*Rushes out L. 1 E*)

GREEN.

His card. (*Looks at his card.*) I don't want to call on him. I don't know him. He seems to be pretty well acquainted with me the way he tossed me about. If I can't get my fifty winks this time, I'll get up and go to some other hotel.
(*Lies down. Col. Thunder enters L. 1 E. with a horse-whip. Goes up to bed.*)

THUNDER.

So, you rascal! I've found you, have I? Run away with my daughter, will you? Take that, and that!

(*Horse-whips him over the bed. Green bounces out of the bed around the stage once or twice, the Colonel after him. The Col. goes off L. 1 E. Green gets up the chimney. (This is accomplished by having a short step-ladder back of set fireplace.) Two or three rush on stage with brooms, hoes, pitch-forks, etc. Search all around the room. Finally Wrench fires pistol up the fire-place, which brings Green down all in dirt. As they make for him he rushes out through wing. Dog's barking is heard and Green comes on with a dog fastened to his back; rushes off into one wing and on from another, crossing stage. Everybody after him. Finally goes through window in flat. Crash outside, and*)

QUICK CURTAIN.

THE WAR CORRESPONDENT.

SKETCH.

CAST.

JAKE BLOTTER, ⎫ Two American War Correspondents for the "Daily Pre-
PETE PENCIL, ⎭   mature."
AGUINALDO.
JUAN, a soldier.
INEZ, a waiting maid.
FILIPINOS, SOLDIERS, ETC.

PROPERTY LIST.

Large box for man to hide in, with hinged lid on top and marked on front "Coal." (A large chest will answer.)

Two chairs, large, old-fashioned cradle, pillow and short sheet for cover, "prop" rag baby.

Table and table-cover with few dishes, knives and forks, tin pudding dish with bread reduced to a soft pulp, large spoon. ("Horse" effect explained in Section 2).

Guns for Juan and soldiers.
Document with red seal for Aguinaldo.
Baby cap in cradle to fit Jake.
Bottle on table containing water.
Two revolvers for Aguinaldo.
A "baby cry," or have someone in wings imitate a baby crying.
Two American flags for Jake and Pete.

COSTUMES.

Jake Blotter and Pete Pencil are attired as "tramps" at opening. They disguise themselves in eccentric military coats, hats and accoutrements.

Aguinaldo is attired in burlesque Spanish military costume.

Juan, Filipino soldier, white pants, white blouse, large sombrerro and gun. Soldiers same attire.

Inez, Filipino girl. Spanish costume.

SCENE—*Cottage near Manila. Plain chamber, door and window in flat. Large box with hinged top, marked "Coal," L. C. Table C. with two chairs. Large, old-fashioned cradle R. C. with "prop" rag baby. Inez discovered arranging table.*

INEZ.

War is going on between this country and the Americans, and I don't know what I'll do. I'm engaged to Juan, who will have to go. (*Mournfully.*) I'll be a widow before I'm married.

(*Enter Juan, door in flat, greets Inez.*)

JUAN.

I just ran in to tell you that I've got to be on guard to-night at the castle, but I will be here about eleven o'clock.

INEZ.

Be very careful, for you know that Aguinaldo has this house fitted up like a military fort. He's a crank on the subject of soldiers and military affairs. So look out.

JUAN.

I'll be careful. He won't catch me over a bomb-shell or in a powder magazine! So, good bye. We're on the lookout for Yankee spies.

INEZ.

Good bye, Juan, good bye.

(*Bus. lovable parting at door and Juan exits*)

The baby is quiet, so I can sneak out for a few minutes and buy something for Juan's lunch. Master would be angry if he knew I left that baby alone, but I can't help it. Love before duty.

Exits door. Lid of box is raised and Pete Pencil looks out, comes from box and whistles as if calling. Jake Blotter also whistles and peers out from under table-cloth and emerges from under table very much frightened, hungry and faint.)

JAKE.

Oh, take me home! Don't let me die in this place.

PETE.

Shut up! Do as I do. Be brave and die for your country. They can only shoot you once.

JAKE.

But I don't want to get shot and die. I want to live. Oh, why, why did you bring me over to this place?

PETE.

To get news for the papers. We can make a lot of money by sending over all kinds of war news. (*Jake shivers.*) Stop trembling! Remember you die in a glorious cause.

JAKE.

You go ahead and die. I want to live. I'd rather have them say " there he goes " than " here he lies." You're always blowing about bravery. I'm not brave. I acknowledge that I was never cut out for a soldier.

PETE.

Listen to me! We are here surrounded by a million blood-thirsty Filipinos.

JAKE. (*Faints*)

Oh, dear! Tell them I'm innocent.

PETE.

You'll be shot before me! There's no use deceiving you. We'll never see the United States again.

JAKE.

Oh, dear! Oh, this is awful You kidnapped me from home. You lured me over here and now I'm going to be shot by Filipinos. I'll tell our President on you.

PETE.

You know we sneaked into this house to avoid the Filipino sentries. Now we must make the best of it. In that room—(*Points R.*)—I saw some military costumes. We must disguise ourselves. It's our only hope.

JAKE.

You stay here and I'll run over to the dock and see if I can swim home.

(*Horse effect—horseman gradually approaching—effect louder and louder until he halts outside. Jake and Pete listen in fear.*)

PETE.

Too late. I hear someone coming on horseback. Quick! into that room, and put on the soldier's clothing.

(*Pushes Jake into R. 2 E. as he protests and shakes with fear and follows after him. Enter Aguinaldo, a military-looking crank, L. 2 E.*)

AGUINALDO.

Where is Inez? Not here! Confound that girl! She is always running after the soldiers, and here we are at war with the Americans. Every man's house is a fort, and every man is a walking arsenal. Ah! the baby is quiet; that is a good thing, for it seldom sleeps. Let me see—(*Examines document.*) American spies in the Philippines. Why, of course, and how can we prevent that? The way is to find them and shoot them. Here's the description of the two who have been followed by our soldiers.

(*Reads as Pete and Jake enter R. 2 E. in misfit military costume. Aguinaldo looks up.*)

Ah! a pair of military gentlemen! What seek you in my house?

JAKE. (*Shaking.*)

He told me to put these on—(*Pete checks him.*)

PETE.

Shut up, you idiot! (*To Aguinaldo.*) We came to your house to—to—

JAKE.

Yes, the two-two of us to-to find out where is the kitchen!

AGUINALDO.

The kitchen?

PETE.

My friend means, has your kitchen been searched for spies?

JAKE (*Aside.*)

Yes, for pies, slap jacks, ham sandwich, anything.

AGUINALDO.

To what are you attached, the Army or the Navy?

JAKE.

Yes, we belong to the Army and the Navy and the Infantry on horseback

PETE.

We are with the fresh regiment just arrived from Iloilo.

JAKE.

Yes, we're *oily* and very fresh! Fresnest lot of ducks you ever saw.

AGUINALDO.

Cavalry or Artillery!

JAKE. (*Patronizingly.*)

Both! If we can't get that, we'll take beer; we don't care.

AGUINALDO.

Where are you stationed?

PETE

Cavite Castle.

JAKE.

He is; I ain't. I'm on my own hook.

AGUINALDO.

I believe you are a pair of imposters.

JAKE.
That's right, mister; give it to him. He's an imposter.

PETE. (*To Jake.*)
Shut up!

JAKE. (*To Pete.*)
That man knows you.

AGUINALDO.
If you are soldiers, you have nothing to fear. But if you are spies or Americans, you must be looked after. I'll notify the guard. (*Exits L. 2 E.*)

PETE. (*Angry.*)
Do you see the trouble you've got me into?

JAKE.
You got me into trouble, bringing me over here.

PETE.
Quick! we must hide. He's gone after the soldiers.

(*Runs for box and gets into it. Jake tries to follow.*)
Get out of this. There's room for one only.

JAKE.
Where will I go?

PETE.
Into the cradle with the baby.

(*Jake runs over to cradle, puts baby cap on and throws baby to Pete. Jake gets into cradle and covers himself with sheet which is short and exposes his feet.*)
Cover those feet. I hear somebody coming.

(*Jake rocks cradle and almost spills himself out of it. Pete yells to him to be quiet. Jake sees bottle on table, dashes out of cradle in spite of Pete's warning and gets the bottle; returns to cradle and drinks from it and then covers himself with sheet. Aguinaldo heard returning. Pete closes lid of chest and Jake remains quiet. Aguinaldo enters with tin dish of bread pulp and large spoon.*)

AGUINALDO.
The soldiers are as hard to find as the police. However, I've fixed everything. I've got my revolvers.

(*Shows them as he sits at table. Pete looks out of box. Jake in cradle alarmed.*)
Where is the bottle I left upon this table?

(*Looks under table. Jake drinks ad lib.*)
Well, never mind. It wasn't fit to drink. It was poisoned!

(*Jake looks amazed.*)
It was poisoned for an American spy, in jail next door.

(*Jake spits out water which he drank from bottle.*)
And a deadly poison it is.

(*Jake spits out more water and groans. Pete laughs heartily from his hiding place.*)
I wonder if these revolvers are in good condition.

(*Examines them. Levels one at the box. Pete slams the lid down.*)
I guess they are all right.

(*Fires a shot as if by accident.*)
Hello! That went off accidentally.

(Pete is heard to groan and baby in box to cry. Aguinaldo has business of looking around.)

I've awakened the baby.

(Comes over to cradle and rocks it. Jake cries like a baby and Aguinaldo tries to hush it. Goes and gets pap to feed it. As he comes over he suddenly discovers the ruse and winks to audience.)

(Aside.) Ah, ha! Playing off the baby, eh? I'll give him the baby's food. *(Aloud.)* Little Sancho wants some dinner?

JAKE. *(Cries baby fashion.)*

Sancho is hungry.

AGUINALDO.

Here's some dinner for you.

(Throws three or four spoonfuls of pap into Jake's face and then the remainder of it in one mass, smearing it all over Jake's face as he bellows, etc.)

Sancho likes his dinner?

JAKE. *(Sobbing.)*

Sancho ain't hungry now.

AGUINALDO.

(Aguinaldo goes to box and raises lid; aims pistol into it and orders Pete out. Pete emerges, holding on to baby.)

I've got one out of that box!

(Then with pistol orders Jake out of cradle. Jake and Pete try to get behind each other to avoid Aguinaldo's pistols.)

Now then, you both die!

(They fall on knees R. shouting "Spare us, spare us." Inez enters door in flat followed by Juan and 4 to 6 Filipino soldiers, who range quickly L.)

There's a couple of Americans. A pair of Yankee spies. Down with them!

(As Filipinos level guns and are about to fire Jake and Pete pull small American flags out of bosoms and wave them at soldiers.)

BOTH.

Fire on this if you dare!

(Music Yankee Doodle. Jake and Pete dancing. Soldiers and rest are cowering. On this picture of astonishment and of Filipinos baffled.)

CURTAIN.

ILL-TREATED TROVATORE.

BURLESQUE OPERA SCENE.

Suitable for After-piece, white or black face, male or mixed minstrels. If played by all males would advise black face.

CAST.

MANRICO, the imprisoned lover.
LEONORA.
THE COUNT.
THE SENTRY.
SERVANT.

Opera-struck ruffians by rest of Company.

Set prison piece R. 2. E. which masks in a step-ladder. There is a grated window in this prison piece and the step-ladder must be high enough for MANRICO *to peer over out window and sing. Wood scene at back and wings used. At opening a funny sentry in eccentric armor is parading before the prison. Lights half down, music pizzicato at opening, which changes into march as enter* COUNT DE LUNATIC *and his servant* MIASMA. *Sentry salutes them and stands at "present" with spear.*

COUNT.

Is everything quiet?

SENTRY.

You could even hear a gum drop, your Highness.

COUNT.

'Tis well. Guard the prisoner and see that he does not eat his way out through those granite walls. (*Servant exits L. 2 E.*)

SENTRY.

I will shoot him with this spear if he attempts to bribe me or come out of that window.

(*Clattering of feet—Horse effect can be introduced—noises, etc., heard L. 2 E. and servant dashes in with a large document with large red seal dangling on end of it.*)

COUNT.

Well, fool! What is this? (*All three frightened.*)

SERVANT.

Take it! Take it!

COUNT (*timidly*).

Who—who sent it?

SERVANT.

I think it's from Washington.

COUNT (*to Sentry*).

Take that document and examine it.

SENTRY.

No, sir! I'm on guard and can't leave my post-office.

COUNT.

Cowards! I'll take this office myself. (*Takes document gingerly.*) I'm not afraid of an investigation or a court martial. (*Trembling.*) All that they can do to me is to retire me for six years on full pay! (*Opens document.*) Go get me some gas.

SERVANT.

All right, your Highness! (*Exits L 1 E.*)

COUNT.

It is addressed to me, and of course must be for me.

(*Servant enters with lighted candles.*)

SERVANT.

Here's your electric light.

(*Count begins to grimace as if reading the document. Servant peers over his shoulder, reading it aloud also.*)

Two pairs of paper collars, one cuff, one bosom and a piece of suspender.
(*Count turns on him.*)

COUNT.

How dare you read my letter?

(*Begins reading again. Servant peers over his shoulder as before. Count turns and they peer into each other's faces.*)

SERVANT.

He writes a beautiful foot, doesn't he?

COUNT.

Mind your own business! Hold up the light.
(*Servant raises it over Count's head.*)
No! no! Lower down! Lower it.

(*Servant lowers it. Count reads until Servant ignites a fire-cracker or two, which are wired securely into the cardboard seat. Soon as they explode Count, Sentry and Servant fall in eccentric manner, sprawling, ad lib.*)

SERVANT.

The candle busted!

COUNT (*rises*).

Get up! There is danger ahead for us. (*Sentry rises.*) There is a plot to steal these woods and kidnap the jail, but they'll never do it.

(*Servant and Sentry repeat all the boastings of Count as he paces stage, they imitating him.*)

I'll have the life of the first one daring to trespass on these lands. I'll show them I'm not a cowardly Spaniard. I am a New York politician. They can't get anything out of me. I wonder what they take me for? No, no, no, never! Follow me, follow me to death if needs be! (*Dashes out L. 1 E*)

SERVANT.

To death if needs be! (*Imitates Count's exit.*)

SENTRY.

I don't care to stay here alone. I wish I knew of some saloon with a side door, but there isn't one in this city

(*Enter Leonora L. 2 E.*)

LEONORA.

The cruel Count has incarcerated the only one I love in that cruel prison. (*Peculiar noise.*) I hear him breathing in his cell and fighting mosquitoes. (*Coyly.*) Ah, there! Manrico.

MANRICO.

Ah, there! Leonora. It's no use, I cannot slumber, although I sigh to rest me. (*Chord.*)

(*MUSIC—Introduction to duet from "Il Trovatore" lower scene* MANRICO *sings. Situation as per above illustration.*)

(*As they conclude Servant enters L. 2 E. Sentry is asleep leaning on spear during duel.*)

SERVANT.

Do you want to get him out?

LEONORA.

Yes ; but how can you get him out ?

SERVANT.

I'll move the jail !

(*Takes hold of prison piece and runs it into R. 2 E. exposing Manrico seated on the step-ladder. Manrico sees Leonora L. C.*)

MANRICO (*descending*).

Leonora !

LEONORA.

Manrico ! (*They embrace and separate.*)

MANRICO.

Once more ! (*Embrace again.*)

(*Chord or discord. Count and funny soldiers enter L. 2 E.*)

COUNT.

What's this? Treason! Seize the prisoner! (*Two soldiers seize Manrico.*)

LEONORA.

Oh, Count, spare him, spare him! (*Kneels to him.*)

COUNT.

Never! (*She rises.*) He dies! (*Servant puts sword into Manrico's hands.*)

SERVANT.

Defend yourself with that.

COUNT.

Traitor!

(*Slashes at Servant who hides behind Sentry.*)

MANRICO.

I'll fight for my life!

(*Short sword combat between Count and Manrico. Servant puts on muzzle and umpires the fight as though it were a prize fight, and Leonora advises Manrico to stab Count, cut his nose off, carve him, use a razor on him, etc., all ad lib. during fight. Finally Count disarms Manrico and runs sword under his arm. All exclaim: "Oh!" Count tries to pull out sword, but cannot.*)

COUNT.

His blood is rusty!

(*Pulls and tugs, puts foot against Manrico's bosom and is thus enabled to pull out his sword accompanied by a long discord in orchestra, made by violins, as he does so, and Manrico falls dead. Leonora runs to him and kneels, sobs and cries in wild terror.*)

LEONORA.

Oh! you have killed him and he's dead. Speak to me, Manrico! Speak to your *Leonora*, who is *leaning o'er* you!

MANRICO (*looks up*).

I can't speak; I'm dead. (*Lies down.*)

COUNT.

I'll bring him to.

SERVANT.

Bring three; I'll have a drink myself.

COUNT (*commandingly.*)

Bring the anvils and the hammers.

SERVANT.

Oh, he's going to "knock him."

(*Soldiers place an anvil on a box or pedestal R. C. and two more place an anvil L. C. in same manner. As they start to do this the music of Anvil Chorus begins, the introduction being kept up until all are ready to sing. Manrico rises as anvils are in position. Count and Servant are at anvil R., servant having a bar of red-hot iron, end of it painted red, and Manrico and sleepy Sentry are at anvil L. They have large or small hammers. Soon as all are in position the Anvil Chorus begins. There are no words used, merely a "gibberish" of supposed Italian. Leonora and soldiers are at ends of circle. With the final strokes of hammers the curtain descends.*) ·

(Here are the Italian [?] words that can be sung as chorus proper begins.)

Tempo di Marcia. (VOICES.)

Piano or Orchestra. Sold to me the bour - ba - zee, De

La - ger Beer from Kan - ka - kee; Sold to me, de Ju - bi - lee, De

Da - go loves de "Mac - ca - ree: Hand case, Switz - er case, Hard case,

Dutch case in a tin case, Go pound de ten - der steak, Go pound de

ten - der steak and call the board - ers in.

N. B.—If desired, a large or small chorus of courtiers, nobles and ladies in costume can be introduced in this finish.

Section X.

SHADOW PANTOMIMES.

This very humorous but mystifying performance will be explained in a simple manner, and the amateur can produce the effects as well in the drawing-room, with its folding doors, as the professional, with all the stage accessories of height and space. No scenery is needed, but plenty of "properties," so arranged that their shadows will be cast upon the white sheet or curtain. With the electrical appliances and calciums of the present time the shadow pantomime is easily gotten up, and will be a source of wonder and plenty of laughter from your audience.

The first thing needed is plenty of light. In the absence of these lights, however, a good substitute for drawing-rooms can

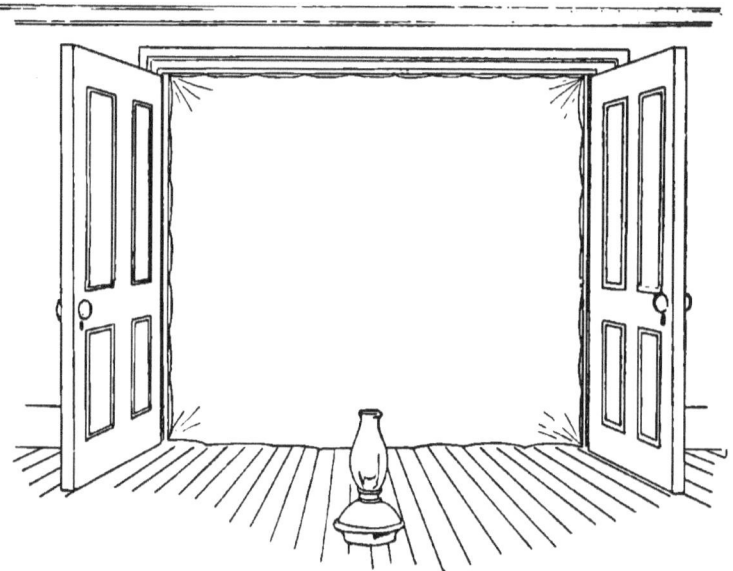

be had in a powerful lamp or reflector. This light is placed on the floor about six feet away from the screen, sheet or curtain. This sheet is secured between your folding doors, and made very taut, top, bottom and sides. In a hall or theatre, it is best to have it of muslin with small seams, and fastened top and bottom, also sides, by tacks or battens ; or in the shape of a window curtain. Let it come flat to the stage, so the feet of the shadow performers can be distinctly seen. The sheet or curtain will then look like illustration on opposite page.

The audience must be seated in the dark; no lights can be used in *front* of the curtain. Behind this curtain get as strong a light as possible by means of a powerful lamp, calcium or electric (carbon) such as are used in picture machines or magic lanterns of the modern style. Having arranged your lamp, light, curtains, etc., you are now ready to begin your pantomime. Remember that coming near to the curtain and in front of the light casts your shadow on the curtain life-size only. Going nearer to the light, and *away* from the curtain, you become larger and assume gigantic proportions. Step over the light from behind it. (Care must be taken during this not to turn lamp over.) You then appear as dropping from the clouds, or space above. Jump over the light, from in front of it, with your back to the curtain and audience, and you appear as if leaping up into the clouds, or space above, and you totally disappear in gigantic proportions. The " prop-erties " used, if signs, they must be of cardboard with letters cut out, so the light will shine through the cut places thus :

Instruments, brooms, hats, fish and articles well-known are easily recognized by their shadows and need not be specially made, except when spoken of in the pantomimes as "special." Then they will be described. It is always best to draw off a front scene to reveal the cur-tain illuminated by the light behind it, in order to begin the pantomime. In the absence of scenes, you can open the doors and get the same effect. Remember to darken the space in front of the curtain, leaving your audience truly "in the dark" before you begin. Music is essen-tial. An overture of popular melodies enlivens the pantomime.

Most important.—Be sure and stand sideways or in profile, during the important business of the shadow pantomime, as *facing* the audience *will not show the outlines of your features*, but when you are sideways the entire profile is distinctly seen. Participants can talk audibly to each other, to convey the meaning of action and simplify matters. Not loud enough, however, for the audience to overhear the speakers. Advise plenty of rehearsals so as to get positions and ges-tures just right.

SHADOW PANTOMIMES AT HOME.

THE LOBSTERSCOPE.

PROPERTY LIST.

Axe.
Imitation log of wood.
Gun for soldier.
Soldier costume.
Purse or wallet with money.
Horse pistol.
Tinker's furnace and soldering irons.
Box, with strap for tinker to carry on his back.
Dummy baby.
Tin dish of sawdust and large spoon.
Police outfit.
Crutches for Cripple.
Money for Cripple.

Chair.
Lot of old tools—hammer, saw, axe, auger, etc.
Stiff cardboard arm to be sawed off from Cripple's body.
Long link of imitation sausages.
Lady's bustle.
Tin pump with live cat inside of it.
Basket, with imitation crabs and a lobster.
(See description in pantomime.)
Cardboard skeleton with legs and arms loose.

MUSIC—Either a 6-8 two-step or waltz, very *piano*.

Clown enters *R*. Pantaloon *L*. Clown yawns showing he is lazy and sleepy. Pantaloon motions to Clown to get his axe and chop some wood. Pantaloon gets the axe from *L*. puts it into Clown's hands and tells him to chop. Clown begins chopping at log of wood *C*. Pantaloon starts *L*. Clown falls asleep with axe raised, Pantaloon turns and comes to Clown and slaps him on the back. Clown begins chopping rapidly, and Pantaloon exits *L*. Clown gazes after him, and in so doing, allows the axe to strike his toe, (apparently) and he drops the axe, hopping about in pain. Enter soldier with gun *R*. Clown about to run away when soldier levels gun at him, and orders him to return. Soldier says Clown has got to enlist, to go and fight for his country .Clown says he's brave, and only too glad to go. Demands the gun, to show soldier how he can drill. Gets the gun and after few movements with it, levels it at soldier, and commands him to take off soldier hat, then coat, and orders soldier out very bravely. Soldier exits *R*. Clown puts on coat and hat and paces stage with gun. Pantaloon runs across from *L*. to *R*. Clown puts out his foot and trips Pantaloon, who falls on his face, then rises. Seeing soldier he is afraid, and about to run when Clown orders him to halt ; then he orders him to "hands up" and throw down his money. Pantaloon throws purse on ground, then Clown orders him to leave. Pantaloon frightened, exits *L*. Clown laughs, puts down gun and begins to count money in the purse; as he is seated *C*. Pantaloon returns *L*. sees clown, and gliding behind him takes the gun and levels it at Clown, who is busy counting money. Clown turns his head and peers into gun barrel, drops money and starts to run *R*., when Pantaloon orders him to halt. Pantaloon compels Clown to take off hat and coat, which he does. Then they agree to divide the articles, put down gun and seat themselves at *C*. The Soldier returns *R*. with a large pistol, points it at Clown, who turns and sees it. He puts all the articles into Pantaloon's lap, saying : "You can have them all." He rises and runs out *R*. Pantaloon laughs and is gathering up the articles, when he sees the pistol barrel close to his face; he peers along the barrel and sees the soldier, and pushes all the articles toward him; then rises and strides off *L*. The soldier picks up gun and articles and exits *R*. Enter Tinker *L*. with furnace and soldering irons in it. Box upon his back. He pauses *C*. Clown runs out from *L*. and greets him. Pantaloon enters *R*. They engage in conversation. Clown steals a hot iron out of the furnace, then Tinker turns to talk to him and Pantaloon steals one. Clown puts his iron into his pocket and it burns him. He capers about and yells, then takes out iron, and hands it to Tinker, who burns his hands as he is seizing the iron. Pantaloon burns himself with his stolen iron, and then burns the Tinker in trying to return it. The Tinker with the hot iron burns both Clown and Pantaloon on arms, legs, back, etc., then in great anger exits *R*. threatening them. Clown and Pantaloon feel the burnt parts of their body and show grief and pain. Enter woman with baby L. They halt her C. While she is talking to Pantaloon, the Clown steals her bonnet and puts it on himself. They both admire the baby. Woman asks Clown to hold it. He says "No; Pantaloon likes to hold babies." She turns to him and asks him to hold the baby, puts it in his arms and exits. Clown laughs at Pantaloon and the baby begins to cry. (Use baby-cry.) Clown is in great glee over Pantaloon's troubles with the baby. He paces the floor with it. Clown says: "The baby is hungry; let's feed it." Clown gets a tin dish of sawdust and a big spoon from R. and shows that the dish is full of "stuff" by stirring it with spoon. Comes to baby and tries to feed it. Baby cries very loud. Clown becomes very angry and forces spoon down the baby's throat. Pantaloon upbraids him for it, when Clown throws contents into Pantaloon's face. Pantaloon throws baby at clown who throws it back again at him, but misses Pantaloon, who dodges it, and it strikes a policeman who is entering L. Clown and Pantaloon scamper off R., pursued by policeman. Woman runs in L. picks up the baby and starts in pursuit also, R. Cripple enters L, comes to C. and pauses. Clown and Pantaloon rush in from R. bump against Cripple and knock him down. They aid him to arise and pick up his crutches, apologizing and trying to soothe the Cripple's ruffled feelings Cripple says he wants to see the doctor. Clown says "there's the doctor," pointing to Pantaloon. Cripple says he needs doctor's attention at once. Pantaloon says "five dollars in advance." They get the money from Cripple and Clown demands half of it. Pantaloon gives him a coin and orders him to get a chair. Clown brings a chair to C. Cripple sits down. Pantaloon orders Clown to get his instruments. Clown returns with hammer, saw, axe, auger. etc. Drops them at Cripple's feet who in terror rises to escape, but is held in chair by Clown. Pantaloon examines Cripple's legs, and concludes that the pain is in the Cripple's arms. Takes the saw and amid much bustle and fright on the part of the Cripple, Pantaloon saws off one of his arms. (This is done by Cripple holding his R. arm close to his side and using a stiff cardboard arm, which Clown slyly brings in and holds close to Cripple's side, or shoulder, while he is seated looking R.) They saw off this arm and Clown holds it up, then throws it over the light. Cripple demands his crutches; Clown gives him but one, telling him he has but one arm and needs but one crutch. Cripple exits L. Clown and Pantaloon congratulate each other on their surgical skill. Enter fat man running and in great pain, L. They capture him and ask: "What ails you?" Fat man motions he has terrific cramps from eating something. Clown and Pantaloon demand money for treatment. Fat man gives money; both grab for it. Pantaloon gets it. They order fat man to sit down; they peer into his mouth. Pantaloon runs his arm (apparently) down the fat man's throat and pulls out long links of sausages (made of muslin.) Then Clown puts his arm down the fat man's throat and pulls out a lady's bustle. These articles are all under fat man's coat and pulled out to seem to come from his open mouth. Clown holds up the bustle and then throws it over light. Fat man squirms and kicks again saying he's worse. They compel him to lie on the floor. Clown gets a tin stomach-pump. A tin pump large enough to hold a live cat. The thick wire as a pumping rod or piston can be on the outside of the cylinder. They force the lower end of the pump into the fat man's mouth, then Clown pumps They raise the pump and open the lid and spill out a live cat. Fat man rises, thanks them, says he feels better, shakes hands with the doctors and exits R. much relieved. Doctors put away the "prop." used, and shake hands with each other. Fish-horn is blown off R. and enter a fish peddler with a basket on R. arm. He comes C. They stop him and demand price of fish. The peddler says he is selling live crabs and lobsters. They express delight and say they love crabs and lobsters. As peddler talks to Clown, Pantaloon steals a crab and puts it in his pocket. Then peddler's attention is taken up by Pantaloon and Clown steals a crab and puts it in his pocket; then he puts his hand into the basket and slips his finger into a ring sewn into claws of a large (linen) lobster and withdraws his hand with the lobster clinging to it. Yells, capers and expresses pain. Pantaloon comes over to aid him and gets the lobster fastened to his hand. He yells and jumps and shrieks for help. The peddler tries to rescue his lobster and gets it fast to his fingers. He yells, jumps and in wild antics exits *R.* with lobster clinging to his fingers or hand Clown and Pantaloon laugh at peddler's misfortune, when suddenly the crabs in their pockets bite them. Clown strikes his pocket, jumps, yells for help, etc., and then puts in his hand and takes out crab from pocket and flings it out *R.* Pantaloon strikes at his pocket and takes out the crab after a violent struggle and flings it out *L.* Policeman followed by peddler enters *R.* Lively music as chase begins. Clown and Pantaloon run off *L.* followed by policeman, peddler, woman with baby and soldier, all running in eccentric manner. Then Clown returns by jumping down over the light from behind it and running down close to sheet and off *R.*; Pantaloon next, then Policeman, Peddler, soldier and woman last. Soon as all are off *R.* Clown returns close to sheet from *R.* at *C.*, he turns and runs up stage and jumps over the light going upwards. Then Pantaloon, then policeman, then soldier, and last of all the woman. Soon as she jumps over the light, Clown and Pantaloon jump back again downward and roll down towards the sheet. Get on their knees, praying for mercy as a cardboard skeleton is dangled *before* the light, by someone stationed there. The skeleton will be of huge proportions and when shaken will appear to be grasping Clown and Pantaloon by the hair of their heads.

CURTAIN.

FROLICS IN THE MOON.

A SHADOW PANTOMIME.

PROPERTY LIST.

Sausage machine.
(See description in pantomime.)
Sign "Sausage."
(Letters cut to allow light to shine through them.)
Money for Pantaloon.
Imitation or live dog.
(If imitation. have it on a thin board to glide along when pulled on by string.)
Link of sausages, 6 or 7 feet long.
Link of two sausages.
Sign "Dentist."
Chair.
Old tools — hammer. mallet, saw, auger, plyers and a large wooden tooth.
(See description in pantomime itself.)

Five profile fishes on a platter or in a pan.
Hoop skirt and dress to be pulled off.
(This dress is made like a large apron. Woman unties the string and "walks out of it" as dress is pulled.)
Cot-bed.
Axe.
Knife.
Cardboard heart.
Cardboard skeleton, to work arms and legs.
(See description.)
Broom.
Boxing gloves for Clown and Pantaloon.
Policeman's outfit for two persons.

NOTE.—It must be remembered that almost everything expressed must be done in pantomime and as noiselessly as possible.

(*Music—Waltz, Very Piano.*)

Clown and Pantaloon enter *L.* meet *C.* and shake hands; point to *R.* and say: "Hello! Somebody's coming." Enter two men *R.* with a sausage machine,

a narrow box about ten feet high. and with a wheel to turn as if grinding. The men place the machine *R. C.* and Clown speaks to first man, asks nature of business machine. Man says: "It's a sausage machine,"and holds up a sign, showing letters "Sausage." Then hands the sign to his partner. Clown asks:

"How much for it?" Man shows with fingers that he wants fifteen dollars. Clown and Pantaloon search their pockets and find money; pay it to man, who exits with his partner, *R*. Clown and Pantaloon, delighted over their purchase, begin to look for "material." Enter a woman *L*., leading dog by a string. Pantaloon engages her in conversation and Clown sneaks behind her and unties

the dog and takes it in his arm. Lady exits *R*. They put the dog in the machine and Pantaloon "grinds" it. Clown pulls out a link of sausages, about six or seven feet long. They are delighted. Clown throws sausages over the light. A fat man enters *l.* They are delighted with hi size, and motion to eac other that he will make great lot of sausages The invite Fat man to come over and inspect the machine; they coax him to peer into it; then they seize him, and amid much bluster they force him into machine, or rather behind it,

where he crouches out of sight. Pantaloon "grinds" but no sausages appear. Clown orders him to grind faster, which he does. Clown peers into end of machine and pulls out two sausages; shows them to Pantaloon and both are disgusted and shove the machine off into *R*. Fat man creeps off with it. Enter dentist *L.* with sign "Dentist" He calls for assistance and Pantaloon enters *R*., takes the sig and exists with it *L.* Dentist rubs his hands as if expecting business. Ente victim with toothache *L.* Pantaloon brings a chair and victim is forced into it *L* Both peer into victim's mouth. Dentist sends Pantaloon after tools and he brings in auger, hammer, plyers, etc. ; drops them at victim's feet, who jumps up i alarm and seeks to escape, but they force him into chair, and demand money Victim pays; then Dentist puts auger into his mouth and works at tooth; the

gets a chisel and hammer and works at the tooth again; then he gets the plyers and puts them into man's mouth and secures a large wooden tooth, which Pantaloon has brought in and holds ready. The plyers catch the tooth by a nail in it's head. Dentist pulls and tugs in all shapes at the tooth; Victim squirms during this tugging. Then dentist puts his foot against the man's chest and with this brace he gives a long pull and draws out the tooth; holds it up to view.

Victim exits *R* ; shaking head over successful operation.   Enter Clown *R.*, Pantaloon *L.*, motioning that someone is coming.   Enter woman with pan on her head, containing four or five profile cardboard fishes.   They halt *C.*, engage her in conversation and Clown steals a fish and Pantaloon steals one, until pan is empty.

Then, as woman (man) starts to exit *R.*, Clown takes hold of her dress and it comes off, exposing her hoops worn over tight pair of pants ; Clown laughs and throws skirt (or dress) over the light, also the fish.   They now show signs of being weary and want to sleep.   Pantaloon gets a cot-bed from *L* , places it *L. C.* and gets into it.   Clown pulls Pantaloon out of the cot and gets into it himself. Pantaloon pulls Clown out and gets into bed.   Clown exits *R.*, and returns with axe ; hits Pantaloon several times on head with axe ; then he gets a knife and pretends to cut into Pantaloon's breast, and pulls out a cardboard heart and holds it up to view. (The heart and knife were on the cot when brought out.)   As Clown holds up the heart, a skeleton dangles before the light, grabbing at Clown, who in great terror sees it and runs out *L.*, partially pursued by skeleton, which

now returns and frightens Pantaloon, who rises.   In great terror, he shoves cot out *L.*, pursued and beaten by skeleton   This skeleton is of cardboard, about three feet high, and the arms and legs are jointed like a "Jumping-Jack ;" this makes the arms and legs work in all shapes.   A stout wire fixed to a block of wood in skeleton's head serves to hold it out over the light   Soon as skeleton drives Pantaloon out *L*., a ballet dancer runs out from *R*. and dances a "Highland Fling," *C*. The dancer wears short skirts like a ballet girl. After the short "fling," the dancer runs out *L*. in eccentric manner. Then a man (dentist) enters *R*., woman *L*. They meet *C* , and begin to embrace each other ; then they kiss. When they kiss for the second time, a woman (supposed to be girl's mother) runs out *B*. with a broom and beats the man and woman off *L*. Then enter Clown and Pantaloon *R*. and *L*., with boxing gloves. They meet *C*. and begin a prize fight. They spar and dance away from each other several times. Then Clown strikes Pantaloon an upper-cut, and Pantaloon becomes a "Giant" in size and strikes down at Clown ; then he comes nearer to curtain and becomes natural size again. More sparring, and Pantaloon strikes Clown an upper-cut and becomes gigantic in size. Clown kicks and steps upon Pantaloon's head.

Then comes close to curtain and becomes life-size. Both strike each other and both become giants ; spar, and come down to life-size ; suddenly, Clown strikes Pantaloon, who falls *R*. *C*. Then there is a shout of "Police !" Clown and Pantaloon run out *R*. Two policemen run across from *L* to *R*., followed by a woman in hoop-skirt   Then Clown comes down over the light, runs down to curtain, then off into *L*. Pantaloon comes down over light and exits same way. Then the first policeman and the second policeman, then the woman with hoops. Soon as she is out, Clown returns *L* , comes to *C*., and runs up stage and jumps over the light ; then Pantaloon ; then first policeman ; then second policeman ; then the woman in the hoop skirt. Soon as she jumps over the light, a pair of hands (one of the policeman) is held over the light ; one each side of it, and they will appear of tremendous size upon the sheet. Agitate the fingers as if grasping at an object, as the curtain descends. ("Hurry" music throughout the finale.)

CURTAIN.

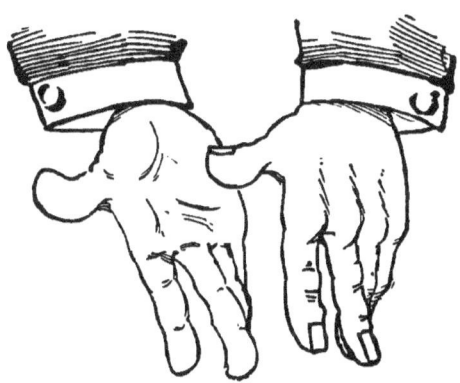

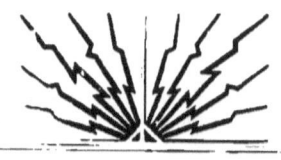

DIRECTORY.

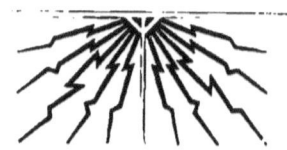

SUITABLE MUSICAL NUMBERS FOR

CAKE=WALKS.

ORCHESTRA

Name	Composer.	10 parts	14 parts	Full Orch.	Piano acc't	Piano solo
Down Ole Tampa Bay	*W. T. Francis*	40	60	80	15	50
Darktown Parade	*J. Henry Fisher*	40	60	80	15	50
Darktown Is Out To-night	*Will Marion*	60	80	——	15	50
Darktown Cyclone	*Edw. Trautman*	40	60	80	15	50
Louisiana Pastime	*J. B. Michaelis*	40	60	80	15	50
Razzer Dance	*E. L. Bailey*	40	60	80	15	50
Dat Blackville Wedding	*Robt. Cone*	40	60	80	15	50
Levee Revels	*W. C. O'Hare*	60	80	1.00	15	50
Sambo Out of Work	*J. A. Silberberg*	60	80	1.00	15	50
Stuttering Coon	*H. Y. Leavitt*	60	80	1.00	15	50
Chrystie Street Brigade	*Max Gabriel*	60	80	1.00	15	50
Rubberneck Jim	*J. W Bratton*	60	80	1.00	15	50
Coonville Jubilee	*C. H. Collins*	60	80	1.00	15	50
Rambling Ebenezer	*Geo. J. Trinkaus*	60	80	1.00	15	50
Mississippi Moonlight	*Jerome Basye*	60	80	1.00	15	50
Darkey Doings	*Effie F. Kamman*	60	80	1.00	15	50
Calk Walk in the Sky	*Ben Harney*	60	80	1.00	15	50
Lucinda's Serenade	*Isidore Witmark*	75	1.00	1.25	20	50
Plantation Pastimes	*W. C. O'Hare*	60	80	1.00	15	50
Up in Nigger Heaven	*Lyn Udall*	60	80	1.00	15	50
Ragtime Society	*Herbert Dillea*	60	80	1.00	15	50
Ragtime Reverie	*Stanley Carter*	60	80	1.00	15	50
Cottonfield Capers (A Kentucky Coon-Hop)	*W. C. O'Hare*	60	80	1.00	15	50
Nigger Alley	*Geo. D. Andrews*	60	80	1.00	15	50
Lumb'rim Luke	*J. A. Silberberg*	60	80	1.00	15	50
De Pullman Porters' Ball	*J. Stromberg*	60	80	——	15	50
My Dixie Queen	*S. L. Perrin*	60	80	——	15	50
Possum Hollow	*Gottlieb-Hopkins*	60	80	1.00	15	50
Colored Delegates	*J. M. Fulton*	60	80	1.00	15	50
Ebony Echoes	*Gus Edwards*	60	80	1.00	15	50

COMPLETE CATALOGUE ON REQUEST.

M. WITMARK & SONS, Publishers.

WITMARK BUILDINGS,   SCHILLER BUILDING,

NEW YORK, LONDON.   CHICAGO.

An Invaluable Reference :—

"WHAT'S WANTED FOR AMATEUR MINSTRELSY."

A complete and illustrated up-to-date catalogue containing thematics and minute information pertaining to this particular line of entertainment. Fifty pages of interesting matter, FREE on application.

MINSTREL OVERTURES, (AN INDISPENSIBLE ACQUISITION.)
The First Impression Generally Counts!

The first impression of a minstrel show is its opening chorus. Realizing this, we have devoted a great deal of time and thought to this particular subject, with the gratifying result that the
WITMARK MINSTREL OVERTURES AND OPENING CHORUSES
are built on the most perfect and practical systems known.

They are compiled on original lines of catchy, popular and specially composed melodies, consistently dove-tailed, harmoniously blended with appropriate "business" that makes these overtures veritable musical kaleidoscopes of interest to all classes.

The Witmark Minstrel Overtures and Opening Choruses are really a long felt want satisfied. The Piano and Vocal Scores, (handsomely bound) contains in a unique, yet comprehensive manner, full instructions and directions for bones, tambos, so as to derive "surprise" effects from them. "Cues" for interlocutor and ends. Particular attention is paid to the voice arrangement of these overtures as demonstrated by the improvement in Nos. 2 and 3, where the male and female voice parts are printed on separate system of staves, thereby greatly simplyfying matters for study. The numbers one and two have been used by hundreds of organizations with the greatest possible success. Letters of endorsements galore. Not one dissenting communication ever received.

 Each Overture is also specially arranged and printed for full orchestra, in a manner not too difficult, but effective.

 Each Overture also contains separate voice parts in octavo form. Handy and expense saving. Only 25c per part.

 Each Overture is so arranged that it can be used for female minstrels.

To arrange an Overture similar to these, would involve a cost of at least $25.00.

 Price of Overtures for Piano, Nos. 1, 2, 3 . . . . $1.00 each.
 Price of Overtures for Orchestra, Nos. 1, 2, 3 . . . . 1.00 each.

 Prices of Bones and Tambos contained in **"WHAT'S WANTED FOR AMATEUR MIN-STRELSY."** Send for Fifty page Catalogue, **FREE.**

"The Serenade of the Blue and Gray" in "Barbara Fidgity," at Weber & Fields'
A Musical Novelty for Minstrel First Part Finale.

THE SERENADE

—OF—

"The Blue and Gray,"

By HARRY B. SMITH and JOHN STROMBERG.

It is invariably the case when amateurs get up a minstrel performance, for them to be at a loss what is appropriate for a good, rousing finale.

We, therefore, recommend "The Serenade of the Blue and Gray," which can be done either with or without costumes. It is arranged for four voices and contains interludes to which any inventive stage director can arrange pretty marches, entrances and exits.

Piano Copies, 50 Cents.

M. WITMARK & SONS, Publishers.

WITMARK BUILDINGS,   SCHILLER BUILDING,

NEW YORK, LONDON.   CHICAGO.

The Witmark Minstrel Overtures explained and illustrated in
"WHAT'S WANTED FOR AMATEUR MINSTRELSY."

TAMBOURINES.

We carry a great variety of tambos of all kinds and prices. The best for the money in the market.

 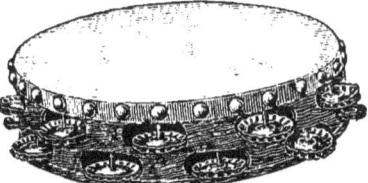

No. 130 10 in., calfskin, 5 sets brass jingles, maple, fancy painted $0.75
No. 170 10 in., calfskin, 4 sets brass jingles. Nickel Plated Rim 1.25
No. 190 10 in., calfskin, 6 sets German silver jingles, professional, Nickel Plated Rim . . . 1.85
No. 200 10 in., calfskin, 7 sets German silver jingles, professional, Nickel Plated Rim . . . 1.85
                Extra Invisible Fastened Head.
No. 310 10 in., one row 14 sets fancy brass jingles 1.25
No. 410 10 in., two row 28 sets fancy brass jingles 1.75
No. 800 10 in., one row 10 sets German silver jingles 1.25
No. 850 10 in., two row 19 sets German silver jingles 1.75
No. 900 10 in., two row 19 sets German silver jingles 2.50
No. 990 8 in., one row 12 sets brass jingles, skeleton model 1.00
No. 1000 10 in., one row 14 sets, brass jingles, skeleton model 1.25

CORK.

There is cork and there is what some call "cork." Good cork is healthful for the skin, while the other is very injurious.

We handle only the best that is used by the most prominent professionals. The difference in price is trivial, but the satisfaction obtained is worth three times the money.

PRICE PER BOX, · · · · **50c**

Our brand especially prepared from the best possible ingredients and we stand ready to guarantee every can purchased.

BONES.

Of various woods and weights, as used by well-known professional end men. Promptly sent on receipt of price.

PRICE LIST PER SET.

No. 00 Black walnut, boys' size, 5½ in., in sets of 4 pieces... .10
No. 10 Rosewood, boys' size, 5½ in., in sets of 4 pieces...... .20
No. 20 Rosewood, men's size, 7 in., in sets of 4 pieces....... .25
No. 30 Cocoa, Boys' size, 5½ in., in sets of 4 pieces .... .30
No. 40 Cocoa, men's size, 7 in., in sets of 4 pieces .... .35
No. 50 Ebony, boys' size, 5½ in., in sets of 4 pieces...... .35
No. 60 Ebony, men's size, 7 in., in sets of 4 pieces......... .40
No. 70 Bone, men's size, fine 7 in., in sets of 4 pieces...... 1.25

There are some excellent effects to be had by end men with bones and tambos, but inasmuch as it requires a little while for some to master the manipulation of those instruments, we suggest that they are ordered as soon as a minstrel show is contemplated.

The Pan-Collegiate Collection of Songs is dwelt upon in
" WHAT'S WANTED FOR AMATEUR MINSTRELSY."

Printed * Uoice * Accompaniments
FOR ORCHESTRA
To all the Successful Witmark Publications.
A GREAT SAVING IN TIME AND EXPENSE.

IT generally costs from $2.00 to $5.00 to specially arrange the accompaniment of a song for orchestra, to say nothing of the petty annoyances, delays and worries involved. To facilitate matters we have had orchestral accompaniments by the best arrangers printed for all our successful songs, and they are sold at the nominal price of 50c. each arrangement. A special catalogue of **Song Orchestrations** free on application.

M. WITMARK & SONS, Publishers,

Witmark Building, New York.

The Paper
The Musician
Appreciates.

Made in America. It stands the most severe tests and gives the utmost satisfaction in each instance.

Tons of "CREST" have been used since its introduction. Can't wear it out.

Every possible improvement in rulings (especially the celebrated Score No. 30,) has been considered and made.

Used by the best musicians in their respective lines, including the following:

Victor Herbert, Julian Edwards, F. W. Meacham, Louis Gottschalk, Herman Perlet, Paul Steindorff, Genaro Saldierda, Gus. Heinrichs, Walter Damrosch, W. H. Mackie, Otto Langey, Wm. C. O'Hare, Watty Hydes, Dave Braham, and one hundred others.

Prices and Samples on Application to

M. WITMARK & SONS, Selling Agents,

Schiller Building, Chicago.   Witmark Building, New York.

MINSTREL QUARTETTES.
WILL FIND NOVELTIES IN THIS LIST.
MALE VOICES.

Dear Old College Days.
GUSTAV LUDERS.

One of the bright spots in "The Burgomaster." A number you are bound to remember and like. Excellent for Glee Club work. Arr. by Chas. Shattuck. Price 20 cents. Also arranged for Mixed Voices.

The Witmark "Coon" Medley No. 2.
Arr. by CHAS. SHATTUCK.

Introducing "Tildy," "Come Back My Honey Boy to Me," "You Am De One," and "Ma Blushin' Rosie." One of the best Medleys on the market. Price 25 cents.

'Tis the Sweetest Song of All.
Intro. Auld Lang Syne.

By ISIDORE WITMARK.

One of the best minstrel songs published. Price 15 cents.

The German Mannerchoer.
By TAYLOR & LEWIS.

From "The Explorers." Price 20c.

Absence Makes the Heart Grow Fonder.
Ballad by GILLESPIE & DILLEA.

Price 20 cents.

Stay In Your Own Backyard.
Pathetic Coon Ballad by LYN UDALL.

Price 15 cents.

Sadie Say You Won't Say Nay
Ballad by WILL R. ANDERSON.

Price 15 cents.

We're All Good Fellows.
ISIDORE WITMARK.

A song in a Bohemian vein—sung with great success as solo with male quartette acc. in "The Chaperons." Meets with approval everywhere. Arr. by Chas. Shattuck. Price 15c.

Dear Old Pipe.
FRED RYCROFT.

A true "Pipe" song. Just the thing for Glee Clubs. Arr. by Charles Shattuck. Price 15 cents:

Chorus of Hussars.
VICTOR HERBERT.

From "The Fortune Teller." Very effective for Tenor and Chorus accompaniment. Arr. by Charles Shattuck. Price 20 cents.

O Wah Hoo.
LYN UDALL.

A comic and descriptive song of the Wild and Woolley West. Bass lead. Arr. by Chas. Shattuck. Price 15c.

Sing Me a Song of the South
Descriptive Ballad by NORTON & CASEY

Price 15 cents.

Ma Blushin' Rosie (Ma Posie Sweet).
Coon Song by SMITH & STROMBERG.

Price 15 cents.

When You Were Sweet Sixteen.
Ballad by JAMES THORNTON.

Price 15 cents.

While Old Glory Waves.
March Song by ANTON HEINDL.

Price 15 cents.

M. WITMARK & SONS, Publishers.

WITMARK BUILDINGS,
NEW YORK,   LONDON.

SCHILLER BUILDING,
CHICAGO.

Send for prices of bones and tambos contained in "**What's Wanted for Amateur Minstrelsy.**" Fifty-page Catalogue, **FREE.**

A Great Number

For an Olio
Turn is an

Illustrated Song Act

The Mountain's Fairest Flower.

SLIDES FOR ILLUSTRATED SONGS.

STAY IN YOUR OWN BACK YARD,	17 Slides	SHE'S KENTUCKY'S FAIREST DAUGHTER,	18 Slides
NOBODY EVER BRINGS PRESENTS TO ME.	15 "	THE FIREMAN'S DREAM,	17 "
WHEN MOTHER SINGS HER LITTLE BOY TO SLEEP,	11 "	MY SUNDAY DOLLY,	12 "
SING ME A SONG OF THE SOUTH,	15 "	YOU AIN'T CHANGED A BIT. FROM WHAT YOU USED TO BE.	17 "
WHEN YOU WERE SWEET SIXTEEN,	16 "	A LETTER FROM OHIO,	18 "
YOU NEEDN'T SAY THE KISSES CAME FROM ME,	17 "	GOLD CANNOT BUY A LOVE LIKE MINE,	12 "
MA TIGER LILY	12 "	COME HOME TO DAD,	16 "
WHERE IS MY BOY TO-NIGHT	18 "	JUST AS THE DAYLIGHT WAS BREAKING,	16 "
OPEN YOUR MOUTH AND SHUT YOUR EYES,	17 "	DEAR OLD SOUL,	17 "
JUST AS THE SUN WENT DOWN	18 "	JUST TIM AND ME.	17 "
THE OLD FOLKS ARE LONGING FOR YOU, MAY	15 "	SHE'S ALL WE HAVE TO-DAY,	16 "
SADIE, SAY YOU WON'T SAY NAY,	17 "	THE BRIDGE OF SIGHS,	22 "
ABSENCE MAKES THE HEART GROW FONDER,	16 "	SIDE BY SIDE,	15 "
		THE SONGS THE BOYS ARE SINGING IN THE CAMP TO-NIGHT,	15 "
PLACE A LIGHT TO GUIDE ME,	21 "	YOU TOLD ME: I NEED NEVER WORK NO MORE.	16 "
WHEN YOU AIN'T GOT NO MONEY YOU NEEDN'T COME 'ROUND,	18 "	WHY DID THEY SELL KILLARNEY,	16 "
		THE MOUNTAIN'S FAIREST FLOWER,	19 "

Sets are Sold at the Rate of 50 cents per Slide.

Deduct One From Number Given For Title Slide, for which No Charge is Made.

The Witmark Minstrel Overtures explained and illustrated in
"WHAT'S WANTED FOR AMATEUR MINSTRELSY."

FREE

A COMPLETE CATALOGUE OF

Standard and Popular Music

——— FOR ———

MANDOLIN	VIOLIN
GUITAR	ZITHER
BANJO	CORNET

TROMBONE

ALSO

VOCAL QUARTETTES FOR MALE, FEMALE AND
MIXED VOICES.

☞ SENT FREE UPON APPLICATION ☜

M. WITMARK & SONS, Publishers,

WITMARK BUILDINGS,   SCHILLER BUILDING,
NEW YORK, LONDON.   CHICAGO.

Prices of Bones and Tambos contained in **'WHAT'S WANTED FOR AMATEUR MIN-
STRELSY.'** Send for fifty page Catalogue **FREE.**

A FINE BOOK OF SONGS

SUITABLE FOR

MINSTREL ENTERTAINERS.

A WEALTH OF

MINSTREL SONG NOVELTIES

CAN BE FOUND IN THIS WORK.

A SESSION "OVER-SHOULDER" READING, AN EASY MATTER WITH THE
"PAN-COLLEGIATE COLLECTION."

The Pan=Collegiate
Collection of Songs

A selection of musical novelties adaptable to all Universities, Academies, Glee Clubs, etc. : : :

Nothing of a local nature contained in this book.

A BRAND NEW IDEA.

Thoroughly up to date in its conception, form and style.

None of the old, stereotyped songs, but the latest, best and most suitable effusions by composers who have declared a new era in college songs. : : : :

PRICE 50 CENTS.

M. WITMARK & SONS,

WITMARK BUILDING, New York.   SCHILLER BUILDING, Chicago.

Prices of Bones and Tambos contained in **"What's Wanted for Amateur Minstrelsy."**
end for fifty page catalogue. **FREE.**

FREE! "OUR SALESMAN."

Containing Violin and Solo Cornet Parts to Our Latest Orchestra and Band Publications
Sent on Application.

M. WITMARK & SONS, Publishers.

WITMARK BUILDINGS,
NEW YORK, LONDON.

SCHILLER BUILDING,
CHICAGO.

Suitable Quartettes are recommended in "What's Wanted for Amateur Minstrelsy."

꙳ ꙳ IF YOU INTEND TO PUT ON ꙳ ꙳

COMIC OPERA WITH AMATEURS

AMATEURS IN "THE MIKADO."

It will Pay You to Consult

The Witmark Music Library.

(M. WITMARK & SONS, Proprietors.)

THE MOST COMPLETE ESTABLISHMENT OF ITS KIND EXTANT.

Representatives of Societies, Lodges, Clubs or Charitable Organizations will receive every attention and advice, gratis, by correspondence with us. We will make you valuable suggestions, and if we close contracts, we will guarantee to do our part toward securing a successful performance. Full paraphernalia for Comic Operas can be arranged for, including

COSTUMES, SCENERY, PROPERTIES, Etc.

We can RENT you almost any musical production written, from

THE WAGNER CYCLUS to "PINAFORE."

Hundreds of comic and light operas on our lists with full or condensed orchestrations, solo and chorus parts, prompt-books, stage manager's guides and dialogue parts.
Send for Catalogues and Prices for everything in the musical line to

THE WITMARK MUSIC LIBRARY,

WITMARK BUILDING,   No. 8 West 29th St., New York.

Suitable quartettes are recommended in "**What's Wanted for Amateur Minstrelsy.**"

Send for our Catalogue of . . . .

Comic Operas
And Musical Comedies

Containing the photographs of the composers,
a List of Songs and Instrumental
numbers from

"THE FORTUNE TELLER,"   "A ROYAL ROGUE,"
"THE SINGING GIRL,"   "THE BURGOMASTER,"
"THE AMEER,"   "KING DODO,"
"CYRANO DE BERGERAC,"   "HODGE, PODGE & CO.,"
"THE VICEROY,"   "THE CHAPERONS,"
"THE JOLLY MUSKETEER,"   WEBER & FIELDS' SUCCESSES,
"THE PRINCESS CHIC,"   ETC.
"DOLLY VARDEN,"

M. WITMARK & SONS,

WITMARK BUILDINGS,

NEW YORK.   - -   LONDON.

SCHILLER BUILDING,   CURTAZ BUILDING,

CHICAGO.   SAN FRANCISCO

An Invaluable Reference :—
"WHAT'S WANTED FOR AMATEUR MINSTRELSY."

A complete and illustrated up-to-date catalogue containing thematics and minute information pertaining to this particular line of entertainment. Fifty pages of interesting matter, FREE on application.

KEEP YOUR LIBRARY STRAIGHT AND CLEAN
BY BINDING YOUR MUSIC WITH
"THE CREST"
MANDOLIN, GUITAR, ORCHESTRA AND BAND COVERS.

Quickstep size, (5x7) . . . . per doz. $1.00
> Single Covers, 15 cents.

Octavo size, (7½x11) . . . . " 2.00
> Single Covers, 25 cents.

Theatre and Concert size (9½x12½) . . . . " 2.50
> Single Covers, 30 cents.

Sheet size, (11½x14½), Piano or Mandolin size . . . " 3.00
> Single Covers, 35 cents.

STRONG, DARK CLOTH BINDING. SEND FOR ONE; AND, IF YOU LIKE IT, SEND FOR MORE.
ABOVE PRICES DO NOT INCLUDE POST, OR EXPRESS CHARGES.

Suitable Songs with Orchestral Accompaniments are given in **"WHAT'S WANTED FOR AMATEUR MINSTRELS."**

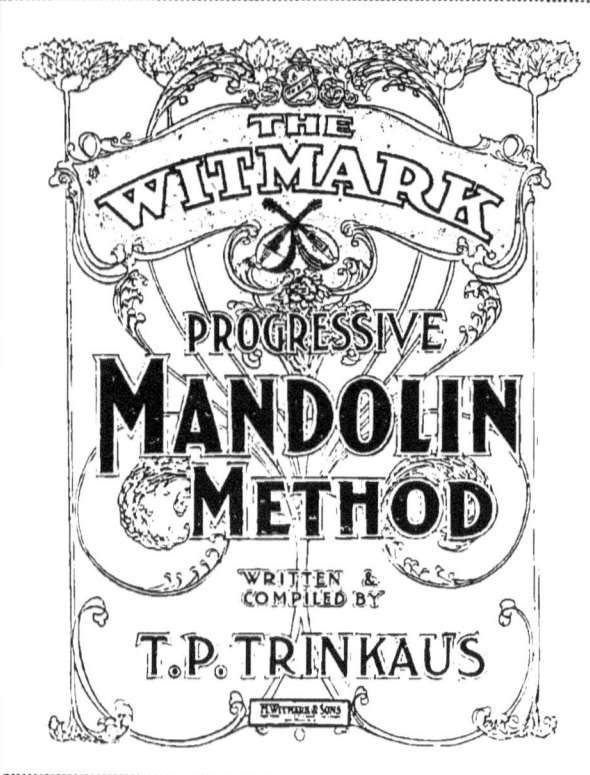
The Pan-Collegiate Collection of Songs is dwelt upon in "**What's Wanted for Amateur Minstrelsy.**"

The Latest and Best 50=Cent Vocal Folio Published.

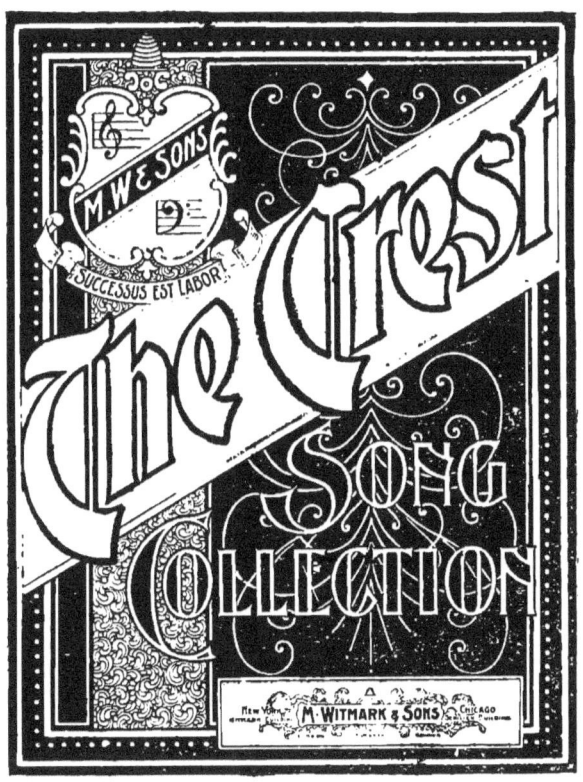

Containing Copyrighted Hits Only (about 50), by the Best Writers. No Cheap Reprints.

THE BEST ARRANGEMENTS

Ballads, Waltz Songs, Duets, Descriptive and Story Songs, Comic and Coon Songs. ⋰ ⋰

ANY OF THESE PIECES SELL FOR 50 CENTS IN SHEET FORM.

⋰ ⋰ Beautifully Illuminated Title. ⋰ ⋰

Price of Burnt Cork, etc., is mentioned in **"What's Wanted for Amateur Minstrelsy"**

CHICAGO TRANSPARENCY CO.,

151 WABASH AVE., CHICAGO, ILL.

———o———

Manufacturers of the Finest Slides

for Illustrated Songs in the World.

The best professional Singers and
Leading Publishers use our Slides
EXCLUSIVELY. ✒✒✒✒✒✒✒✒✒

List of Illustrated Songs Furnished on Application.

JUST THE THING FOR MONOLOGUISTS.

"Jim Marshall's New Pianner"

AND OTHER WESTERN STORIES.

BY WILLIAM DEVERE, "TRAMP POET OF THE WEST,"

" He is to the wild and untutored West what Will. Carlton has
been to the folk of the East, a mouth-piece through whom is spoken
their sentiments and their experiences. The language is that of
their every-day life, they know the speaker, recognize the character
and accept as Gospel truth all that he says."—*Tacoma News*.

"THE BOOK OF A PEOPLE."   "A BOOK FOR THE PEOPLE"

Specially Adapted for Public Reading.   **An Acquisition to any Library.**

Appropriately Illustrated by DOLPH LEVINO and JOSEPH MORNINGSTAR.

CONTENTS.

Black Hills Sermon. (A)	Horse Philosophy.	Throw the Inkstand at 'em,
B. P. O. E.	Jeff and Joe.	Johnny.
'Ceptin Ike.	Jim Marshall's New Pianner.	Two Little Busted Shoes.
Charity, Justice, Brotherly	Kinder Susp'shus.	Ten Mile or Bust.
Love and Fidelity.	No Opening, Write Again.	Tragedy. (A)
Case Equal. (A)	Oofty Gooft's Methuselaism.	That Beautiful Snow.
Give the Devil His Due.	Parson's Box. (The)	"Walk."
Hey Rube.	Queen of Hearts. (The)	Wat T'ell.
His Letter.	Roger.	You're Jest Like Yer Mother,
Higgins.	Spokane.	Mandy.
He Can—Like Kelly Can.	That Queen.	

M. WITMARK & SONS, Publishers.

WITMARK BUILDING, New York.   SCHILLER BUILDING, Chicago.

Price of Burnt Cork, etc., is mentioned in **"What's Wanted for Amateur Minstrelsy."**